Head over Heels by Paige Winsh
Nicole Ryan doesn't realize that the bogus love poem written for her daughter's amusement has landed in Jason Roth's possession. While he fusses with a way to handle her seeming infatuation, Nicole goes about her business. Jason becomes exasperated that Nicole isn't falling at his feet and has to admit that he might be the one with the secret crush. Will these two figure out their mutual admiration before they drive each other crazy?

The Princess and the Mechanic by Pamela Griffin
Zak Blodgett finds an unsigned love poem at the garage where he works and is sure Ellie Merriweather left it for him. Now that he thinks she's attracted to him, as he is to her, he gets up the nerve to ask her out. Unaware of the poem, quiet Ellie is surprised when Zak shows interest. Despite a disastrous first date, love grows. Will Ellie's prestigious parents and snobby friends drive a wedge between them? Or will Zak's zany act of love save the day?

Matchmaker, Matchmaker by Lisa Harris
When Samantha Kinsley slides off the roof and into the arms of good friend Garrett Young, Sam's younger sister, Mandy, decides to play matchmaker. Believing a love poem to be the perfect first step in transforming Sam's nonexistent love life, Mandy plans her strategy. Can Garrett and Sam find love despite the phony love poem, or will Mandy's overzealous matchmaking schemes backfire?

Ready or Not by Pamela Kaye Tracy
When Callie Lincoln moves back to Whiterock, she's looking for a place to lick her wounds. Darryl Meester's wife died six years ago; his wounds should be licked, but they're not. Then he receives a love poem and thinks Callie wrote it for him. Can a case of mistaken identity collide with a series of wrong turns and result in two lonely souls finding true love?

SWEET HOME
Alabama

ONE ANONYMOUS LOVE POEM
MISTAKENLY FINDS ITS WAY
INTO FOUR COUPLES' LIVES

PAIGE WINSHIP DOOLY

PAMELA GRIFFIN

LISA HARRIS

PAMELA KAYE TRACY

BARBOUR
PUBLISHING

ISBN 978-1-59789-354-1

Cover image © Getty Images
Photographer: Ferguson & Katzman
Illustrations: Mari Small

Published by Barbour Publishing, Inc., P.O. Box 719, Uhrichsville, Ohio 44683, www.barbourbooks.com

Our mission is to publish and distribute inspirational products offering exceptional value and biblical encouragement to the masses.

ecpa Member of the
Evangelical Christian
Publishers Association

Printed in the United States of America.

Head over Heels

by Paige Winship Dooly

Dedication

To my husband and kids—thank you for your patience
and help while I was juggling projects. I love you!

And to my coauthors—all of the crazy e-mails
back and forth paid off. We did it!

Listen to my instruction and be wise; do not ignore it.
PROVERBS 8:33

Chapter 1

Jason Roth heard the Kinsley Landscape truck drive up to his bed-and-breakfast and went around back to supervise the placement of his new sod. The day was flying by, and while he felt as if he were running in circles, he figured he could combine a break with this very important project.

He greeted the crew before walking down to the dock, where he stared out at the lake. He missed his grandparents immensely, and though he'd hired an old friend to help him out in the kitchen, he was overwhelmed by having to run the inn on his own. His grandmother, Rosie, had managed the kitchen and juggled that job with cleaning rooms. Of course, that was before Jason had added the diner to increase cash flow. Grandma Rosie had only prepared the complimentary morning breakfast buffet served in the Rose Room.

His grandpa had been in charge of upkeep and landscaping. Jason hadn't realized how much they'd let things go as his grandpa's health deteriorated until he looked at the grounds with new eyes after both of his grandparents passed away.

Jason swallowed the lump in his throat. The elderly couple had died within weeks of each other, his grieving grandma letting go after his grandpa's death. Now it was up to Jason to pick up the pieces and bring the Lakeview Rose back up to their earlier standards. He owed them that.

He glanced over at the Kinsley crew and saw that the sod looked good and would be a huge improvement over the sparse grass it replaced. He took a deep breath and forced himself to really look at his surroundings. The February sun was warm on his back, and the small waves on the lake chased each other playfully before lapping against the dock where he stood. This was his favorite place to hang out when he needed a breather.

It had been his favorite spot growing up, too, and he could never come here without thinking about his childhood friend Nicole. She'd been a couple of years behind him in school, and though she'd taken his heart from a young age, he never let on, not wanting to scare her off. He'd planned to tell her how he felt after her graduation, but instead, she ran off with another guy. Jason had been heartbroken and had buried himself in work.

He stuck his hands in his pockets and watched a small boat sail across the water, pushing the depressing thoughts out of his mind. He wanted to enjoy this beautiful day, to move forward and not dwell on what could have been. The past was the past, and it was time to face the future.

"Hey, stranger."

Jason froze. He'd recognize that soft drawl anywhere. For a moment he thought he'd willed her up from memory, but as he slowly turned around, he stared into the beautiful face of the woman who'd broken his heart seventeen years before.

Nicole Ryan held her breath, waiting to see how Jason would react to her return. He had matured into a striking man—not that that surprised her. He'd been good-looking in high school, too. She'd worked hard to keep her crush a secret from him, not wanting to face the pain his rejection would cause her. Though she'd dated now and then, no one held a candle next to Jason. On the night of her high school graduation, when he didn't seem any more inclined to romance her than usual, she made a rash decision and ran off with the guy she'd been dating off and on during her senior year. They'd had a decent life, but he'd been killed seven years before in a motorcycle accident, doing what he loved. She'd been left alone with his repair shop, their young daughter, and more than a few regrets.

Now she was back home, ready to pick up where she'd left off—if her friends would have her.

Jason gave her a slow but formal smile. "Nikki. I never thought you'd make it back down this way. I thought you'd shaken the dirt from your shoes and headed off to fame and fortune."

Nicole returned his smile. "Yeah, well, it didn't quite work out that way."

They stared at each other, drinking in the changes.

Nicole broke the silence first. "I'm sorry to hear about your grandparents. I know you must miss them terribly."

He looked away. "Yeah. Yeah, I do miss 'em. But I don't

9

dwell on that. Missing them won't bring 'em back. Life goes on, right?"

She nodded. "Uh-huh. That's what I learned when Jeff died."

His expression softened briefly. "I didn't know. I'm sorry."

Nicole shrugged. "We had a good life. He always lived in the fast lane. I don't want to sound uncaring, because I did love him, but I never thought it would last forever. He always burned too hot. Everything was hard and fast with Jeff. He had to push the limits, and that last motorcycle ride, he pushed too far."

She smiled. "But I didn't come here to talk about all that sad stuff. I just wanted to say hi and see what you'd been up to the past seventeen or so years. Abby filled me in on the Lakeview Rose. It's looking good!"

Jason smiled at the compliment. "We've worked hard to get things in order. I feel like I'm right at the breaking point—it's been hectic. Speaking of. . .I'd better get back inside. I've been out here longer than I'd planned. The lunch rush will start at the diner soon, and I need to have things prepped."

"You have a diner?" Nicole was happy for him. Jason had dreamed of putting a fifties-themed diner, complete with booths and a long countertop, in the bed-and-breakfast for years. She was glad to see he'd stuck with his plans.

"I call it Rosie's Diner after Grandma. It's doing well, but it keeps me hopping." He paused, his sweet smile morphing into something distant and unfamiliar. "It's been real nice seeing you again. I hope you find your return home to be whatever you're hoping it will be."

Just like that, a wall went up, and their friendship was dismissed. Jason turned and walked back to the inn. Nicole watched him, feeling as if a piece of her walked away with him. She didn't know what she'd expected, but she had missed his friendship through the years and had often wished she'd done things differently.

✉

Jason walked quickly, trying to outrun his thoughts. Just because she was more beautiful than ever, with new curves and a new maturity that made her even more exotic-looking, didn't mean he had to hand his heart over to her again.

Her visit to the inn unnerved him. He'd never imagined she would come home, let alone as a widow. He'd have to work overtime to guard his heart, because there was no way he was ever setting it out to be hurt again. He'd keep his distance from her and continue to bury himself in his work.

✉

A few days later, Nicole stared at the glum faces across the Formica table in Jason's diner and smiled. "Come on, girls, the assignment can't be that bad! Get on it and whip it out."

Her teenage daughter, Shannon, raised an eyebrow. "Mom, it's an old-fashioned love poem. What do we know about stuff like that? Shakespeare should have had this assignment, not us. It's totally a lame idea."

Nicole laughed at the melodrama in her daughter's tortured voice. She glanced around the busy diner and thought for a moment before returning her gaze to Shannon and Shannon's two closest friends, Mandy and Poppy. "I'll tell you what. Give me a piece of paper. We'll write one together, and then, using my model, you can do your own. You have to make them original, though. Not carbon copies."

Mandy quickly pulled a piece of paper from her notebook and passed it across the table to Nicole, while Poppy dug a black pen from her purse.

"It has to be handwritten in ink, and Ms. Dremmel gave us paper and envelopes—*red* envelopes—to turn in for the completed project. She gave us extras, because even she knows we're going to mess this up royally." Poppy's voice was every bit as tortured as Shannon's.

"Perfect. I'll use one set, you guys can write your rough drafts on regular paper, and then you can transfer it onto the fancy stuff for the final copy. This will be fun!" Nicole quickly began scribbling words on the stationery, pausing only to make notes on the lined paper Mandy had given her. She peeked up in time to see the girls exchange dubious glances, which quickly turned to flirtatious smiles as Jason walked toward their table.

"What can I get you ladies?" His tone was gruff, as if Nicole had never left town and hadn't recently returned. His glance roved over the paperwork on the table.

Nicole belatedly remembered her love note and hid the red envelope under the scrap paper. She had no problem with the assignment, even thought it could be fun, but she didn't need the most eligible bachelor in town, especially one who had once held her heart in the palm of his hand, to see her writing a corny love poem. Since he now stared at her with raised eyebrows, she'd apparently hid it a tad too late. "We'll take the daily special with four Cokes. We have some grueling work to do here, and we need nutrients."

"Grueling work. Right. Try running a restaurant single-handedly while the phone rings off the hook in your front office with no one to answer it." Jason huffed his disbelief, as if their notes couldn't possibly be as frustrating as his crazy schedule. "And for your information, the daily special is a cheeseburger, fries, and a soda. There isn't much in the way of nutrients anywhere in that combo. Are you sure that's what you want?"

He paused, giving Nicole time to change her mind, but she only smiled at him and nodded. Rolling his eyes, he tore the top sheet off his pad and stalked toward the counter, slapping the paper up onto the carousel with the others. "Order!" he barked before hurrying to the next table.

Nicole pulled her note paper back out and grinned at the girls. "Whew, I think I'll write my love poem about him! With all that charm and charisma leaking out, how can I resist?"

The threesome snickered but quickly stopped as Jason brought their sodas. With a disgusted shake of his head, he plopped them on the table before stalking off once more, muttering about empty calories.

"Mom," Shannon said, her confusion apparent, "if he hates junk food so much, why does he serve it?"

"Beats me," Nicole answered, her mind once more on the bogus love poem. "I'm too busy writing my love note to him to have time to analyze him. I've learned through experience, anyway, that it's better not to probe the male mind too closely. It will only cause you *mucho* frustration."

The girls nodded their agreement, already—at the tender age of sixteen—too familiar with the unpredictable workings of the male mind.

The poem was taking shape, and the girls were having fits of laughter over Nicole's zany comments on Jason's charisma—how it shone through his gruff exterior and how it made her determined to break through his shell to his teddy bear heart that lay beneath. She described his strong manly shoulders and dreamy blue eyes. She finished the Shakespearian poem with the promise that if her love was unrequited, she'd perish.

As Jason approached with their tray of food, Nicole thrust the completed note into her purse beneath the table, this time blushing as brightly as the red envelope that held the secret project. Jason shook his head.

"Am I ever gonna get a refill on this coffee?" called a cantankerous customer from across the room. "Or are you gonna just stand and stare at the beautiful ladies?"

Jason closed his eyes as if mentally counting to ten and then walked over to the coffee urn and crossed the room to fill the man's mug.

Nicole followed him with her eyes, concerned now that she was done with the note, and wondered why Jason was so understaffed on this Thursday afternoon. She watched him work as she coached the girls on their writing project. Writing was her passion, and she wanted to instill a love for the craft in her reluctant daughter. She wanted all three girls to discover the joy of writing.

She waited until Jason had a lull, then called out, "Hey, Jace!"

He walked over, exhaustion apparent in his every move.

"What's up with the lack of help? I thought you hired Abby for the kitchen in order to make your life easier."

He snorted. "Yeah, right. Abby's back there creating her next prizewinning dish for the breakfast buffet and can't be bothered by making measly meals for the actual patrons we have present."

Abby was Nicole's childhood best friend, and Nicole had been sure she'd be the perfect complement to Jason's bed-and-breakfast. "So she's not working out?" She tried to hide it, but her disappointment was evident.

Jason shrugged. "It depends on how you look at it. She's working out great as far as wonderful pastries and casseroles for the complimentary buffet for our overnight guests. Our phones are ringing off the hook with new potential customers as word gets out, but I haven't had time to answer them, so I'm losing business with each missed call. I rely on the paying customers at lunch to make ends meet right now. I can't afford to ignore them to answer phones, so the new business isn't going to pay off. In the long run, the overnight guests are worth more, but in the short run, where I'm at now, I need the daily lunch crowd to pay the bills."

Nicole hated seeing Jason so overwhelmed and frustrated. A new crowd of late-afternoon diners entered the café, and Jason walked off to greet them and get them settled. Nicole returned her attention to the girls. They had been carefully copying their finished poems onto the fancy paper provided and now stuffed them into the bright red envelopes.

"Ladies, I think you did a great job on these! Why don't you put them away and save them for tomorrow? Sleep on what you wrote; then in the morning get them out and reread them, and see if you want to make any changes. If there's anything you want to tweak, make the final changes on your extra paper." Nicole knew there would be no tweaking and that the assignment wouldn't be touched or even thought about again until the moment it was handed in. "For now, we have a mission."

The girls happily slipped their cards into their backpacks, all except Shannon, who had left her backpack at school. "Mom, could I put my two copies in your purse until we get home? I don't want to get them lost or messed up. I'll look at them later and decide which is best to turn in."

Nicole agreed. "Okay, now that you fair maidens hath done Shakespeare right and have this assignment off your chests, let's see if we can't help Jason for a bit. Are you guys game?"

The girls looked skeptical.

"You mean, like, work?" Poppy asked dubiously. "I can't even clear our table at home without breaking something. My mom makes me stick with unbreakable stuff."

"Then this will be right up your alley," Nicole quipped. "Jason uses baskets for most of his food, and even the cups are plastic. Not breakable."

Mandy looked over at the man who'd bellowed for his coffee.

"I won't take him. He scares me."

"I don't want him, either!" Shannon hurried to add. "I want the nice customers."

Nicole looked around at the scowling faces at various tables. "I'm not sure there are any today. Let's do this. Y'all seat the people and clear their mess when they leave. I'll wait the tables and handle their wonderful personalities. Jason really needs us. Are you in?"

The girls all agreed and headed to the back room, stopping Jason in his tracks. "What's going on? Why are they heading to the kitchen?"

"We're here to help. Put us to work." Nicole put on her cheeriest smile, sure Jason would attempt to shoot down any ideas they had.

"Uh-uh. No way. They're just kids, and I can't afford to irritate the customers any more than I already have. I appreciate the offer, but I'd rather you all just stay out of the way."

Nicole raised an eyebrow and snorted. "You *can't* irritate them more than you have already. Look around! You have a roomful of people ready for mutiny. Let's turn it around. The girls are plenty old enough to work, and it will be good for them. Give them a chance. You have nothing to lose and everything to gain. Now, show me the way to the aprons."

Jason knew her well enough not to argue, and she smiled smugly, secure in that knowledge. She followed him to the kitchen, taking inventory of the way his usually strong shoulders drooped and his usually neat brown hair hung in a disarray of curls at the nape of his neck. Actually, she thought as she watched him pass through the swinging door, the rough-and-tumble look had to be considered an improvement. He looked good with the slightly messy style.

Bringing herself back to the present, she reached out for the apron he handed her and waved at Abby. The girls giggled as Jason showed them how to wrap the strings around their waists and back to the front to tie. They went out front herd style to begin clearing the tables covered with dirty baskets and cups.

Nicole turned to follow them. "I'm off to take orders, Jace. You're now free to cook and plate the meals. Enjoy!"

"Nikki." Jason stopped her by calling her name. She swung around to see his smirk. "Don't you think it would be a good idea for me to give you a rundown of how it all works?"

"Nope. I'll be fine." She waved and went through the swinging door.

"Hey, Nik. . ."

With an exasperated sigh, she popped her head through the opening once again. "Yeah?"

Jason offered his first real smile of the day. "Thanks. I appreciate it. I think."

Nicole grinned and walked toward the war zone. She called back over her shoulder, "You will. I promise."

In the dining room, Nicole looked around, trying to determine where to start. She hadn't waited tables since before she'd had Shannon. After her marriage to Jeff, they'd both worked to make ends meet while Jeff edged his way up the career ladder at the garage where he repaired motorcycles. By the time Shannon had been born, Jeff was making enough money that they could squeak by on his salary, allowing her to stay home with the baby.

Jeff eventually managed the shop, and when the elderly owner had died, he'd left it to Jeff in his will. Those had been the best years of their marriage, which wasn't saying much. Jeff hired a good staff and spent his free time riding his motorcycle through the countryside, the hobby that had resulted in his death.

Nicole had debated going back to work, but the shop was doing well and she had a good management team, so she stayed home to be available to Shannon while doing the shop's books when needed. She'd only recently felt that the pieces of her life were enough in order that she could return home to the town she'd grown up in, daughter in tow. No longer the rebel who had run away, she had her life together with God and wanted her daughter to have roots with family and friends around.

"Hey, Mom, are you going to work, or are you just going to stand there while we do everything?" Shannon's feisty voice called softly as she passed by with a tray full of dirty dishes.

"I'm working, I'm working!" Nicole replied as she grabbed a water pitcher and headed toward the tables.

Mandy had the coffeepot, and Nicole cringed until she saw the teen pour it carefully into the first mug without a drop spilled. She should have known that cautious Mandy would do fine. Poppy was the one they'd need to keep away from the coffee urn. Who knew where the coffee she poured would go? The girl was a walking accident waiting to happen, but the trio of girls balanced each other well. Where Mandy was cautious but outgoing, and Poppy was klutzy but funny, Shannon was the brain. Shannon needed her two new friends to bring her balance and teach her how to be a teen. She'd always been too serious for her own good.

The bell tinkled as new customers entered the diner, and Nicole hurried to seat them. Mandy was right behind her with silverware and cups of ice water as Shannon and Poppy finished clearing the last of the dirty tables. Jason slapped his hand down on the bell, calling out an order number, and Nicole was happy that his voice was back to his normal gruff instead of weary and worn out.

Awhile later during a lull, the phone rang in the front office, and Nicole slipped out to answer it. An irritated voice said from the other end, "It's about time! I've heard great reports about your inn, but I've tried all day to get through and haven't been able to. I understand with your great reputation you're bound to be busy, but I am determined to get a room."

Nicole wanted to laugh. Instead of being upset that no one had answered the phone, the caller assumed the lack of response was due to the high rate of business, and that added to her determination.

Glancing around, Nicole spotted the reservation book to her left and flipped it open. "What dates do you need?"

The woman rattled them off, and Nicole paged through the listings, found the correct page, and studied Jason's notes. "Hang on. I'm checking to see what we have available."

She'd never booked hotel rooms before, but how hard could it be? Jason obviously wasn't into computers, which worked in Nicole's favor. She'd never figure out his system if he was. But in the book, the room numbers were listed in the first column and dates were jotted above the adjacent columns. In the slots that had already been filled, Jason had penciled in the last name of the party, as well as the number of guests who would be staying in the room.

Nicole found two rooms available on the dates the customer wanted and, using a chart taped to the front desk, she read off the description of each room's theme and location and then penciled in the woman's name in the slot by the room she chose.

She put the woman on hold and dug around the disorganized countertop, knowing there had to be some type of customer sheet around. She found it, took down the woman's information—name, address, and credit card number—and then said they'd look forward to her arrival in two weeks.

Dashing back into the café, she saw that the girls had everything under control. Jason stood outside the swinging door, watching in disbelief as people enjoyed their meals in the peaceful, clean room.

Shannon sidled up to Nicole and held out a handful of money. "This is off the tables. We have more that we put under the counter. What do we do with it?"

Nicole walked over to the counter, picked up a tip jar, and put the cash inside. "We'll put the money in here and ask Jason what he wants done with it."

Jason overheard her comment. "You all can split what's there. You earned it. I don't know how to thank you enough. I think the rush is over for the day, too, so you're free to go if you want to."

Shannon grabbed the tip jar and let out a whoop, then went off to tell her friends, who once again sat in their booth now that things were slowing down. They split the money, then called out good-byes to Nicole and Jason as they hurried through the door.

"I'm impressed," he added as he turned to Nicole. "I had no idea girls that age could do such a good job. They seem so flaky most of the time." His face reddened. "Oops, sorry."

Nicole laughed, waving off his apology. "No, you're right. They can be flaky but, when needed, they can pull together and get a job done."

Jason looked contemplative. "Do you think they'd like to split the job after school? I could really use the help. I'll pay them a fair wage, including for today, and of course they'll keep their tips."

"I'll talk to them about it and see what the other parents say. I know Shannon would enjoy it, and it would be good for her to earn some spending money on her own. She's very into buying clothes now and wants to go to design school. Maybe two days a week each or so would be okay. I'll get back to you." Nicole hesitated and then blurted out the next words that popped into her head. "How would you like to hire me? I could use a job to fill my days, and you most definitely can use some help. Please don't say no."

Nicole could tell that Jason weighed his decision carefully. She was dismayed that he didn't immediately jump on the idea. Instead, he actually looked a bit pained. But in the end, he agreed. "I can't keep this up on my own. I have no idea what skills you

have, but we can work that out as we go. You dem...
me today that you can work under pressure, and that al...
worth a lot. Can you start tomorrow morning?"

He looked relieved now that the decision had been made and added, "I don't think I can handle another day like today. Have Shannon come in after school, too, if you'd like."

Nicole echoed her daughter's earlier whoop and threw her arms around Jason's neck in a spontaneous hug. "You won't be sorry. I promise. I'll see you in the morning."

Jason watched Nicole jounce out the door with a wave. The woman oozed energy, and a perpetual happiness radiated from her. His life seemed to brighten when she walked into the room, and it now dimmed when she walked out. He brushed away the corny thought, dismissing it with the excuse of impending darkness outside, and headed to the table where a red napkin had fallen to the floor when Nicole had grabbed her purse from the booth seat. As he reached down under the table and picked it up, he realized it wasn't a napkin but a bright red envelope.

He remembered Nicole's blush as he'd walked up to deliver their food, and the note she'd tried to hide in her purse. Apparently she'd missed when she'd stuffed it in. It wasn't sealed, and he couldn't help but take a peek. He felt the color drain from his face as he read the words that were surely about him and declared Nicole's apparent love.

This was great! He'd just hired the woman and now had to work with her and her crush every day. He needed her as an

so about wanting the job that he
ed the money to make ends meet. He

love note would have been an answer to
ugh he was still attracted to her—and though
he green eyes, accentuated by long, silky dark curls,
still intrigued him—he didn't have the dad gene in him and had
no intention of taking on a child, half grown or not. After all
these years of bachelorhood, he didn't even intend to take on a
wife. The question was, how was he going to deal with Nicole's
infatuation?

Chapter 2

Nicole drove her SUV down the road, enjoying the balmy Alabama air that blew through the open windows. Winter in the Deep South was the best. Most of the time, the late February weather was mild like today, though sometimes temperatures dipped down into the lower digits, making the weather just cool enough to remind people how blessed they were to live in such a great climate.

Her car slowed suddenly and jerked before shifting back into gear. She loved the vehicle, but it was acting a bit unpredictably, and she had hoped it would behave until she could settle in and look for a newer model. Though she'd lived in the town for a few months, there had been a lot of unpacking to do, along with enrolling Shannon in school and spending time with old friends and family.

The car's problems had taken a back burner to settling in, not a good thing for a woman who owned a car repair shop, though fortunately the shop was so far away that she wouldn't be a poor advertisement for the place. So the car was having an attitude, but in the meantime she felt blessed that she lived in a town where nothing was too far away. At least there'd be no more worries of breaking down on a deserted highway, miles from anywhere! Then again, before moving, she'd always had the guys from her garage available for a tow and a quick fix. They'd been telling her for a year that it was time to upgrade to a newer-model vehicle, and now that she was settled, she needed to make that a top priority.

Nicole rounded the curve, and the Lakeview Rose came into sight. Though the inn was beautiful in and of itself—wraparound porches and towers on all three levels—the view of the lake beyond took her breath away. Tall pines and oaks could be seen all the way down to the lakefront dock where she'd finally run into Jason several days before. Four boats for the guests' personal use lined the dock's edges, while private, sheltered sitting areas were strategically placed among the trees so patrons could enjoy the lake view without being on the water. She'd always loved the area while growing up, and Jason was doing a lot to improve it even more now that he was the owner. She looked forward to working here. She pulled into the parking area and turned her car off, cringing as it shut down with a bone-jarring clunk originating from somewhere under the hood.

"That certainly didn't sound good," she muttered, making a mental note to ask Abby or Jason for the name of a good mechanic. She'd need a local shop for emergencies.

As Nicole entered the inn, Jason stood in the lobby, on open space with a hallway leading to the large back deck, discussing breakfast ideas with Abby. Exhaustion etched lines around his eyes, and his relief was apparent when she walked in the door. But he quickly replaced the look with a scowl. Nicole was confused. While Jason had always been more on the serious side, especially after his parents abandoned him, leaving him in the care of his grandparents, he'd seemed content after moving in with the elderly couple. Now he looked tortured, and Nicole had to wonder if his pain was caused by the loss of his grandparents or if there was something more.

Though she'd run off with Jeff fresh from high school, she'd always loved and missed her family and taken comfort from the fact that they were less than a day's drive away. She didn't have the nerve back then to make contact—other than a brief note to let them know she was okay—but she knew if she'd needed her parents, they'd have been there for her. Now she'd come home and made peace with her family, and it hurt her to think of Jason being all alone.

"Hey, boss, I'm here bright and early, ready to get to work. Just show me the way!" Her voice sounded overly perky, even to her ears, but she couldn't help it. She was excited.

"Early? We're done with most of the breakfast rush." Jason edged past her and headed for the counter. "Things start hopping at dawn around here. The guests like to get an early start on their day."

Nicole's happy bubble burst. "I'm sorry. I should have been clearer yesterday on when I'd be in. I had to get Shannon to school." She paused. She hated the instant tears that formed in her eyes at his gruff words. "If this will be a problem, I can find a job somewhere else."

Jason pulled off his Alabama baseball cap and distractedly smoothed back his hair. His eyes didn't meet hers. He stared out the back foyer door toward the balcony that looked over the lake. "No, it's fine. Breakfast is a buffet affair, and I didn't expect you to do anything with it, anyway. Abby sets things out before the guests arrive, and they help themselves for the most part."

He plopped the cap back on his head and met her eyes for the first time. "Let me give you a quick tour, and then you can get to work."

Nicole sent Abby a troubled look, and Abby shrugged. Obviously this wasn't normal Jason behavior, but Abby wasn't going to be any help. Briefly, Nicole thought of the note she'd penned that was still somewhere in her cavernous purse. Surely he hadn't seen any of it as she'd worked with the girls at the table. She couldn't even remember exactly what she'd written, just some silly things to make the girls laugh and have more fun with their project.

"We'll start with the diner." Jason led the way into the now-darkened room. "You might remember this as an extra dining room when my grandparents ran things. They liked to serve a light breakfast in the morning room—which we now call the tearoom or the Rose Room—then they served lunch and dinner in here. After they. . .uh. . ." A cloud of grief moved across his face. "After they passed away and the inn was left to me, I thought it made more sense to open it to the public as Rosie's Diner to increase sales and exposure. I offer the inn's guests the traditional complimentary breakfast in the Rose Room and then allow them the choice to dine here for lunch or to eat out wherever they might be."

He glanced around the room.

Nicole moved into the space where she'd worked the day before and smiled. "I like the fifties atmosphere. It looks like an old soda shop. You did a good job."

"Thanks. Business is up. As you noticed, we offer a good variety of sandwiches. I originally cut out dinner since there are so many nice restaurants nearby, but I've recently hired someone to work the evenings for me. We'll be open nights starting next week. The afternoon shift ends at four, so you can be out of here soon after. Will that work with Shannon's schedule?"

Nicole nodded. "I told her to head over here when she gets out of class, if that's okay. If it isn't, I'll make other arrangements for tomorrow. She and her friends do want to job-share and can work several days a week each, as long as their grades stay up. They're all coming this afternoon to talk to you about hours and to do whatever paperwork is required."

"That's fine. I still hesitate to rely on teens, but we'll give it a shot." He moved toward the kitchen area.

Nicole promptly tripped over the doorjamb, and Jason's arm shot out to steady her. His grip was strong, and she felt momentarily safe—until the swinging door swung back and caught her upside the head.

"Ow! Oh! Ow, ow, ow!" She gasped, pressing her hand against her forehead while bending forward and doing a little dance of pain. "Maybe it isn't the teens you need to worry about."

Jason let out a chuckle. "Maybe not. Are you okay? I'm so

sorry. Let me find you some ice."

He hurried off and returned with a damp cloth filled with ice, which she promptly held against the rapidly forming lump.

"Here are a couple of pain relievers, too." Jason reached behind him for a glass and filled it with water. "From the looks of it, you'll need them."

"That bad, huh? This'll make a great impression on the customers. I'm going to look like a klutz and scare everyone away." With a wry smile, she took the pills from his hand and swallowed them down with the water. "Continue on with the tour. I'll be fine."

Jason didn't look so sure, but he moved forward, anyway.

"This is Abby's domain. Now that you're here, I'll cook while she creates. She wants the breakfast buffet to be renowned." He grinned at this comment.

"And that's a funny thing?"

"Not really. It's just that she has big plans for this tiny place. But she does a great job, and the customers are raving, so it works."

"For your information, it isn't such a tiny place." Nicole glanced around, taking in the space and layout so she'd know her way around later.

"Well, maybe not, but I'm not sure it's on the scale she envisions." He led the way to a door that opened out into the back end of the main hall. "Watch the door. It doesn't swing, but we don't want to take any chances."

Nicole grimaced at his dry humor, and though it was at her expense, she was happy to know his wit still lived on somewhere inside that serious head.

"Nikki! What happened to you?" Abby rushed to her side, reaching to pull the cold pack from her head.

"Nothing, really. I'm fine." Nicole pulled the ice away in embarrassment, and Abby gasped.

"It's that bad?" Nicole glanced around for a mirror.

"Oh, it's really not, now that I think about it." Abby recovered quickly while raising her eyebrows toward Jason. She lowered her voice to a dull stage whisper. "What did you do to her?"

Jason ignored her and led the way to the ornate, open stairway. "I'll show you the upper floors next."

"Oh, it's breathtaking!" Nicole ran her hand across the smooth wood of the banister. "I'd forgotten how beautiful it is. I bet it looked gorgeous decorated for Christmas."

"It could," Jason hedged. "I haven't had much time to decorate since Grandma died."

Nicole placed a hand on his arm. "Jason, I really am sorry about your loss. I wish I'd known. I would have called or sent a card or. . .something."

Jason brushed her off. "It was a long time ago. C'mon. The guest rooms are this way."

Nicole felt the wall go up between them and played along. "Okay, so what do I need to do up here?"

Jason stopped momentarily. "Well, we usually have a maid to clean the rooms, but our last one ran off with a guest two days ago, so it would be great if you could help clean rooms until I can replace her. I have an ad out, and it should only be for a day or two."

"That sounds easy enough. Not a problem."

Jason showed her the laundry located on each floor and the family-style reception areas on both levels, complete with fireplaces. "I tend the fires, so you don't need to bother yourself with that. We send our laundry out, so all you have to do is gather the dirty laundry, hang up new towels in the bathrooms, and put new linens on the beds. The laundry rooms are for the guests to use during their stay."

They returned downstairs and walked into the tearoom. Jason hesitated. "Have you eaten breakfast yet?"

Nicole looked sheepish. "I'm not a big breakfast eater."

Jason took her arm and led her to the buffet. "Well, you need to learn to be. Plan to take a few minutes to grab a plate of food when you get in each morning."

He picked up a plate and handed it to her. "Help yourself. Things don't start hopping in the diner until midmorning, usually around eleven, and the lunch rush lasts until about one. Guests check out at ten in the morning, so you have an hour or so there to do the rooms, and you'll have some more time after lunch. Most guests leave earlier, though, so they can get a good start on their travel. I keep the ledger up front and will note who has checked out so you can start on their rooms as soon as you get to work. As I said, it will be hectic until we get another maid, but that won't be for long. Things pick up again in the diner around two thirty with the after-school crowd, and then the rush tapers off at four. Check-in starts at four, so I'll be free by then to handle things out front."

Nicole was having a difficult time concentrating with Jason

so close. His unruly hair flipped over his forehead, and his blue eyes sparkled in the dancing light from the fireplace. Yesterday, she'd joked with the girls about his attractiveness, but now she had to admit he still had a piece of her heart from their high school days. Though he hadn't had the time of day for her back then, other than as a friend, the crush she'd had on him was obviously rearing its annoying head even now. She forced herself to focus on the breakfast delicacies that lay before her, with the silent reminder that Jason was not on the menu.

After filling her plate, she followed Jason to a quiet table near the fire and began to eat.

Jason continued with his dissertation of her duties. "If this works out, I can answer most of the phone calls from the kitchen as I cook. You can keep an eye on the front desk until the girls get here to free you up. If guests arrive early and their rooms are ready, they can go ahead and check in. I'll show you how we do that after breakfast."

Nicole couldn't hide her smile. "Is that it?"

"I think that's about all." He grinned back.

"'If this works out. . .' I like a guy who sets high goals for his staff," she teased.

Jason shrugged. "From the looks of the bump on your head after less than an hour officially on the job, I have to wonder what you'll look like after your first day. I have to keep my options open."

"Very funny."

Nicole tore bite-sized pieces off her pastry while thinking. "You know, if you switched things over to computer and joined the modern world, you could access a computer in the kitchen for scheduling while I could have access to another one at the front desk. As it is, we'll be running back and forth with the reservation book, which will be a pain if we're both fielding phone calls."

Jason stood and abruptly pushed away from the table, their camaraderie broken just like that. "Don't start messing with my system an hour into the job. You'll have your hands full as it is. Meet me at the front desk when you're finished."

With that, he stalked off toward the lobby, leaving her and her partially eaten food behind.

Abby walked up and plopped into Jason's vacated seat. "Whew, I'm ready for a break. So what do you think about our boss?"

"I'm not sure, Abs. One minute, he's human, and the next, he's a brick wall."

Abby sighed. "Yeah. He's changed a lot in the past couple of years, ever since he lost his grandparents. He sort of shut down back then." She looked at Nicole through narrowed, inquisitive eyes. "I saw the first spark of life in two years, though, the moment you walked through that door."

Nicole felt her face redden. "What's that supposed to mean? He's barked at me nonstop! 'You need to eat breakfast to start your day. You'll get no nutrients out of a cheeseburger and french fries. Don't try to change my business style. . . .' Everything I do seems to irritate him."

Abby smirked, "Exactly what I'm talking about. He's just been placing one foot before the other, day after day, for two years. Since you walked back into his life, he's finally showing some emotion!"

"I didn't 'walk back into his life,' Abby. I came home to *my* life. I want Shannon to grow up with family, and I wanted to make things right with my parents. That's all. This job is just the icing on the cake of my boring life. And the emotion Jason's showing is the frustration I, for some reason, bring out in him, which can't be a good thing."

Abby smirked again and patted Nicole's hand as they both stood to return to work. "You just keep telling yourself that. I saw the way you looked at him at the buffet while plating up one of my specialty pastries. I think that emotional door swings both ways, if you know what I mean. No pun intended. Just be careful so you don't get hurt."

With a laugh at her joke, Abby headed down the back hall toward the kitchen.

Nicole reached up to touch the goose egg on her forehead as she headed for the lobby.

"Just for your information, Abby, this bump is due to a door swinging freely back to hit me. It had nothing to do with my staring at Jason," Nicole called after her.

Jason's expression was pained as he looked at her from behind the front desk. "All righty then, now that we have that all cleared up, how about we get some work done?"

Nicole was mortified. She hadn't seen him sitting there. The impression she was making on Jason had nothing to do with anything positive. Abby was wrong about that. At the rate she was going, she'd be fired before nightfall, and the day was young.

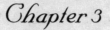

Chapter 3

The first few weeks on the job flew by, and Nicole found a comforting routine in her work. The girls were doing great in their afternoon job slots and were even taking on the bulk of waiting tables. Nicole was able to focus on the front desk, check in guests, and prepare rooms.

Cooler weather had briefly caught up with the season, but now spring had arrived. Nicole was humming as she peeled soiled sheets off a bed in one of the guest rooms when she heard a chuckle from the doorway. She glanced up to see Jason lounging against the doorjamb, watching her work.

"What?" she questioned, looking at the bed to see what he found so humorous. He was usually so serious that hearing him laugh was a major event.

Jason nodded toward her hands. "Purple latex gloves? Very stylin'. You're going to start a fashion trend."

Nicole grinned, waving her purple-clad hands in the air. "It's called 'infection control.' I prefer to keep my hands as sanitary as possible when cleaning. Deal with it."

"Aren't there nice, ordinary white gloves for such a thing?"

"Sure, if you're a nice, ordinary kind of girl, which I'm not. I like to pep things up a bit."

Jason pushed away from the doorpost, filling the space with his wide shoulders and height. "So I've noticed."

Nicole glanced at him, trying to figure out if he was joking or serious—most likely the latter. She watched as the invisible wall slipped up between them again. Jason was a master at distancing himself from her—from everyone, for that matter.

She tossed a pair of purple gloves his way, determined to put the smile back on his face. "Wanna match? We can be the purple posse, cleaning team extraordinaire."

"Are you going to get back to work or continue to stand there and flirt with me?" Jason stared at her hard, a muscle working in his jaw. Before her stunned mind could form or voice a retort, he'd turned and strode from the room.

Nicole spun back around to the bed, peeled off the purple gloves, and jammed her hands into a boring white pair. Tears forced their way out of her eyes, infuriating her as she slapped the fresh sheets in place on the stripped bed. She hadn't been flirting! She'd just wanted to see a smile replace his ever-present frown. She had no idea where he'd come up with such an idea. She only knew that she was done trying to break through his shell and that from now on, she'd make sure to steer clear of the heartbreaking man. Grabbing up the dirty bedclothes, she stuffed them into the laundry cart in the hall.

Nicole returned to the room to place the inn's new trademark chocolate mints, which she'd had Abby custom-order, on the next guest's pillow and checked the room once more to make sure it was ready. The room looked warm and welcoming, totally opposite of the owner she'd just dealt with. After a peek into the bathroom to make sure the basket of private-labeled shampoo, conditioner, and soap was in place on the bathroom counter, she swiped at a final tear and resolutely closed the door.

As he stomped down the stairs, Jason called himself a hundred different names for the rude comment he'd just made to Nicole. She'd done nothing but brighten his day, and he'd ground her into the floor. The look of devastation that had crossed her face at his words would keep him up for nights, but at least he'd put her in her place, and she would no longer want to carry a torch for him.

He didn't deserve her adoration. He wasn't the person she apparently thought he was. He was a loner and a grump and perfectly happy with his life as it was. The inn took up most of his time, and he didn't have much left to invest in a relationship. He didn't want to acknowledge the fact that with Nicole, Shannon, Poppy, and Mandy working with him, he had more spare time than he cared for. But even if he had the time, he didn't have the energy for a relationship. Relationships hurt too much, anyway. He'd learned that first as a small child when he was dumped on his grandparents, then seventeen years ago when Nikki ran off with another man, and yet again two years ago when the two people he'd loved most in the world had been taken from him.

He stormed into the kitchen and barked orders at Abby.

Instead of hustling to oblige him, she studied him with knowing light blue eyes. "Trouble in paradise?"

"I have no clue what you mean, and I'm not in the mood for guessing games," he snarled back. "I just want the order called in and tomorrow's buffet prepared."

Abby waved around her. "The order has been called in, the pastries are ready for the morning, and the girls are tidying the diner. What else would you like me to do?"

Jason rubbed his hand across his eyes. "I don't know. I'm sorry, Abby. I don't know what's gotten into me."

Abby leaned on the counter, her position implying she was ready to give Jason a dose of her endearing, if unsolicited, advice. Fortunately for him, she was interrupted when Shannon burst through the kitchen doorway, barely missing the same fate that had befallen her mom as the swinging door swung back and just missed her as she flew through. Jason made a mental note to adjust the door so it would close more slowly now that the Ryan women worked for him. He wanted their pretty features to stay intact.

"Abby!" Shannon squealed, the decibel level making Jason cringe. "He's here! He came back! He's right out there in the diner! What do I do?"

Jason strode toward the door with purpose. A good confrontation would do him good and would rid him of the anxiety that had built up after snapping at Nicole. "I'll get rid of him. What did he do? Whatever it is, I assure you he'll never do it again."

Shannon stopped in her tracks, horrified, and Abby grabbed

Jason's arm. "You aren't going anywhere—and Shannon, you're going back out there to take his order! Get ahold of yourself, girl! Your Romeo awaits."

Shannon nodded, started out the door, and then froze. "I can't. I get all nervous when I'm around him, and I know I'll say something stupid. You go."

Jason rolled his eyes. All this over a guy? "Shannon, you'll be fine. Just act like he's any other customer and play it cool. Go on."

Shannon looked doubtful, and Jason hid a grin, wondering if he'd ever caused a female such grief. He felt his face warm as he remembered one he'd just destroyed not thirty minutes earlier. He needed to apologize but didn't know how to approach Nicole. By now she'd surely worked up a royal fit, and he would be mincemeat by the time she got through with him. Worse, she might burst into tears, and he'd have to figure out how to comfort her. Dealing with teen hysterics sounded better by far.

He entered the diner and saw Shannon talking to a table full of gawky football players. They were giving her a hard time, but she set them in their place and took their order with all the skill of a seasoned waitress. He wondered which one was the special guy, then noticed that the quietest one let his gaze linger on Shannon a tad longer than the others, who had already gone back to their dissection of their latest game.

Shannon looked dreamy as she hurried past. "Thanks for hiring me, Jason. This moment has made the whole job worthwhile!"

Jason laughed at her innocence but quickly sobered as he

wondered if she'd feel the same when she saw her mother's mangled heart hanging by a thread. As if he'd willed her into the room, Nicole bustled in, passed right by him, and called out to Abby and Shannon that her friend Ellie had arrived and she was taking off a bit early to run an errand. With a distracted wave of dismissal toward Jason, she was out the door and gone.

Once in Ellie's car, Nicole wilted against the seat and closed her eyes against the memories of the painful afternoon. "Floor it and get me out of here," she said, peeking over at her friend. "The faster the better."

"If I go too fast, especially in this rain, I'll end up in the same boat as you, with a car that sits dead in the shop. If you'll remember, I still have to get that dent in my door fixed." Ellie gave Nicole a knowing look as she cautiously drove away from the Lakeview Rose on the road that curved in front of the entrance. "Bad day at the inn?"

"The worst. I don't know what I've done to rub Jason the wrong way, but I think it's safe to say he hates me. I've decided I'm going to write my resignation tonight. I hope he'll keep Shannon on after school. She really loves her job."

Ellie was quite a bit younger than Nicole, but they'd become good friends. "I thought you loved your job. Are you sure you should do this?"

Nicole sighed. "I did love my job. I do. I just. . ."

She waved her arm in dismissal. "I can't work with Jason. He really dislikes me, and I don't know how to change that."

Ellie laughed. "I can't imagine anyone not liking you! There must be more to it. Maybe he's just going through a bad time?"

"If he is, it's only a bad time when he's with me. He's sweet with Abby and patient with the girls. I walk into the room, and he's like a time bomb waiting to go off."

"Ah." Ellie smiled. "Maybe he doesn't hate you. Maybe it's the complete opposite. He likes you too much and doesn't know what to do with that. He's had a hard time the past few years, you know."

"I've had a hard time the past few years. That doesn't make me send poisonous darts out to one innocent person with the expectation that it will make me feel better!"

"But you have God, and though Jason was brought up in church, he hasn't been back since his grandparents died. He's a hurting man."

Nicole smiled, reached over, and patted Ellie's hand. "How'd you get so smart at such a young age?"

Ellie snorted. "Young. I feel older every day! But the smart part rubbed off from you. You've been a great friend and mentor."

"You can leave that comment at the friend part. Mentor makes *me* feel old. Speaking of mentor, how are things going at home?"

"Same ole thing, as always. Daddy and Mother are still harping on me to go out with Cassandra's cousin, Larry, but I'm not at all interested. Just because he's a rising star in his father's law firm and will inherit his daddy's millions someday isn't enough pull for me. But I don't want to talk about me today. I want to hear about you and Jason." She changed lanes and headed toward the shop where Nicole's recently repaired SUV sat waiting.

"There is no 'Jason and me,'" Nicole hurried to point out. "As I said, I can't think of a thing I've done that might have rubbed him wrong, but since day one, he's been on my case."

She hesitated as a horrible thought occurred to her. Grabbing up her purse, she began to dig through it. She saw a red envelope and sighed with relief. Her relief quickly turned to panic, though, as she slid out the piece of stationery and saw her daughter's handwriting. "Oh no. This can't be. Oh no. . ."

"What is it?" Ellie slowed the car. "Do we need to run back to the inn?"

"No. Keep going." Nicole continued to search for her bogus love poem, finally emptying her purse in desperation on the seat of Ellie's car. "If I don't find what I'm looking for, I'll never want to go back to that place again."

Ellie put on her blinker and pulled to the side of the road. "What are you looking for? Maybe I can help."

The red envelope with her poem wasn't there. She didn't need Ellie to help her figure that out. She'd gone through every nook and cranny in her purse and had pulled out each item one by one. Other than the envelope holding the poem that Shannon had decided wasn't as neatly written as the one she'd turned in, Nicole's purse held no poem. Her worst fear was realized as the thought that had been in the back of her head finally pushed its way forward. She must have left the note at the diner, and Jason must have found it. That's why he'd been acting so weird.

If Abby or the girls had found it, they would have returned it to her.

"What is it, Nikki? You look like you're about to pass out." Ellie's face creased with concern. "Do you feel okay?"

"If I'm right. . . Oh my. This can't be happening to me. Tell me it isn't happening to me. No wonder Jason thinks I'm a nutcase."

Ellie stared at her blankly.

"A few weeks ago, the girls had an assignment at school where they had to write an old-fashioned love poem. I wrote a fake one to show them how to set it up, using Jason as my unrequited love." Nicole paused as her friend's hand flew to her mouth in disbelief. "Yeah."

Nicole took a deep breath. "I think it fell into Jason's hands. I remember him walking up with our order, and I quickly stuffed it into my purse. In the heat of the moment, I sort of remember thinking I'd missed, but Jason was talking and I was distracted. I meant to check before we left, but then we started helping out in the diner, and I didn't give it another thought. A few times, the thought tried to press back into my muddled mind—I guess when I'd get into my purse and just see the one envelope that was left—but before the thought took root, I'd be on to something else and would convince myself that Shannon had taken her envelopes out and the remaining one was mine. Instead, I have her extra card and mine is nowhere to be found!"

She ended the spiel with her voice on a high note, just like Shannon did when she was upset.

Ellie didn't say a word.

Nicole waited. "Say something. Anything. Tell me this can't be happening."

"Oh my," was all Ellie said. A smile twitched at the corners of her lips. "Oh, Nicole. Um. Oh my. I don't know what else to say."

Nicole felt her lips twitch in response to her friend's. "This isn't funny. Not in the least. If Jason found the note, he thinks I have this fatal love for him and that I must be daft. He's been walking on eggshells so as not to encourage me or push me over the edge. Oh, this is so embarrassing."

"Well, the good news is, maybe Jason isn't as far gone as we'd thought. He's probably just a normal guy, trying to do a job with a psycho woman in his employ. We can stop worrying about *his* well-being now!"

Nicole tossed Shannon's rejected envelope at Ellie, who let it fall between the seats. As Nicole began to stuff the other items back in her purse, she muttered, "That's very funny. And in the meantime, *I'm* the psycho woman he's afraid of!"

"Sorry." Ellie's voice showed she wasn't sorry at all. She was enjoying this.

"Just wait until something similar happens to you. I'm going to enjoy every moment," Nicole bantered back. There was no sense in getting angry at her friend. It wasn't Ellie's fault Nicole was in this mess.

"These things never happen to me." Ellie grinned. "Remember, I'm the princess. I make it a habit never to write bogus love notes that will be found by the person whom I wrote said note about."

Nicole groaned and sank down into the seat. It was true. Ellie's father was the mayor, and she came from a family of socialites. She'd been raised better and never made the social blunders that Nicole seemed to make continuously. Nicole spent the rest of the short drive to the shop in silence, trying to figure a way out of this mess.

Ellie dropped her off at the garage with a shy wave at Zak, the cute mechanic. "I'll be praying for you as you decide how to approach this. I'm sure things will turn out fine."

Nicole thanked her, but she wasn't so sure. She thought gathering Shannon up and skipping town sounded like the safest idea. Though how she'd do that when Shannon was with Jason was beyond her! She could walk up to Jason and come clean. Just sum up the situation, have a good laugh, and go on. But what if he *didn't* have the note? Then she'd be more embarrassed than ever! And what if he didn't believe her?

Or she could go with plan C and go into work as if nothing had happened, keep her distance, and do her job. In time, surely Jason would realize the whole thing was a big mistake and get off her case. Though she'd left work that afternoon with plans to resign, she decided plan C was her best option. It might kill her, but she'd hold her chin high and move forward as if nothing was wrong. She just hoped she wouldn't trip over anything while her chin was up in the air!

It was bad enough facing Jason after his devastating comment. She'd barely gotten out of there without bursting into tears, and the effort had given her a piercing headache. Now, when she picked up Shannon, she had to go back and face him and act as though all was well. The night couldn't end soon enough. As soon as she was in the privacy of her bedroom, she'd free the tears and let the dam burst. After a good cry, she'd be better able to face the new day.

The SUV drove like a dream, much to Nicole's dismay. The one time she'd be thrilled to be stranded on the side of the road—indefinitely—the lump of metal ran perfectly, driving her straight back to her worst nightmare.

Chapter 4

When Nicole swung by the inn to pick up Shannon, she did what any self-respecting woman in her situation would do. She pulled up in front of the diner's entrance and honked her horn, motioning to her watch as if in a hurry when the occupants peered outside.

Shannon came bustling out, still stuffing things into her backpack, and plopped down onto the passenger seat. "What's up? I didn't know we had plans tonight other than you picking up the SUV. How's she running?"

"Just perfect, like a dream," Nicole said, her jaw clenched as the car burned rubber; she had to make herself slow down to be a good example. "So how was school today?"

Shannon stared at her. "Same as it was the last time you asked me. Are you feeling okay, Mom?"

Nicole sighed, pushing her hair back with one hand. "Yes. No. I don't know. If we can move anytime in, say, the next twelve hours, I'm sure I'll be just fine."

"Oh no. What did you do now?" Shannon gave a little

bounce of frustration in the seat. "Mom, I like it here! I have friends! I'm going to Gramps and Nana's on Friday night." She gasped. "You paid for the car repairs, right?"

Nicole looked over at her daughter as if she'd lost her mind. "Of course I paid for them! What's that supposed to mean? I've never bailed on paying a bill in my life!"

"Whew. Okay. But the way you peeled out back there and all and are wanting to skip town, I thought maybe you—we—were on the run." Shannon looked relieved.

"You have *got* to stop reading those spy novels. I've warned you about that," Nicole teased.

Shannon ignored her. "So why are we running?"

Nicole told her about the missing note and explained that she vaguely remembered stuffing it in her purse and thinking she might have missed, but with her excitement over helping Jason out at the inn, she'd forgotten to check to see if it was there. And now that she had checked, it wasn't, which meant Jason probably had found it.

"Oh, Mom, that's bad! It's so bad it's funny! All this time, he's thought you had this major crush on him and if he makes a wrong move, you'll flip out on him! I'd want to skip town, too!"

Nicole glared at her daughter. "Then you're in? We can pack up and go? Because I'm finding no humor in this."

Shannon was already shaking her head. "No way. What is it you're always telling me? You can't run from your problems; you have to face things head-on."

"Wise advice when it doesn't pertain to me—especially

when it's me in this particular situation. This is what is called an extenuating circumstance."

Shannon wasn't buying it. "Seriously, Mom. I know it's embarrassing and all, but it isn't the end of the world. Have you prayed about it? Maybe something will come to you."

"Out of the mouths of babes," Nicole muttered, not able to believe Shannon had played the prayer card. All of Nicole's motherly advice was coming back to haunt her now.

"Kasey and his guys came into the diner tonight! I'm pretty sure he was flirting with me!" Shannon gushed, changing the subject as only teens know how to do. "They didn't leave a tip or anything, but he left this napkin with all sorts of sketches on it."

Shannon pulled the slightly greasy item from her backpack, sighing dreamily.

"How come flirting sounds like such a good thing when you say it and can sound so. . .awful when Jason says it. Ohhh, I cannot go back to work at that place."

Her daughter stepped back into the mother role. "Yes you can, Mom. You'll go in there and say, 'Good morning,' and walk on by as if nothing has happened and start your day. You've done it every other morning of the four weeks or so that we've worked there."

"But I have knowledge now. Knowledge is a powerful thing. I've lost my innocence. I will never be able to find it again." Nicole knew she was being dramatic, but the situation called for it.

"Maybe God has a plan in all this. You've taught me to

face all things with that in mind. Even if we don't understand something, God always can and does make things right. He can use everything to His advantage." Shannon smirked.

"How come that excellent advice sounds so much better coming from my lips to your ears?" Nicole couldn't help but be proud of her daughter and the maturity she'd gained in the past few years. She sighed. "Okay, you're right on all counts. I'll hold my head high, walk through those doors tomorrow, and resume my job as if I haven't done countless things to make my old friend think I've gone daft during my years away."

"That's the spirit, Mom! I'm proud of you."

Shannon wouldn't have been nearly so proud if she'd been with Nicole the next morning as she stealthily made her way through the front entrance of the inn.

"Wimp." She berated herself as she peered around the corner and slipped into the tearoom. Seeing no sign of Jason, she moved silently to the breakfast buffet, planning to grab her items and eat them in the privacy of an upstairs lounge or guest room.

"Morning, Nik," a voice boomed from behind her as a firm hand slapped her back. Nicole jumped a foot in the air, and her plate went flying, food splattering all over the buffet. Only one person called her that. She turned to see Jason's stunned expression. "Oh. . .I didn't mean to startle you. Let me grab Abby, and I'll be right back."

Nicole made herself stand there when she wanted to run

away and hide. So much for being invisible for the next decade or so. She picked up the larger pieces of food as Abby rushed forward with a damp towel and slid the mess into an empty pan.

Jason stood sheepishly behind her. "Do you have a minute to grab another plate and sit down?"

Nicole shook her head. "No, I need to get upstairs and get started on the rooms. We have a lot of guests leaving today, and we're booked this afternoon, so I need every moment I can get. I was just going to grab a plate and eat upstairs."

A wave of disappointment crossed Jason's face, but he quickly recovered. "Surely you have time to eat down here. It won't take any longer."

Nicole forced a smile. "No, really. I just need to get things going. Maybe another time."

"Oh. Well. I needed to tell you. . . No, I wanted to tell you. . . I'm really sorry for my attitude yesterday. That was uncalled for. I'm the one who walked in and distracted you, and then I bit your head off with my stupid comment. It made no sense, and I'm sorry."

Nicole's face burned. She knew he had reason, or at least he thought he had reason, to think she had a crush on him and had been flirting the day before. If she really analyzed her actions, she probably *had* been flirting. She'd always cared deeply for Jason, and now that she was back home and around him again, she'd realized those feelings hadn't gone away. But just as when they were kids and teenagers, his feelings toward her apparently hadn't changed, either. She was a fun person to hang out with, but. . .nothing more.

That was probably the most humiliating part of this entire mess. The note that she'd written in jest really bared her heart, though she'd never admit it to anyone. She'd only just admitted it to herself.

She waved a hand in the air and forced another smile. "Don't worry about it. I'm not." She cringed inwardly at the untruth. Her vulnerable heart was being torn to pieces, and only she knew how painful it was. She wanted Jason to like her, to care about her, and all she'd done was botch things. "We all do things we regret. The best thing is to move on and not let it get to you. Today's a new day."

Her life motto. She knew she spoke to herself as much as to him. Once again, here she was spewing out wonderful advice that sounded good when presented to others but about killed her to follow herself. "I really need to be going now. I'll talk to you later. Hey, Abs, sorry about the mess."

Nicole slipped around Jason, not bothering to fill another plate. She had no appetite, anyway. The job she'd enjoyed so much had lost its shine, and she knew she needed to move on. She didn't need the job financially. Though Jeff had started out on a rough note, they'd done okay, and she and Shannon were fine. She'd just needed the job for her sanity. She hated sitting around doing nothing, and this job was a perfect outlet for her creative energy and free spirit. But there were other jobs, or perhaps she could volunteer somewhere like Ellie did. Maybe brighten the lives of some of the stodgy old citizens who never thought she'd amount to anything back in the days before she'd left town.

Hurrying upstairs, Nicole wondered how she'd gone from feeling total complacency after she and Shannon had moved home to feeling as though she had a huge hole in her life. Something was missing, and this time it wasn't God. She and Shannon had been careful to keep Him at the forefront of their move, their choice of house, their new church, and their relationships with others. She hesitated as she realized that since starting this new job, she hadn't been as faithful in her daily prayer and Bible study time. She knew that was part of her problem lately. Giving a real smile for the first time in days, she felt a bounce return to her step.

Her routine tasks throughout the morning gave her a good chance to catch up with God since the duties required no thought. She felt again that she had purpose and vowed to use part of that time to talk to God about Jason. Shannon was right. Maybe God had a plan in all this, and if nothing else, at least she was getting back on track.

Jason watched Nicole hurry out the door as if he were a contagious disease. For someone who couldn't live without him, she sure didn't seem to want to spend a minute extra in his company. It was irritating. He had promised himself he'd avoid her, but he really didn't want to avoid her. When all was said and done, he sort of liked the thought that Nicole had a thing for him. Just because she had a thing for him didn't mean they had to get married. Couldn't they simply resume their friendship, grab dinner now and then, and let it go at that?

Jason's laugh was sardonic. He knew that wasn't what would happen or even what he wanted to happen. He wanted to spend every moment in Nicole's company, and now he saw that he'd invented every excuse he could come up with to spend time with her or be in her presence. While he'd mentally tried to bury his head in the sand, his heart had taken the plunge and was sinking fast. But instead of enjoying his company, Nicole seemed nervous in his presence, or even worse, she ignored him.

He began to realize that maybe Nicole wasn't the one with the crush. . .he was. The thought wasn't new. He'd fallen in love with her when he was just a boy, but she had a free spirit that even at the tender age of ten he'd known would be crushed by his serious disposition. It had broken his heart when she'd run off with Jeff but hadn't surprised him. He'd been content to hang out with Nicole, basking in the energy that radiated from her, but he'd never let on how he felt.

If he was honest, he now realized it was his way of protecting himself from being abandoned again. He'd built a cocoon around his heart, and only his grandparents had gained access to that spot. He kept Nikki out while at the same time craving her friendship. The loss of his grandparents had sealed that spot for good, and now he didn't want to let anyone in again.

He traveled back to the philosophy of his youth. Now that he realized why he'd been such a grump with Nicole and he'd faced reality, he was free to resume their friendship with his self-imposed boundaries in place. If he'd been that strong as a child, surely he would be better able to keep their relationship at a surface level now. His countenance relaxed considerably, and he even began to whistle as he headed to the diner to begin his lunch preparations.

Abby glanced up from the prep table as he whistled his way to an apron. "Okay, I give. What's up?"

Jason knew this was the first of many tests he'd face regarding his new take on life. "Nothing is up, Abigail. Can't a man be happy when he wants to be?"

"Sure, most men can be, but if you want my honest opinion, I haven't seen you happy for a long, long time. Seems something, or someone, has brought a smile to your face, and it's been a long time coming."

"I don't think I did ask for your honest opinion—or any other type of opinion, for that matter—but you're right, it has been a long time since I've felt this way, and I intend to capture the feeling more often from now on." Jason noticed that Abby wielded a huge knife and wasn't about to tell her anything else about minding her business. Besides, with the mood he was in, he was too happy to worry about her questions, anyway.

"You're sure it doesn't have to do with a special someone who has come to work with us lately?" Abby continued to probe, not one to let things drop without a fight.

Jason feigned innocence. "Who? Shannon? She's a bit young, don't you think? Or were you referring to Poppy or Mandy? They're so spazzy they seem even younger than Shannon. So no, my mood has nothing to do with them, though they're working out well, and I do enjoy their antics. They make work fun. I appreciate them."

Abby had a smug smile on her lips. "I guess there's no reason you left out the most obvious choice of new employee, Nicole, in your essay on why you suddenly have a new lease on life?"

Jason realized his mistake too late, but that was okay. He felt fresh, powerful, as if a bright light had been turned on in his life. Nothing, and no one, could mess with his mood on a wonderful day like this.

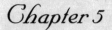

Chapter 5

J ason's euphoria lasted approximately five hours and thirty-four minutes. He was in the kitchen, cleaning up after the afternoon rush, when Shannon came stiffly through the swinging door.

"Um, is my mom around?" she asked, her voice strained.

Jason had a bad feeling about this. "No, she left a bit ago to run errands. She said to tell you she'd be back to pick you up when your shift was over." He hesitated, seeing her eyes well up with tears. "Uh, is there something I can do?"

Shannon made a concerted effort to control her emotions, but Jason could tell she was about to lose it. Of all times for Abby to take off early, too! And neither of Shannon's friends was working today. Only he and Shannon were working, with Shannon about to erupt. This was exactly the not-close-to-a-father moment he'd lived to avoid.

A sniffle leaked out from Shannon's tightly reined emotions, then another, and finally she was shaking with sobs, a look of pure mortification on her face. Jason hurried to her side and gathered her in his arms.

"Come on, now. It can't be that bad! Are you hurt?"

Shannon shook her head against his chest, her sobs coming harder.

"Did something happen in the dining room? Do I need to go out there?"

Shannon jerked away from him. "No! Oh no, please don't do that. I'll be fine."

Jason stared at her, trying to figure out the right thing to say. He couldn't let her continue to work as upset as she was. If he could just talk to her a bit or calm her down until Nicole got back, he thought she would be fine.

"You sit over there in that chair by the pantry, and I'll get you a glass of water. You'll feel better in a moment." He handed her his cell phone. "Try calling your mom. Tell her you're free to go when she's ready to come back."

Shannon looked doubtful but did as he said and took a seat. He filled a glass and handed it to her, then excused himself to go out front to see if any customers needed his attention. The diner was empty, save for a couple of high school students, and they looked ready to leave.

"Can we get our ticket and pay? Our waitress took off and didn't come back."

Jason was pretty sure the kid was the one Shannon called Kasey, the one who'd been flirting with her. Now he sat cozied up in the booth with a cheerleader type, waiting for Shannon to come back and have their relationship thrown in her face once more. Poor girl. Either she'd misread his intentions, or he was a jerk and had yanked her chain, only to turn around and break her heart.

"No problem. Shannon needed to make a call, so I told her I'd take care of her table until she got back." There. That ought to cover for her in case the scrawny kid took joy in the fact that he'd just stomped on Shannon's heart.

Jason locked the door after they left, then returned to Shannon. She sat with silent tears coursing down her flushed cheeks. "Are they still out there?"

"Nah. I shooed 'em out the door."

Shannon attempted a smile, but instead, more tears forced their way free. "I'm so sorry. I didn't mean to get this upset. I'll go clear the last few tables while I wait for my mom."

"No you won't. Go sit down. I'll make us a bite to eat, and you can tell me all about it. Sometimes it helps to have a guy's opinion, but I can't promise I'm any good with this teen stuff."

Shannon smiled through her tears and, with a hiccupping laugh, went through the doors while Jason whipped up a couple of cheeseburgers and a large order of cheese fries, placing them on a tray. Though he didn't usually eat this way, the unhealthy meal seemed to be Nicole and Shannon's favorite comfort food. He added two glasses of soda and carried the tray out to her.

She'd cleared the last tables while he cooked and now sat waiting as he'd suggested. He joined her, and she took a fry, dabbing it halfheartedly in the ketchup. "I feel so stupid. It's bad enough that I fell for a total jerk, but then I had to let myself fall apart over him. I really, really am sorry. I promise it won't happen again."

Jason chuckled. "Yes it will, probably more than a few times. A broken heart's a part of life. But you can choose not to let it get to you, and each time you'll be a bit more prepared."

Jason felt like a fake. Here he doled out advice, and he was the master of not letting a broken heart affect him. He refused to admit he even had a heart! Shannon needed to talk to anyone but him.

"So. . .you've had your heart broken before?"

This wasn't where the conversation was supposed to go. He'd planned to talk her through this first teenage crush and broken heart, not vice versa!

"I once had a friend who I lost in a big way. I wanted her to be more than a friend, but I knew it wasn't meant to be."

"So you never pursued her? You just let her walk away? Did she even know how much you cared?"

Jason had forgotten the romantic streak teens carry, and he had a feeling he'd underestimated Shannon. "Uh, yeah, kind of. We drifted apart. She wanted to see the world, experience life outside the boundaries of our quiet little town. I was the opposite, wanting to dig deep roots and never leave. I didn't want to hold her back."

Shannon gasped. "You're talking about my mom, aren't you? You had a thing for her when you guys were growing up, and you still have a thing for her now! Tell her!"

"Whoa, hold on there." Jason knew his face had gone red, and he hoped the darkening room hid that fact from her. "I never said it was your mom."

"But you didn't deny it, either. What's wrong with it, anyway?

My mom's a great lady, and I like you enough. Why not tell her how you feel and see what happens?"

"Sure. As soon as you tell—Kasey?—how you feel and see what happens."

Immediate tears filled Shannon's eyes, and Jason knew he'd just made a mistake. "I'm sorry. Scratch that last comment. Guys can be royal jerks, even at my age. Want to talk to me about it?"

"Y–yeah, I guess." She sipped her soda, her sad green eyes so like her mother's. "I thought he was interested in me. He flirted every time he came in the diner, and if his friends got out of line—which was all the time—he'd set them straight and apologize to me. A few times he waited for me in front of school and walked me to my locker. His was just a few lockers down. I thought we were friends and that he was interested in more, and then he came in here tonight with Janice and acted like I was a total stranger."

"I'm not going to pretend I hold the secret to the workings of the male mind. I can't even figure myself out half the time. But I will say that time heals all wounds, cliché as it sounds, and you'll feel better about this in a few days. Maybe he'll come around or maybe he won't, but I promise you, as pretty and sweet and tough as you are, before you know it, there will be a flock of guys chasing you down, and you won't even remember what ole Kirby's name was."

Shannon giggled. "Kasey."

"See how it works?" Jason reached across and snatched a french fry out of her fingers and popped it in his mouth. "Guys can be annoying, but there's always another one waiting in the wings."

Shannon took another fry and ate it before he could grab it away.

"I see the annoying part. At all ages," she added with a pointed glare at him. "By the way, why do you serve this type of food when you clearly hate it so much?"

Jason grinned at her. "I don't hate it. I actually love it. But I know it isn't the healthiest stuff around. I once tried to switch over to a more health-friendly menu, but the natives rebelled. I had to go back to this before the town of Whiterock declared mutiny on me."

"Oh." She took a bite of her burger and chewed in silence for a moment. "So, about another one waiting in the wings, is that what happened to you? Someone was waiting in the wings and off my mom went? Was it my dad?"

Jason sighed. Here they were again, back to him. "Your dad was probably better suited to your mom than I was. He was a free spirit, too. I would have clipped her wings, and she would have hated me."

Shannon smiled. "Ya know, I doubt that. My mom's been happier since she took this job than she's been in a long time. Well, until this last week or so, anyway. Did something happen between you two?"

She was getting too close to the truth. "I thought I was supposed to be counseling you, not the other way around. How'd we get back on the topic of me and your mom?"

"It's a topic I like much more than Kasey the Creep. I don't even know what I saw in him."

Jason wondered at the ever-changing teen mind. The female teen mind at that. Shannon appeared to be as resilient as her mother.

She waved a french fry in his direction. "You know, you'd make a cute couple. Your looks complement each other."

"They do, huh? Is that a prerequisite to dating these days?"

"Dating! You admit you want to date my mother? That's so cool!"

"Now wait a minute, I didn't say any such thing! You're putting words in my mouth. Your mom hasn't even talked to me all day. She came in and did her job and went out those doors as fast as she could get through them." Jason ran his hand through his hair in frustration. "If I didn't know better, I'd say she was about to fly the coop just like she did after high school."

"We aren't flying anywhere. We both love it here, and this is home. I think you just need to ask her out and see what she says."

Jason stared at the jukebox on the far wall, wishing he could let go and do as she suggested. She made it sound so easy. But the cocoon around his heart was too tight, and he was afraid if he let it loose and his heart was trampled, he'd never get it to work again.

"Why are you so scared?" Shannon's eyes peered into his, and he felt she could see into his soul and identify with his pain, wise beyond her years.

"I'm not scared. I'm. . ."

What? he asked himself. *What are you? The woman of your*

*dreams walked through that door less than two short months ago,
and ever since, you've been running scared.*

"I know I'm young, Jason, but I know how it feels to be
scared. I was scared when my dad died, but my mom was there
for me. We ended up in church, and I learned that Jesus was
there for me. I'd never be alone or have to face things alone
again. Mom packed me up and moved me back here where I'd
have other family around, and Abby, and you. I felt like a piece
of my heart was chipped off when Kasey walked in with that
girl, but you know what? I already know that he was a mistake.
My heart didn't want to admit that, but when you had me sit
down, I had time to think, and I knew in my head he wasn't the
guy for me."

Jason stared at her across the table. "And maybe your mom
won't think I'm the guy for her. I'd rather keep her as a friend
than ever take that chance."

Shannon smiled, and her entire face lit up. "My mom would
never think you were a mistake." She tore her red napkin into
tiny pieces. "Kasey was a mistake because I didn't take time to
know his heart. He isn't the kind of guy I want or need. I'll
be okay. I want to find a guy like you. A much *younger* guy, of
course, but still. . . You'd make a great dad, though!"

Her grin was impish, and he returned her smile. Teens
weren't so bad, after all. The dad comment caught him off
guard, but this past hour had been pretty intense, and he'd put
a smile back on her face. They'd both survived. Maybe he really
did have a dad gene in him.

He wanted to talk to her some more about their life before

returning to Whiterock, but Nicole picked that moment to appear. He let her in the locked door and waved her on toward their booth.

"Hey, Mom! Sit down and have a burger with us." Shannon's eyes were still puffy, and Nicole looked suspiciously at Jason. "Please?"

Jason started for the kitchen, not wanting to take no for an answer. "I'll be back with your food in a moment."

While he cooked, he thought about his talk with Shannon. He remembered back when Jesus was at the forefront of his life. But since his grandparents' deaths, he hadn't darkened the door of a church. His grandmother would be dismayed to know he'd fallen so far away, and she was the one woman on earth he'd most wanted to please. Well, until Nicole came back to town. Now she'd joined Gram in that place of honor.

Shannon was right. He needed to tell Nicole how he felt. At worst, she would turn him away. Jason could live with that. He could go on. He felt the need to return to church, where he could draw strength from others around him. He'd be okay. He wanted to get his focus back on God and get his life back on track. He felt as if a huge burden had been lifted and a veil had been pulled from over his eyes. All because of a certain smart-beyond-her-years teenage girl.

Nicole sat with Shannon and listened as her daughter bared her heart, sharing how Jason had taken care of her. Nicole was touched and happy to see signs that her old friend was still in there, somewhere. He had been through a lot of pain, and maybe he was healing. She dared to hope part of that healing was due to her, but after the way he'd talked to her, she doubted that was the case. Regardless, he'd salved her baby's broken heart, and that meant a lot to her.

Jason returned with her steaming burger, cheese melting out the side. She tipped up the bun and saw pickles, onion, and mustard, no ketchup.

"Just the way I like it!" she quipped, as if amazed that he'd known her style.

"You order the same thing as often as I'll serve it to you. If I didn't balk now and then, you'd eat it every meal. It's ingrained in my mind."

Nicole grinned. "I'm not that bad."

"Yeah, you choose the chili cheese Coney dog now and then, just to try to throw me off. But that's even less healthy than this." He stood beside the table, not wanting to intrude now that Nicole was here with Shannon. He felt like an outsider.

"Come on. Sit." She patted the booth seat beside her as she scooted in toward the wall. Shannon motioned with her head so violently that Jason was afraid she'd end up with whiplash if he didn't sit down. "My daughter tells me you helped her out today, and I appreciate it. This is why I moved home. I knew when I couldn't be around there'd always be someone to care for her. Thanks for confirming that."

Jason shrugged. "I think she gave me more good advice than I gave her. You have quite a girl there."

Shannon's eyes sparkled with the compliment, and Jason

found himself thinking Kasey had made a mighty poor decision to alienate such a great person. But Kasey's loss would be some other guy's gain. Next time her heart would go out to a great young man who would appreciate and deserve her. Jason would make sure of that. He smiled at the thought, again thinking that the dad gene might be somewhere deep inside.

Nicole and Shannon chattered away, and Nicole seemed to be relaxed around him for the first time in a long while as they finished their meal. Content, Jason watched the women talk. This was how it should be. He could get used to meals in their company, listening to Shannon tell about her day while her mother exchanged glances with him over the table.

Jason had some serious praying to do.

Nicole stood too soon, and Shannon hurried to the door. "I'll get the car started. Take your time, Mom."

She was about as transparent as air.

Nicole grinned at him. "Ignore her. I have no idea what she's up to. But I do want to thank you."

Jason put his hand out to wave away her gratitude, but she continued on.

"No, don't. Hear me out. It means a lot to both of us. We've been alone for so long that it's new to have anyone else take interest in our lives or to care about us. I've missed that. I know I've upset you lately, and I'm sorry. I'd love to have you join us for dinner tomorrow night—my way of saying thanks for tonight. I miss being your friend."

Jason couldn't get an answer past the knot in his throat, so he nodded. Wild horses couldn't keep him away from dinner with his two favorite girls. Though suddenly he wanted to be much more than Nicole's friend, he'd take that as a start. He had let her get away once before, but he wouldn't let it happen again.

He watched them drive away and smiled at the irony. The love note he'd found from her had originated in his own heart long ago. Now he had to make it real.

Chapter 6

Jason drove his truck down the narrow lane of Sweet Gum Street, checking house numbers to find the right one. Though nervous, he was excited about this glimpse into Nikki's life and the chance to be a part of it.

As he rounded a bend in the road, he smiled. He knew Nicole's cottage without even reading the numbers painted on the curb out front. Every other home in the neighborhood was painted white, but Nikki's Cape Cod had been touched up with a soft yellow and surrounded by a white picket fence.

The wraparound porch and small yard burst with color. Bright red flowers overflowed from planters strategically hung along the edge of the porch roof, their blooms toppling over the planters' sides to almost reach the porch rails. Small white flowers surrounded two large trees that stood guard over the front walkway. Well-trimmed bushes flanked both sides of the porch, stopping only at the steps that climbed to the leaded-glass front door.

Jason took a moment to whisper a prayer. He wanted this

night to be perfect. He realized he was like the stodgy old citizens who had judged Nikki years ago for her free-spirited personality, and now he wanted to be a free spirit, too. He'd closed himself off from life long enough. Now it was time to live again. He hoped that the future would hold a place for Nikki at his side, but if not, he'd be okay. He'd take one day at a time and see what God had planned.

The front door swung open, and Nikki stood in the opening, welcoming him in with a smile. Storing a picture of the warm house surrounding Nik in his memory bank, he exited the truck and loped up to the porch.

"Hey." Nicole greeted Jason with a lame wave, feeling awkward now that he was at her home. She wondered if he thought it was too small after the inn and found herself hoping he'd like it.

"Hey, yourself!" Jason stopped a few feet away and looked up at her with a smile. She returned the look before remembering her manners and stepping back to invite him in. This was more awkward than any high school date had ever been. She wanted so much to have him approve of her house, her choices, and how she turned out. She wanted to bypass where their friendship had ended and move into the relationship she'd always dreamed of.

As they entered the hall, Shannon burst down the staircase, her momentum throwing her into Nicole, which in turn plowed Nicole into Jason's arms. He steadied her with his strong grip, his spicy masculine aftershave making her senses reel.

"Oops, sorry!" Shannon quipped, not sounding very sorry

and not slowing in the least. "I'm off to Mandy's. We forgot about a quiz tomorrow, and we're going to get a pizza and study."

Nicole could feel the color creeping up her neck and across her cheeks. The ploy was so horribly obvious; she didn't know what to say. "But I have dinner ready. Jason's here."

"Yes, so I see. You guys go ahead without me. I'll be home later. Behave!"

With that, and giggling at herself, she rushed out the door and was gone.

Nicole realized she was still in Jason's arms, and if she was really honest with herself, she didn't want to move. But decorum and embarrassment kicked in, and she pulled away.

"Oh. . .um. . .sorry." She gave a little wave toward the stairway. "Shannon doesn't usually rocket down the stairs like that. Or leave without asking my permission. Especially when we have a guest and dinner's ready."

Her voice trailed off as she realized she was rambling. And that Jason hadn't let go of her waist.

She glanced up at him, and he had a funny look on his face.

"Oh no. I'm sorry! Did I hurt you? Do you want to sit down?" Nicole motioned toward the sofa in the living room. Hurting the man she was trying to impress didn't bode well for the relationship. He was probably thinking he wanted out of this craziness that extended from his diner to her home. He was already planning his escape, and her dream bubble was about to burst.

Jason's voice was hoarse when he spoke. "No, what I actually want—and of course you can say no—is to kiss you."

"Kiss me? Right here? Right now? You want to kiss *me*?" Nicole's heart began to beat faster. She'd dreamed of this moment, sharing a kiss with Jason, ever since she'd watched *Gone with the Wind* in seventh-grade English class.

Jason had the nerve to chuckle. "Yeah. Right here. Right now." He kept his arms firmly around her and pulled her close.

"Shannon planned this. I really didn't know she was going to literally throw me into your arms or duck out on us. I promise it wasn't planned. I had no idea. I'd only planned spaghetti."

"Nikki."

Nicole bit her lip. She was rambling again. "Yeah?"

Without answering, he pushed her hair back from her face and stared at her a moment. She lost herself in his blue eyes and then had to remind herself to breathe, taking in a gulp of air with a loud gasp. Jason just smiled, the corner of his mouth tipping up. She wanted to kiss that mouth into a full smile. As if reading her thoughts, he slowly lowered his head and pulled her close, briefly touching his lips against hers. Fireworks went off in her mind.

She reached up to keep him from moving too far away, and he leaned back to meet her lips again, this time savoring the kiss a bit longer. Nicole's knees buckled. If he hadn't been holding her close, she would have melted into a puddle on the floor. Just like in the cartoons.

Nicole gasped out the only word that came to mind. "Wow." Oh yeah. That was profound. At this rate she'd win the Romantic of the Year award. Rambling chatter, a gasp for breath after she'd forgotten how to breathe, and now her first comment about one of the most significant moments of her life sounded like something Shannon, Mandy, or Poppy would say.

Jason laughed and snuggled her close, where she gratefully buried her face against his chest. The action did double duty. She could hide, and she could stay in his arms a bit longer. She savored the moment.

"I hoped to renew our friendship tonight. I've missed you, Nik."

Nicole leaned back and looked into his eyes. He was breathtaking. Maybe not in a movie-star way but in a way that suited her heart. He was her Jason, and she'd missed him, too.

"Come on." She tugged at his hand, and he followed her to the couch. They sank down onto the soft cushions, and Nicole sat sideways, leaning back against the armrest so she could face him. "I've missed you more than you'll ever know."

Jason reached out and caught a lock of her hair in his hand, twisting it. "I had a thing for you in high school."

"High school?" Nicole sat up straighter with a squeal. "Only since high school? I fell in love with you when I was ten years old!"

She dropped back against the sofa arm as soon as the words escaped from her mouth. Surely she didn't just say that. If she had a net, she'd sweep the words right back in and hide them away forever. How she'd gone from inviting him in for a simple dinner of spaghetti to declaring her love for him was beyond her. She jumped up from the couch. "Spaghetti time!"

Jason captured her arm and pulled her back down beside him. "Not so fast. This is just getting good. Love, huh?"

"I was ten," Nicole stated patiently. If you couldn't beat them, avoid them, she always said. "I was talking in past tense, in case you didn't notice."

"Hmm, I think your exact words were, 'I fell in love with you when I was ten years old.' There was no disclaimer."

"I have garlic bread, too. Homemade. And salad."

"I still love you, Nik. I knew it the moment I turned around and saw you step onto the dock at the inn. I was going to tell you after graduation, but you ran off with Jeff. You broke my heart."

Nicole tried to remember where she'd last seen the brown paper bags. On TV people always breathed into them when hyperventilating, and Nicole was just about there. How come even a simple spaghetti dinner didn't work out so simply for her?

"I didn't know." Her words were soft, tears threatening to overflow onto her cheeks. Sad tears for the wasted years and for the pain she'd caused, and also tears of happiness that they were having this moment and conversation. "I liked Jeff a lot, but you were the one I wanted. When you didn't say anything personal at graduation, I thought you didn't care. Jeff had asked me to go with him when he left town, and I knew I could never live here and not be with you. So I ran. So many wasted years!"

Now she was crying.

Jason pulled her into his arms and held her close, whispering into her ear. "No, not wasted. We both had a lot of growing up to do. And you have Shannon to show for it. She's a wonderful girl."

Nicole sniffed. "She is, isn't she?"

She sat back so she could see his face. "I loved Jeff, but not like I loved you. I should have done things differently. I should have waited to see what God had planned. I never consulted Him about what He had for me. I just did my own thing back then. I hurt my parents, my friends, and I hurt you. I'm so sorry."

Jason leaned down and kissed her softly on the lips again. Once, twice, three times.

"Does that mean yes? You forgive me?" She hiccupped.

"I forgive you, but on one condition." He gently tugged at a strand of her hair.

"A condition?" Was he going to ask that she stop working at the inn, maybe to give him some space or time to think? She didn't want to be away from him another moment.

"We've lost a lot of years. I want to make up for lost time." He stopped, his blue eyes twinkling at her. He looked happier than at any time she'd seen him since she'd returned home. "I've grown to like Shannon very much. I know you like the inn. We could have a good life together." He sighed. "Now I'm the one rambling."

"It's okay. Go on!" Nicole wasn't about to miss what was coming next.

"I've been around you enough to know you're the same girl I fell in love with years ago. I want to court you, but I don't want to be apart for long. Can you see us together, forever, in the near future?"

Nicole let out a whoop that would put the teens to shame and threw herself into his arms.

"Does that mean yes?" He mimicked her earlier response with the question.

"I want to walk down that beautiful stairway at the inn wearing a simple wedding gown, and my dad can give me away." Her voice was muffled against the front of his shirt. "The wedding can be in the Rose Room. Abby can provide the wedding feast. We'll just have a small gathering. . . ."

Her voice drifted off. "You *were* talking about getting married, weren't you? I didn't mean to move too fast."

Jason let out a full-blown laugh. "I guess if you've been planning this since you were ten, it really isn't all that fast. It's actually way past time to get this wedding on the road."

He was serious for a moment. "I'm glad Jeff treated you right. I was worried he'd dump you off in some town far away and I'd never see you again, but I just wanted you to be happy. I'm glad to know he turned out to be a good guy."

"He loved us both the best way he knew how," Nicole agreed. "He liked to keep busy, though, and wasn't home much. Shannon and I did okay."

"Well, I'm going to make sure you're better than okay. I love you, Nikki, and I'm glad you're home. Your note scared me, but I'm happy you wrote it."

Nicole laughed. "The note was a fake, but my love's the real thing." She explained about the girls' assignment. "I guess I have to admit I meant what I said, though."

"Oh." Jason's mouth quirked sideways. "Well, regardless, I guess it served its purpose and made me analyze where my life was at."

Nicole could smell the garlic bread burning in the kitchen. She pulled him up off the couch with a smile. She doubted either one of them had much of an appetite, anyway, after what they'd just discussed. They had a lot of past to catch up on and a future to plan.

After turning off the oven and stove, she placed the spaghetti in the fridge while Jason dumped the bread in the garbage pail out back.

"Feel like a drive?"

"Now?" Her curiosity piqued, she nodded her head.

After scribbling a quick note for Shannon, she followed him out to his truck and settled into the middle of the bench seat. She watched as he did the familiar routine of years ago of placing his wallet—with the new twist of the cell phone—in the cubby under the dash. There were so many things she couldn't wait to see if he still did. And other things that would be new to discover.

The warm sun was setting over the lake as Jason led her down to the dock. Out of habit, they both kicked off their shoes as they walked along the path. He settled her on a bench, knelt on the wooden dock that had seen so many of their growing-up days, and took her hand in his.

"We fished here while still in grade school and swam here with our friends through middle school. In high school, we lay back on these wood planks and spent hours talking about our dreams. . .all except the one that was most guarded in our hearts. I think it's only right that I ask you this here. You're the best thing that ever happened to me, Nicole, and I never want to lose you again. Will you marry me?"

This time Nicole didn't try to hold back her tears, definitely tears of happiness. "I will. And I'll marry you as soon as we can get the plans made. I don't want to miss another moment with you. I'm so glad to be home."

✉

Jason watched as Nicole glanced over at the inn, and he knew she meant at home with him. With that comment, Nicole jumped up and dragged Jason to the edge of the dock. The moonlight glistened on her hair, and a daring grin lifted her lips. In the past, anytime their talks got too heated, she'd drag him into the water, whether in swimsuits or fully clothed. It used to make Jason crazy. He'd rather hash out whatever they were "discussing," but Nikki always avoided the issues and jumped.

This time, he grabbed her by the hand and took the plunge, pulling her into the cool lake along with him. They broke the surface of the water at the same time, and she swam over to him for a kiss.

"I see you have some surprises in store for me. I didn't think you'd jump."

"There are a lot more surprises where that came from," he promised as he helped her climb up the ladder to the dock. They settled at the edge, feet dangling into the lake, with her head against his shoulder, and watched the moonlight dance on the waves. With Nicole by his side, the fun had just begun.

PAIGE WINSHIP DOOLY

Paige enjoys living in the warm panhandle of Florida with her family, after having grown up in the sometimes extremely cold Midwest. She is happily married to her high school sweetheart, Troy, and they have six homeschooled children. Their oldest son, Josh, now lives in Colorado, while the newest blessing, Jetty, rounds out the family in a wonderful way. Paige has always loved to write. She feels her love of writing is a blessing from God, and she hopes that readers will walk away with a spiritual impact on their life and a smile on their face.

The Princess and the Mechanic

by Pamela Griffin

Dedication

Thanks to my friends, fellow writers,
and crit buds on this project—Paige, Pamela, and Lisa.
It was such fun to work with you on this collection,
despite all of the last-minute craziness!

Thanks also to my mom for her help,
and to Therese, a good friend and great writer.
Both of you are wonderful!

To God, I give my love, my thanks, my all.
Without Him steering my life,
I would have lost direction long ago.

Plans fail for lack of counsel,
but with many advisers they succeed.
PROVERBS 15:22

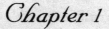

Chapter 1

E llie Merriweather rued the blush that heated her face as her gaze penetrated the glass walls of the garage's office and connected with the soul-shaking blue eyes of Zak Blodgett. Breathless seconds of rapid pulse transpired before he looked back down at the counter where he stood and picked up his hamburger.

Drat. He'd caught her staring. Again.

Ellie shifted her attention to Andy, the garage attendant who stood outside with her. She reminded herself she was now a twenty-year-old adult, a confident, mature adult, and no longer some googly-eyed junior high student with a crush as wide and deep as Whiterock Lake. Back then, she'd been just another innocent, hopeful angelfish in a school of many who'd dreamed of the day Zak might hook them by asking for a date. Of course it never happened, and Ellie had contented herself with staring at him from afar and wishing she were one of those lucky girls whose hand he held.

With his sandy brown hair, ocean blue eyes, and roguish

good looks, Zak had been and still was a heartbreaker. His mischievous smile set off some serious heart palpitations, and when framed by two deep, boyish, irresistible dimples in lean cheeks that now often bore a hint of five o'clock shadow? A girl didn't stand a chance. If one could expire from too many heart thuds, Ellie would have been history as far back as seventh grade.

"Zak'll be back from break soon if you wanna ask him how long he thinks it'll take, Ellie. But with a dent like that, I can tell you right now, it'll take some sandin' and some poundin' out, and then there's the repaintin'. . ."

"Huh?" She brought her mind back to the present. "Oh, right. Thanks, Andy. I'll check back tomorrow."

Out of the corner of her eye, she noticed her niece move from the soda vending machine against the outside wall and dart into the dark garage. "Crystal!" she called, but the seven-year-old either didn't hear or ignored her.

"You really need to watch where you park your car," Andy continued, rubbing the nape of his sunburned neck. With his back to the building, he hadn't seen Crystal run into the open garage. "People tend to ram into cars parked closer to buildings than those parked farther away. I remember when my Pop-Pop took the closest parking space at the Palace Theater one time late last summer. . . ."

Darting frequent glances at her speedy niece and listening to Andy's meandering conversation, Ellie tried to keep track of both. Her heart skidded to a stop when Crystal banged into the edge of Zak's rolling cart. It flew halfway under her car. Instead of pushing the cart out of her way, Crystal stepped onto the wheeled platform as if it were a stair and hauled open the passenger side door. Ellie's eyes widened when the child climbed inside. Her carrot-red hair appeared briefly as she scrambled over the console to the backseat, then flopped to the front again.

Wondering what mischief her niece was carrying out, Ellie glanced at Andy, her mouth parted, waiting for a spot to break in. Not finding one, she looked back at Crystal and almost laughed aloud when she saw her niece emerge from the car holding Snuffles, her white stuffed cat.

Of course. The constellations would fall from the sky and the sun would cease to rise if Crystal didn't have Snuffles.

Ellie hid a smile and refocused on Andy.

". . . And then with the fender bender just the week before, it like to have drained my Pop-Pop of his entire savings."

"That's awful, Andy. I try to be careful of where I park, but thanks for the advice." She held out her hand and wiggled her fingers in a silent message to Crystal as she spoke. Once the child rejoined her, Ellie withdrew her wallet from her pocketbook. "Do I owe you for anything today?"

"No, Ellie. Not till the job's done. Sure you don't want to stick around and talk to Zak? He should return any minute."

"No." She refrained from letting Andy know that Zak *had* returned. "We need to get back to Merriweather House."

"Oh? Planning a special event for the Fourth of July?"

"You know it." She grinned. "I'll see you, Andy."

"Will do."

Ellie strolled with Crystal down the shady sidewalk for the

seven-block trek to her family's ancestral home.

"Crys, next time you do something crazy like run into Mel's Garage when my back is turned, I might not be so quick to say yes when your daddy and mama ask if I'll watch you. You could've gotten hurt, sweetie! I saw you almost fall over that cart, and other dangerous equipment is in there, too."

Crystal hung her head. "I'm sorry, Aunt Ellie. But you were talking to that man, and I had to get Snuffles. He would've been scared if I left him there overnight."

"I see." Ellie tweaked the cat's plush ear and gave her niece a smile. "Well, okay this time. At least no harm was done."

Zak wiped mustard off his fingers with a rag from the back pocket of his coveralls and left the office to return to work. He'd been surprised to see Ellie still at the garage once he returned from Rosie's Diner with his to-go meal.

Then again, with Andy working today, he should have expected Ellie's presence. The man talked more than anyone Zak knew. From the first day he worked with him, Zak resisted calling the man Barney, since in looks and character he resembled the sheriff's deputy from his grandfather's favorite rerun. Funny that the sheriff's name on that show was actually Andy.

As Zak approached Ellie's new Dodge coupe, he thought about the petite brunette with the big brown eyes. He'd caught those same eyes on him three times today, and wondered about that. The first two times he'd noticed her stare, he'd nodded and smiled and hadn't missed the pink that flushed her face. She had the type of skin, close to the color of milk, that blushed easily. The third time, minutes ago when he sat on the stool behind the counter during his break, he'd felt someone watching him eat and had looked up. Sure enough, from five yards away and standing in front of the island of two gas pumps, Ellie stared at him through the glass.

She seemed eager to get her car fixed, and since that task had fallen to Zak, he assumed that's why she'd kept track of his movements.

He walked around to the passenger side of the vehicle and stopped in surprise. The wheeled creeper he used to work under cars had slid halfway beneath Ellie's car, and he saw a red envelope laying on top—a blank red envelope.

Zak bent to pick it up, opened the flap, and withdrew a note. He opened his eyes wide at the flowery verse, and his face grew hot.

"Whatcha got there?"

At the sound of Andy's voice, Zak jumped and quickly refolded the unsigned poem, stuffing it back in the envelope. "What?" he turned around, slipping it in his pocket. "Nothing." He shrugged.

Andy's eyes narrowed at Zak's jerky reactions, but he didn't push. "She sure was in an all-fired hurry to get out of here."

"Who was in a hurry?"

Andy regarded Zak as if he'd lost all sense. "Our only customer this morning. Ellie. Remember her? The pretty young thing whose car you're working on?"

"Oh." Zak gave a close-lipped grin. "Right."

"What did Jason put in your shake, anyway?"

"I just had my mind on other things, Andy, like fixing this car." Zak turned and ran his fingers across the foot-long deep scrape that marred the metallic green paint.

"Uh-huh. Well, I'll let you get back to work. I need to get back to the office."

Once Andy exited the garage, Zak let his mind travel to the love poem—and what a poem! He could scarcely believe it, but the evidence sat concealed within his pocket.

Ellie Merriweather had a thing for him.

Back in high school, he'd thought she was cute, quiet with a sweet personality. But a janitor's son didn't date the mayor's daughter. It just wasn't done.

He'd seen his friend Clint publicly lambasted when he showed interest in a wealthy rancher's daughter who hung in the same clique as Ellie, and Zak hadn't wanted to risk the humiliation of being put in his place. Not that he thought Ellie would have been cruel if he'd asked her out on a date. But he didn't see a reason to invite rejection, either. And so he'd concentrated on the girls in his league, pushing any further thought of Ellie out of his head.

Zak would have to be blind not to notice the attention he garnered from the ladies, but a superficial attraction didn't interest him now that he was older and somewhat wiser. Back in high school, dates spurred by physical attraction were the norm. Now he wanted much more.

He'd received a few simple anonymous gifts and notes back in his school years, and he recognized the sign of a secret admirer. It wasn't difficult to add the numbers. Ellie had been their only customer, she had been anxious to leave once Zak returned from the diner, and minutes later he'd found the note.

Ellie secretly liked him—more than liked him. She had a heart thing for him.

Zak smiled. At one time, he wouldn't have dared entertain the thought of pursuing Ellie Merriweather, but this love poem changed matters. And his plan of action wouldn't be at all secret.

Chapter 2

Sunshine flickered through the long rows of trees border-ing each side of Azalea Street and created white coins of light on the swept sidewalks. Happy to be alive, Ellie breathed deeply of the warm air wild with blossom scents of every kind. She missed her car, but walking did have its merits, and since almost every street in Whiterock boasted sidewalks, thanks to her granddaddy who'd been a member of the city council years before, transportation on two legs had been plea-surable, if slow.

An earlier call to Mel's Garage brought Zak on the line instead of Andy, whom she'd expected to answer, but she'd managed to ask her question about when her car would be ready with some presence of mind. At the memory of Zak's warm, easygoing voice over the phone, chills of delight raced across her arms.

Really, this had to stop. She hadn't been able to quit think-ing of Zak since she'd dropped her car off at the garage two days ago.

With her mind wrapped up in that embarrassing memory, she barely took notice of the footsteps coming from behind, but when they quickened and someone fell into step beside her, Ellie turned her head—and almost stumbled. She halted, sure her legs wouldn't carry her farther, anyway.

"Hi." Zak smiled. "Where you headed?"

"I. . .uh. . .the library." Flustered, Ellie hardly knew what she said. "I"—she glanced down at the books in her arms, surprised she hadn't dropped them yet—"need to dump these fish down the chute before I go to my brother's book fry." She realized her mix-up of words and winced.

"Ah. That's quite a stack of fish." Zak grinned, not unkindly. "Need some help?"

Help? She didn't think she could make her legs work with him walking beside her the whole two blocks there. Her mouth had already mutinied against her, as well as her brain. At the thought of his close company, her arms jerked, and the top books began to slide.

"Whoa." He saved the hardbacks from crashing onto his work boots and then hoisted the rest of the stack from Ellie's arms to his. "No one available to drive you?"

She managed to shake her head.

"Well, like I said on the phone, your car should be ready Friday. I would've stayed to work on it, but the boss doesn't like us to put in overtime."

"Oh, I wasn't expecting you to stay just to be with my car. I mean. . ." She took a deep, steadying breath. "I know you have a life, too."

His smile was gentle. "Library closes soon."

"That's okay. I'm not in any real hurry. I don't plan on going in; I just want to dump these in the drop-off chute outside." She realized he was the one holding the heavy books. "I mean—yeah, we should go."

She turned to resume her walk before her mouth made her into even more of a fool than he must already think her.

To his credit, he didn't laugh at her behavior or mock her tongue-twisted words. But then, he probably was accustomed to such muddle-headed reactions from infatuated females. Ellie felt much as she had in junior high when Zak was a sophomore and he'd joined her to walk to the bus stop one morning. He'd helped her carry her science project—a huge model of an eye—and seemed impressed by it. Then as now, she'd stuttered and flubbed her way through their entire conversation before his girlfriend had appeared, and Zak had left to go with Stacey.

Their two-block walk to the library progressed better than Ellie had thought it might. She didn't fall on her face and didn't have to speak again, two big pluses in her favor. He talked about work and his home life with his grandfather, and when they arrived at the brick building, Ellie was surprised to realize she felt somewhat relaxed.

"Hey, Ellie!"

At her friend Beth's cry, Ellie turned to see the tall blond wave. Zak strode to the outside wall to dump the books through the metal door of the chute. Beth approached, her eyes wide as they went to Zak.

"Hi, Zak." Beth's tone reeked of curiosity.

"Beth." Zak looked at Ellie. "I should be getting home. Enjoy the book fry tonight." His soft, teasing smile and the look in his eyes seemed personal, as if they shared a private joke, and Ellie found herself returning his grin.

"Thanks, I will."

"Enjoy the book fry?" Beth repeated after he walked away. "What's he talking about?"

"Nothing," Ellie said, still watching Zak.

If Zak had been hard to like, if he'd been full of himself, then it would have been easy to write him off as not worth the time. But Zak was neither of those things. The man didn't have a mean bone in his body. In high school, he'd given the same friendly greeting to the nerdy girl with bottle-thick glasses as he did to the cute captain of the cheerleading squad. Little wonder that all of Ellie's peers had practically drooled at his feet, hoping for a word or a smile. He'd been voted most popular, and no doubt Zak's yearbook picture had more penned hearts around it than any other boy's picture.

"Ellie," Beth gently warned as Ellie watched Zak cross the street and stride away, his gait smooth and confident, "think about this a minute. The mayor's daughter dating the local mechanic? That wouldn't go over well with your folks."

Ellie looked at her friend, unhappy to be reminded of what she also realized was the truth. "He just walked me to the library, Beth. That's all."

"Maybe." Beth's gray eyes were kind. "But you have that look."

"Oh? What look is that?"

"The same look Satine gave Christian when he opened his mouth and first sang to her. Or when Christine saw the Phantom for the first time."

Ellie laughed at the crazy comparison. "You watch too many romance musicals."

"Yeah, that's what my mom says. But I don't want your story to end as tragically as some of theirs did."

"My story? You're comparing my life to fictional characters in a movie, Beth. Do you realize how crazy that sounds? You're blowing this way out of proportion." Ellie shook her head and chuckled. "Come on. After that walk, I could use a soda. My treat." She headed for the ice cream shop nearby.

But Ellie couldn't resist darting one last glance down the street in Zak's direction.

✉

"Hey, Gramps, you know you're not supposed to drink that stuff." Zak took the beer bottle from the table and poured the remainder down the drain. "Among other things, the doc said it's not good for your liver."

"Don't tell me what I can and can't do in my own home," his grandfather griped as he did most of the time. "Only your grandmother could do that. . . . I miss her."

Zak frowned and tossed the bottle in the trash can. Ever since he'd moved in with his gramps to help after his grandma passed away two years before, life had been like this. For two years in high school, Zak indulged in party drinking, but he had never turned into an alcoholic like his grandfather. Then in the summer of his junior year, Zak volunteered his time in helping with the canoeing at a church youth camp, and there he'd encountered God. During a nightly worship meeting, he'd had a soul-shaking experience that transformed his life.

He wished he could get his gramps to discover what he'd found, but the man was just plain stubborn when it came to listening. Often Zak felt his role was more a caretaker to a child than a grandson helping with the upkeep of his grandpa's home and spirit, which turned out to be the most difficult of caring tasks.

He put a hand on his grandfather's bony shoulder in silent support. Gramps didn't look at him; instead, his rheumy blue eyes latched onto a stain on the wall.

"After I clean up, how about I make us some oven-gourmet pizza?" Zak asked. "The three-meat deal. Then we can kick back and play some Scrabble or just watch reruns if you'd like."

"Your grandmother was the Scrabble champion in her ladies' group. She won a blue ribbon."

Zak closed his eyes and sighed. "Yeah, I know, Gramps." He also should've known better than to bring up the game when Gramps was in the doldrums like this. "Hey, remember Ellie Merriweather?"

A spark of interest made his grandfather turn Zak's way. "The mayor's daughter?"

"Yeah." Zak cleared off empty bottles and food containers from the countertop. "I ran into her earlier. I'm working on her car at the shop—did I tell you? Anyway, I'm thinking of asking her out."

"You're kidding me."

Zak tensed at the skeptical amusement in his grandfather's tone. "No, I'm dead serious."

"Son, Clifton Merriweather wouldn't let you come within ten feet of his daughter. He's had her future pegged from the moment they popped the pacifier in her mouth."

Zak drew his brows together. "She's an adult with a mind of her own. She's not a kid anymore. Besides, I've got good reason to believe she'll go out with me."

Gramps scoffed. "What good reason?"

Zak busied himself preparing dinner. He wasn't ready to share the love poem, especially because of his grandfather's disgruntled mood, and Zak felt relief when Gramps didn't press him.

That night, doubts about asking Ellie on a date pummeled Zak and carried through until morning. But after another look at the poem, which he'd stuffed far beneath the shirts in his drawer, Zak prayed and felt encouraged to try.

The next day, he glimpsed Ellie through the diner window and smiled to himself. It would seem he was getting help from above with his pursuit. He'd never seen Ellie eat at Rosie's Diner on his lunch breaks before, and he walked the few blocks from work every day.

The diner simmered with the smells of well-done hamburgers and just-cooked fries. Some of the regular customers waved to him or nodded hello, and he returned their silent greetings in a similar manner. Normally, he took his meal to go, but today he approached Ellie's booth, ignoring the sole empty table in a far corner. She looked up from eating her sandwich and froze midbite, her big brown eyes widening even more.

"Mind if I share your booth?"

She barely shook her head in affirmation. Zak smiled his thanks and slid into the seat across from her.

"Hey, Zak," Nicole said, walking up to the table with a menu. "Need this, or do you just want your usual?"

"You know it," he said with a grin, and she laughed.

"Can I get you anything more to drink, Ellie?"

"Please." The word came out in a rasp. "Just water, Nikki. Thanks."

Sensing he'd thrown her off balance by his unexpected arrival, Zak initiated the conversation, keeping it light and focused on current events. After a few minutes, she visibly relaxed and stopped shredding her napkin with one hand. She even began to make easy eye contact and smiled.

His order came, and he concentrated on making quick work of his burger and fries, giving her a chance to talk, though at first it didn't appear she would.

"Gramps told me you take part in the Civil War reenactments at Merriweather House." He phrased the statement as a question.

She nodded shyly. "We've been doing them every weekend for almost a year now—just short skits my cousin mapped out. We do a different one each month. The tourists love them. Of course, we stay in our roles the whole time, which adds to the fun."

"So you get to dress the part, huh?"

"Yes. And I'm so glad Merle moved here last year and opened up that small costume shop in the square. She also gets business from theaters in Montgomery and from the Internet. She's been invaluable to us in locating authentic period costumes. We're an official tourist site now; Daddy even had a pamphlet made to distribute to area hotels."

"I can't believe I've lived here eight years and have never been to Merriweather House. What part do you play in the skits?"

Pink tinged her face. "My ancestor, Luella Mae Merriweather. They have a daguerreotype of her in the parlor of Merriweather House, and I resemble her. I think that's why I got the part, since Papa hired real actors for other roles." She laughed. "Luella was a character, and her husband—Captain Orville Merriweather? Well, let's just say he wasn't shy. He wasn't afraid to stand up for what he believed in to get what he wanted. During a garden party celebration at the very start of the Civil War, he rode up to Luella's father's house, and in front of the eighty or so guests gathered there, he knelt down in front of Luella on the lawn to ask for her hand in marriage."

"Sounds pretty courageous."

"Oh, you don't know the half of it. Captain Merriweather and Luella's father had opposing views on the South and slavery, and her father forbade Luella to see him. But he was on his way to join the war, and he came to state his heart cause." She grinned.

Zak found her story about her ancestors intriguing and encouraged her to tell him more. After a while, and with his hamburger long finished, he glanced up at the wall clock that resembled a vinyl record and fit in with the rest of the diner's "ducktails and bobby socks" fifties theme.

"I need to get back to work." He drank the rest of his soda in one quick swig, then set the glass down and looked at her. "Would you like to go out with me tomorrow night and catch a movie at the Palace? I'm not sure what movies are showing, but there's bound to be something good."

Her mouth fell open. "You want me to go to a movie—with you?"

He nodded.

"Like a date?"

"That's the general idea, yeah." He grinned.

A dawning of comprehension stole across her face, and her eyes shone. "Okay."

"Okay." His smile grew wider, and she gave a soft, shy laugh. He rose to go. "I'll pick you up at your house. Seven o'clock all right?"

She gave a nod that seemed both overwhelmed and disbelieving. He wondered why she should be so surprised he would ask her out, when revelation hit. Of course. The love poem had been unsigned; she didn't know that he knew she'd left it for him. So unless she brought it up, Zak decided to keep his knowledge a secret, too.

Chapter 3

I can't believe you're going out with him," Beth said over the phone. "I knew you were getting yourself in trouble that day at the library. I *knew* it."

"Aren't you supposed to be my best friend and offer support instead of criticism?" Ellie was talking on her earphone as she stood in front of her full-length mirror and held first the hanger with the blue-flowered cotton shirt under her chin—too casual—and then the hanger with the sunny yellow silk top—too dressy.

She threw the rejects onto the foot-high stack of other rejects on her bed and reached into her closet for another.

"I *am* being your friend; I'm trying to get you to see reason. You're so love-struck with your high school crush, you're not seeing beyond the small, sweet, rosy picture you've painted to the huge, glaring, black-and-white one involving your parents."

"I can handle my parents."

"Really? And when have you ever stood up to them? Even for your junior prom, they more or less arranged your date!"

Ellie sighed. "It was my choice to go out with the son of Daddy's friend, especially since no one else asked me."

"Right."

Frustrated, Ellie threw the soft cocoa brown top onto the pile and snatched a lavender airy blouse from the closet. Unlike the extroverted Zak, she'd always had trouble making friends in school because of her shyness. And the few friends she had, excluding Beth and Nikki, associated with her mostly because of her money—or rather her daddy's money.

"I am a grown woman," Ellie stressed. "I can date whom I please. It's not like he has some morbid dark history and might be an ax murderer or something. He coaches the junior softball team at our church, for crying out loud!"

"Yeah, I know, and he's devastatingly handsome, has a terrific personality, and is good with kids. Nothing I don't know or haven't heard before. But that doesn't change the fact that he works at the local garage, probably doesn't have more than ten bucks in savings, if that—*and* his grandfather is the town drunk."

Ellie clenched her teeth. "Zak can't help what his grandfather is—and he shouldn't be blamed for someone else's misfortune!"

Beth sighed. "Listen, I'm not saying this to tick you off. I'm bringing it up because that's exactly how your parents are going to view this situation, and you know it."

"Okay." Ellie calmed down. "Sorry I snapped."

But later, she couldn't prevent Beth's words from having free rein inside her mind, and when Zak arrived at seven, she felt thankful her parents had business in another part of the mansion. He complimented her appearance, and she was glad she'd decided to go casual in her emerald green silk jersey top and black jeans. Zak looked striking in jeans and a sport shirt that almost matched his sky blue eyes.

When they arrived at the Palace Theater, Ellie noticed Beth and three acquaintances step into line a short distance behind them. Immediately, Ellie tensed. Instead of waving a friendly greeting, Shelly, Tara, and Cassandra, all daughters of wealthy and prominent businessmen, made it clear by their disparaging glances toward Zak and then Ellie that they disapproved of Ellie's choice of a date. Ellie pressed her lips together, ignoring them.

Of the choices offered—a horror film, a WWII movie, and a romance musical—Ellie asked to see the musical, hoping Zak wouldn't mind since he was a guy. He gave a slight, unenthusiastic grin but agreed.

Inside the theater, Ellie almost wished she'd chosen the war flick. Of course Beth would choose the musical, too, and when Ellie's four friends took a seat directly behind them, she could have choked on her soda.

She darted an angry glance over her shoulder. Shelly only shrugged. Beth looked down at her lap. As if unaware of Ellie, the other two girls studied the screen while the previews started to roll. Ellie twisted back around, determined to ignore them.

Ten minutes into the movie, Ellie groaned at her choice. The historical musical told of a mismatched couple, a seamstress's daughter and a cotton plantation owner's son, whose ill-fated romance ended tragically. Ellie's so-called friends' whispered remarks of "Serves him right" and "He should've known better" only further increased her irritation. Tense already, when Zak slipped his arm around her shoulders, Ellie jerked her hand back. Soda splashed onto his lap.

"Oh, sorry!" she whispered. "I'll get some paper towels."

Before he could reply, she hurried to the ladies' room, not at all surprised when her four tormenters soon appeared.

"Are you crazy?" Shelly greeted, dark eyes flashing. "What are you doing here with Zak Blodgett?"

"Not that it's any of your business," Ellie retorted, ripping off the first towel and plunging the lever for another, "but I happen to like him."

"What about Larry?" Cassandra asked. Her petite voice matched her frame. "Your parents like him, and he likes you."

"No offense, Cass, but I don't want to date your cousin."

"Well, he's sure a whole lot better suited to you than Zak is," Shelly insisted.

"In your opinion."

"And I'll bet your parents share that opinion. The guy may be a looker, but he doesn't fit into our class."

Ellie halted her task and looked at the slender brunette. "You are such a snob—all of you."

"Yeah, well you're one of us," Shelly countered. "You were born into this life. Your ancestors were town founders, and you have a reputation to maintain."

"I am *not* a snob."

Shelly shrugged. "You saw what happened in the movie. That type of scenario can't have a happy ending. The guy usually turns out to be a gold digger or vice versa. And you've always been a daddy's girl. I'll bet your father was upset when he learned Zak was your date."

Ellie didn't mention that her father didn't know, realizing that would just lead into another spin-off of their heated debate.

"I think Shelly's right. You should reconsider." Tara withdrew a brush from her leather handbag and pulled it through her waist-length auburn hair. "Zak's fine to date once or twice. The man's hot, no two ways about it. I had a crush on him in high school, too. But to consider him for a long-term slot?" She shook her head. "Uh-uh."

"Thanks, ladies, for all your advice," Ellie said dryly, "however unwelcome it may be. Now, if you'll excuse me, I need to get back to my date." She resumed her task, yanking towels from the holder.

"Whatever." Shelly expelled a disgusted breath. "Come on, girls."

Tara and Cassandra trailed behind like the obedient followers they'd always been. Ellie grimaced. Their families socialized together, and Ellie had been childhood playmates with all four girls, but Beth was the only one she considered a true friend. In the mirror's reflection, she saw Beth hadn't left with the others. "Why'd you bring them here tonight? Couldn't you have let me enjoy my dream-come-true in peace?"

"Bring them here?" Beth grunted in disbelief. "When Shelly found out, she lit a fire in the others. I couldn't stop them." Beth put her hand on Ellie's shoulder. "But even though they were tactless and cruel and as shallow as always, they were right about one thing. Your dad's never going to agree to let you see Zak."

Tears welled up in Ellie's eyes. "It's just one date, Beth. One lousy date."

"So look me in the eye and tell me you're not hoping for another," her friend countered quietly.

About ready to explode from the anger, disbelief, and uncertainty rushing through her, Ellie held eye contact with Beth in the mirror as long as she dared, then spun on her heel and left the room.

✉

Zak paced in his upper-story bedroom, using the afternoon light from the open window to read over the poem again.

> If I could gather my dreams, one by one, and hold them inside my heart, they would reflect you.
> Bright as the stars on a midsummer's night, your smile chases the clouds away.
> Gentle as the rain that falls at midday, your voice reaches into my soul.
> Sweet as the wildflowers that sweep through the valley, your laugh sends quivers through my heart.
> In your eyes, I see my future.

He couldn't understand how the author of such a poem would reject a second date from the one she'd composed the poem for. . .unless Ellie hadn't written it.

Zak thought that over. Impossible. No one else had been in the garage, and though he knew a child could have a crush on a young man, Crystal was too young to come up with something like this. It had to have been Ellie.

So why, after he'd taken her home and asked for another date, had she refused? She'd seemed unhappy when she told him she couldn't see him again, even looking at him as though she hoped he might argue and try to change her mind. When he'd first arrived for their date in his pickup, her nerves had resurfaced, but after five minutes she'd relaxed and seemed to enjoy herself. Until her friends showed up and sat behind them, that is; then she'd been as tense as a baby calf surrounded by wolves. He'd watched her friends file out from behind him after Ellie left to fetch paper towels and knew they might have had something to do with her attitude as well as her jumpy behavior all through the movie. Later, when he was alone with her, she'd relaxed again and even smiled.

"Hey, Zak, you up here?"

Hearing his friend Clint shout up the stairs and the heavy thuds as he took the steps by twos, Zak frantically shoved the letter back into the envelope, looked around, then slapped the poem on the windowsill and sat on it, almost knocking his head on the upraised sash. His ball cap went askew, and he tugged it back down with an impatient jerk. A chair and desk stood at the opposite end of the room. The bed stood against the other wall, too far away to shove the letter beneath the pillow in time.

"Zak?" Clint burst through the door. Even when they were childhood pals, he had never knocked.

"Hey, Clint."

Clint's brows sailed up when he saw Zak sitting in the window, and he looked toward the empty chair, then back again. "What's up?"

"Nothing. Just getting some fresh air." Zak leaned forward so his head didn't smack against the sash. With his back to air, and the sill too narrow for comfort, he knew he must look anything but stress free.

"You look like something's eating you," Clint said, not buying Zak's excuse. "Anything wrong?"

Zak thought it over. Clint had been flamed by one of Ellie's wealthy friends, but Zak needed his buddy's advice.

"If you knew a girl liked you and for the most part everything went pretty well on your first date, but then she refused a second date when you asked her—though you felt she really did want to go out with you—what would you do?"

Clint shook his head in amusement. "Girl trouble? You? That's a first."

"I'm serious, Clint."

"So am I." Clint pulled the chair from the other side of the room and straddled it backwards, his arms across the top. "I guess it would depend on how I felt about the girl. If I liked her, nothing would stop me from trying to see her again."

Zak nodded; he felt the same way but needed to hear it from another source.

"So who is this mystery girl?"

Zak could hedge, but in a town as small as Whiterock, Clint would find out sooner or later, and Zak felt a little surprised he hadn't heard sooner. "Ellie Merriweather."

"Ellie Merriweather?" Serious, Clint straightened. "You're asking for trouble, Zak. Forget what I said—forget her."

"Clint—" Zak shifted and leaned forward. "I know you went through a bad experience with Beth, but Ellie's not the same."

"They're all the same." Clint's jaw hardened. "We might as well be two different species—them, the wealthy somebodies, and us, the poverty-stricken nobodies—for all the good it'll do you to get serious about Ellie."

"I wouldn't call us poverty-stricken, and who said I was getting serious?"

"You did by your own words. You've never given this much thought to seeing a girl and never asked my advice about one, except back in ninth grade."

Zak sighed. Clint was right. "You ever wish you would've tried again with Beth?"

For a minute, Clint looked as if Zak had struck him, then he shrugged. "Yeah. Sometimes."

"I've watched her with Ellie. Beth's nice, not like the others; she seems to care about people—it's no wonder she and Ellie are best friends. Maybe you should talk to her. She might've just been having a bad day that day."

"She told me flat out we weren't cut from the same cloth. That she wasn't interested."

"Four years can change things, Clint—can change people."

Loud laughter from outside made Zak look over his shoulder. Four young boys stood on the lawn beneath his window, laughing over something they held in their hands.

"Oh, no." Zak shot up and stuck his head out the window. "You give that back to me right now, Billy Reese! It's not yours!"

The freckle-faced scamp and ringleader of the gang of neighborhood juvenile delinquents grinned up at Zak and stuffed the love poem in his back pocket. "Make me!"

"All right, you asked for it," Zak muttered. He charged from the room, past Clint, and barreled down the stairs. By the time he reached the front door, the boys were fast pedaling away on their bikes.

"Great." Zak ripped the ball cap from his head and threw it to the grass. "Now what?" The mischief Billy could cause with that love poem in his hands sent dread prickling down Zak's spine. If word got out that quiet Ellie wrote it, it would embarrass her and possibly kill any further chance he sought with her. If gossip linked the poem to Zak as the author, he would never be able to stare his friends in the face and could already hear the ribbing he was sure to receive every time he walked into the diner or garage. Not that he thought poetry was lame; he sort of liked it. But even if he'd known how to write a poem, he would keep it between Ellie and himself—not broadcast it for the entire town's entertainment. And Billy's grandma was the town's chief gossip.

"What was that all about?" Clint moved through the door to join him outside.

"Nothing, nothing at all." Zak snatched up his hat and shook his head, resigned to the fact that all of Whiterock would soon know he had a new love interest.

Chapter 4

er eyes on the illustrated page, Ellie barely noticed that someone had taken the opposite seat at the library table. She finished the last sentence of the paragraph, judging its content for suitability, and glanced up as she turned the page.

"Zak!"

"Shh." The teenage boy next to her shushed her.

"What are you doing here?" she whispered, hiding her elation at seeing him. Four days had passed since their date, and his smile set her pulse racing and her heart thumping.

"How's your car running?" He kept his voice low. "Andy told me you had problems."

"Better. It's so crazy. First you fixed that massive dent, and then when I drove home from the garage, the car stalled and wouldn't start. If I didn't know better, I'd say whatever got hold of Nikki's car is contagious." She giggled.

"Shh!" The boy beside her glared daggers at both of them.

Ellie barely managed to restrain another giggle. "Sorry."

"Have you got a minute?" Zak whispered. "I'd like to talk with you." His gaze dropped to the illustrated hardback cover of the children's book she closed, and his brow rose in perplexed curiosity.

She slipped the book on her stack of three and nodded. "Maybe we should take this outside."

"Brilliant idea," the teenager mumbled, his eyes on his thick tome.

She and Zak shared a smile. Ellie took a few minutes to check out her books and met Zak at the door. He opened it for her, then turned toward her as the glass door swung shut.

"Ellie, I'm not sure what went wrong the other night, but I'd like to go out with you again. Would you give me another chance?"

"Oh, Zak, it wasn't you. You were perfect. I loved our time together." Shyness still threatened to unbalance her. But sprinklings of reality had begun to settle around her fantasy-come-true of being with Zak, dimming the spectacular brightness of awe to a pleasant glow of satisfaction. She felt better able to relate to him now that she'd spent time in his company and had gotten to know him better.

"Then can I ask a question?"

"Sure."

"Why didn't you want to see me again?"

His frank query left her chastising herself, as she'd done for days. She couldn't tell him that brief insanity on her part had forced her to take her snobbish friends' advice. They'd battered her defenses that night, and she hadn't thought things through—instead allowing their words to sway her reasoning as to how her parents might react. But after having had time to think, she'd reached a decision. As she'd told the girls, she was a grown woman, and she would approach her parents as an adult, telling them how she felt.

She grinned at Zak. "You busy now?"

"No, today's my day off."

"Then would you like to come with me while I run some errands? We'll have to walk, though. Until my car's fixed, I don't have wheels."

"Sure, I'll come. And you don't have to walk. I have my truck."

"Great." She hoisted her book selections closer to her chest.

Zak's brow grew quizzical as he looked at the children's book. "What are those for?"

"You'll see." Her grin matched the one he gave. "Let's go."

✉

Zak leaned against the doorjamb and stared in amazement at the picture of Ellie sitting in a chair beside a child's hospital bed. Earlier she'd told him that he could drop by the restaurant in the lobby while she visited with a patient for about twenty minutes, but he knew as he watched her now that he couldn't leave even if he were starving.

He'd thought he had her figured out—quiet, introverted, keeping to herself—but each moment that passed in her company proved to Zak how mistaken he was. She continually surprised him, though he'd always suspected she wasn't the spoiled rich girl his friends claimed, despite her not having a job like everyone else. She didn't need one, since her daddy took care of "his princess."

But as Zak witnessed Ellie read a fairy tale to the little girl with the bandaged eyes, he realized that while she may not have a paying job, her volunteer work was just as important if not more so than any paying job out there.

As she read about a lonely prince and a peasant girl and their happily-ever-after ending, her soft, melodious voice both soothed Zak and made him more aware of her than ever before. He couldn't take his eyes off her sweet face with the sun highlighting her pretty features and bringing out gold flecks in her brown hair. Even when a nurse cleared her throat for him to move out of the doorway so she could sweep past, Zak at first stood unaware of the woman's presence.

"I liked that story better than last week's," the little girl said. She couldn't have been more than ten.

Ellie closed the book as the nurse set a lunch tray on the table, smiled, and left. Ellie said a short prayer with the child, blessing the meal.

"Will you come next week and read me another story again, even though I'm getting my bandages off?"

"Of course." Ellie shoveled up a spoonful of corn. "They have your favorite—sweet corn." She guided the spoon into the little girl's mouth.

"And will you come when they take them off?" the child asked, her mouth full.

"If you want me here, Lacey, I'll be here," Ellie soothed.

Lacey became quiet a moment. "What if I still can't see?" Fear trembled in her voice.

Ellie took a deep breath and shared a helpless look with Zak before looking at Lacey again. "Honey, I know it's scary. But no matter what happens, remember you have a mommy and daddy who love you. I love you, too. And God promised always to be with us, no matter what. When I worry about the future, I like to draw close to Him and ask Him to hold me."

"Does He really hold you?" The child's voice filled with awe.

"It feels like He does." She guided more food into Lacey's mouth.

A pause. "What's it feel like?"

Ellie laughed. "All warm, soft, and peaceful."

"You think He would hold me?"

"Oh, sweetie, I know He would."

"Will you ask Him?"

Zak watched Ellie kiss the child's forehead and then pray with her for God to hold her and make her feel safe.

"She comes in to visit twice a week," a nurse murmured near Zak, having stopped to peep in. "Everyone here thinks highly of Ellie; she likes to visit those who don't have visitors, and we've given her the name Angel of Whiterock Hospital."

Zak nodded in approval. It fit.

"Lacey's parents don't visit?"

"They were in the accident, too, and the child was alone for days. Now that her parents have been discharged, they visit as often as they can, of course. But those two"—she nodded toward Ellie and Lacey—"they bonded."

Zak figured Lacey was one lucky kid to call Ellie a friend.

Fifteen minutes later, at Ellie's direction, Zak drove to a retirement center on the outskirts of town. They walked through the carpeted corridors, and she carried another book. He recognized the title of the classic from his high school days.

"Thanks, Zak. If you hadn't driven me, I wouldn't have been able to walk this far. These new slippers are killing me." She giggled as they walked to a sunny room. "It probably wasn't smart to wear them, but I'm trying to break them in for this weekend."

"This weekend?"

"At Merriweather House."

They said no more as they entered a room full of elderly people playing dominoes or just chatting. One man played a waltz on the piano. Zak watched Ellie approach a woman in a wheelchair. She wore a smart white pantsuit, and Zak recognized her as a friend of his grandmother's.

"Mrs. Friedman," he addressed the widow, taking her hand in a gentle shake. "It's good to see you again."

"Zak." Her brown eyes sparkled. "How's that rapscallion grandfather of yours?"

"The same. He won't go outdoors and won't talk to anybody."

She shook her head. "Poor man. I understand how he's feeling. After my Jim died, I didn't want to see anyone for months. Things will get better as time passes."

Zak didn't mention that his grandfather had buried himself in deep grieving for almost two years and not a matter of months. He worried about him.

"So," Mrs. Friedman said, looking at Ellie. "What did you bring for me today?"

"*Pride and Prejudice.* You mentioned you liked Jane Austen the last time I was here."

"Oh my, yes. I saw that movie at the Palace last month. That Mr. Darcy certainly could make a girl's heart throb. What a guy!"

Zak noted the hint of pink that flushed Ellie's face and the quick look she darted his way before turning her attention to her book.

"I don't know what I'd do without you, Ellie. I suppose I could always invest in audio books now that my vision's grown bad, but I do so enjoy your company."

"I enjoy yours, too, Mrs. Friedman."

Wanting to learn more about the facility, Zak excused himself. His findings over the next ten minutes intrigued him. The sunny, spacious rooms looked as if they belonged to a resort, not a nursing home. The residents lived in their own apartments and had a choice of eating in their own place or visiting the dining room at night. Myriad activities from shuffleboard to lessons in ballroom dancing to senior aerobics were offered, and the number of outside activities available also impressed Zak.

His grandfather needed socialization. Zak had tried but felt he came far short of what his gramps needed. He might consider bringing him here to check out the place.

Thirty minutes later, Zak and Ellie left the retirement center.

"So, you make this a bi-weekly habit?" Zak asked as he drove out of the lot.

"Yes. I have oodles of free time on my hands, so I use what talents I have by volunteering. I like to read, and I've been told I have a voice that's easy on the ears." She shrugged with a self-conscious laugh.

"You amaze me," he said, his admiration growing by steady strides. "What you did for Lacey and Mrs. Friedman is really commendable."

"Thanks, Zak." Her smile was soft. "I have to get home now, but I'd like to ask—will you come to Merriweather House this weekend and watch the new skit?"

"I wouldn't miss it for the world."

Chapter 5

Once Ellie saw Zak's face, even the discomfort of the corset that pinched her waist faded to nothing. Strange how at one time his presence disrupted her breathing, and now knowing he'd come to Merriweather House only created a blissful contentment.

She floated through the nineteenth-century skit, which took place in the grand ballroom and included a dance, a cotillion, which brought an enthusiastic burst of applause from the tourists at its conclusion. Zak's expression of admiration made all the dance lessons Ellie had needed to take these past weeks worthwhile.

"Good evening," she said as she approached him. Mark, the tall, redheaded reenactor who played Captain Merriweather, came up beside her and inclined his head in a brief welcome to Zak.

"It is indeed an honor, sir, to have you visit our home," he said.

Ellie noted the slight confusion on Zak's face. "Perhaps our guest would care for refreshment on such a humid day as this?" She directed her formal words to the captain, then looked at Zak. "Why, your throat must be simply parched, sir! A glass of Cook's lemonade will provide a wonderful cool refreshment."

Zak's eyes lit up, and he smiled, catching on. "Ah. . .yes. Thank you for your kind offer. Captain, it's a pleasure to meet you." He shook the man's white-gloved hand, then turned to Ellie. "Mrs. Merriweather." He took her glove but didn't shake her hand, and tingles coursed through Ellie as he bowed over it with all the suave aplomb of any nineteenth-century gentleman.

Ellie forgot all about lemonade.

"You must be Mr. Zachary Blodgett," Mark said. "My wife has told me a great deal about you, sir." He glanced at Ellie. She felt her face warm, wishing Mark had omitted that particular revealing comment. "But I don't think she mentioned how you make your living."

"I'm the town blacksmith," Zak said without missing a beat. "I take care of the horsepower here in Whiterock."

The captain laughed at the pun, and Ellie relaxed.

"Well, we certainly could use more of your kind, Mr. Blodgett. My wife will show you our home, if you would care to view the rooms. I have matters of business to attend to."

"A discussion on the strategies of war?" Zak asked.

"Of course." Mark smiled, nodded farewell, then moved to talk with a small group of tourists.

Noticing that two young girls still watched—their eyes mostly on Zak—Ellie stayed in character.

"Mr. Blodgett, which room in particular would you care to visit first? All twenty-three downstairs rooms of our mansion are open to the public." She took hold of his arm, walking him over the parquet floors and past the small gift shop, which contained inexpensive Merriweather House mementos.

"Do you have a stable?"

"A stable?" She looked at him, puzzled, then grinned. "Oh, I see. Because you're a blacksmith, you'd naturally want to see that, wouldn't you? Well, we do have a stable, but no horses. The troops took every one of them for the cause," she quipped.

"That's too bad. I enjoy riding. My sister, Jill, married a rancher."

"Really?" Taken aback, Ellie halted. "I didn't know your sister was married. A rancher, you say?"

"Yes, but their homestead is nothing as fancy as that of your friend Beth's father. It's just a small spread fifteen miles from here."

Ellie nodded. "I could show you the garden, if you'd care to see that, Mr. Blodgett?" She smiled at a young guest who stood within hearing distance. "It's this way."

"I would be most honored, Mrs. Merriweather. . .only. . ."

"Yes?"

"I can't help feeling guilty, as if I'm keeping time with another man's wife."

Ellie burst out giggling. "I assure you, sir, you've nothing to fear. When absent from Merriweather House, I find my affections do not lie with the captain, nor do his with me." She wasn't certain if it was the nineteenth-century gold and green ball gown that made her feel silly and flirtatious, the act in which she'd been enmeshed, or her role as her ancestor Luella Mae. Zak played his part well, and Ellie was enjoying her performance as a Southern belle.

"Really?" His brow arched. "Would it be inappropriate to ask why not?"

"Oh yes. Frightfully so." She giggled again. "But regardless, I shall tell you." She leaned in close, as if to divulge a secret. "The captain deceives people into believing we're married," she explained, "so as to gain respect from his commanding officers. I, after all, am known and admired as far north as the Mason-Dixon Line—and beyond even that."

Zak laughed. "And may I be so bold as to ask with whom your affections do lie?"

"Did I say they lie with any one man, sir, or that I admired any one man in particular?" She pulled out her lacy fan, suddenly glad for the prop, and fanned her hot face. His question seemed more serious than fun.

"No, you didn't. But I can understand how you would be the object of any man's admiration."

All answering quips flew from her mind as, with the debonair gesture of a gentleman, Zak again lifted her white-gloved hand to his lips. This time he kissed the back of it, maintaining eye contact with her the entire time.

Ellie forgot to breathe, then took in a swift lungful of air when she noticed her mother approach from the opposite end of the corridor. Her upswept blond hair was a great foil for her costume, but her snapping dark eyes seemed as formidable as the nineteenth-century black satin dress she wore as she played the elder Mrs. Merriweather.

"Luella Mae, your presence is required in the ballroom," she announced.

"I was just about to show Mr. Blodgett the garden," Ellie countered. She made quick introductions, but her mother's eyes didn't lose their bite.

"I apologize for bringing your tour to an abrupt end," Ellie's mother said to Zak. "Perhaps one of the other girls can show you around the mansion."

"Thanks, but I really need to get going." His smile seemed forced, yet his eyes were kind as he turned to Ellie. "Walk me to the door?"

"Of course." Anger warred with embarrassment at her mother's cavalier treatment of Zak. Ellie didn't dare look at her for fear of what she might say.

At the door, Zak again took Ellie's hand but didn't kiss it. "Would you like to go fishing with me Saturday morning? I don't go into work until the afternoon."

"Fishing?" Of all things she thought he might ask, this hadn't been one of them.

"Ever been before?"

"With my granddad, when I was a little girl, but that was a long time ago." Even then, she and a fishing pole had never gotten along well together.

He gave his irresistible dimpled smile. "Come on, it'll be fun."

With Zak for company, she didn't doubt it. "All right. Saturday then."

She couldn't wait for Saturday to roll around.

✉

Ellie was great company—most of the time. But when it came to fishing buddies, she didn't rate at the top of the list.

With amused tolerance, Zak watched her splash, barefoot, into the shallow water.

"Eek!" she raced back to the bank. "It's still too cold for late spring, even if the sun is shining and it's warm outside."

He nodded his agreement.

"I don't suppose it's really swimming weather, you think? And that rain yesterday probably chilled the water some, too."

He gave a slight shake of his head along with a close-lipped smile.

"What?" She grinned, walking closer. "You're awfully quiet. I've done all the talking since we got here. Everything okay?"

"Sure." His grin grew larger as he looked up at her. "But talking scares away all the fish."

"Oh!" she said in a sudden loud whisper. "I'm sorry, I didn't know. I mean, what with the birds squawking as loud as they are, I didn't think us talking would do any damage. As you can tell, I'm no fisherwoman." She sat down beside him on the grass. "Why didn't you tell me to be quiet earlier?"

"I enjoy listening to you. The fish aren't biting this morning, but I doubt it's *all* because of you." He grinned to show he was teasing.

"Hmmm. Maybe they're at a book fry on the other side of the lake," she joked. "I really doubt they'd be at a catfish fry."

Zak chuckled and leaned back against a boulder. Each time he was with her, Ellie relaxed around him more. He enjoyed the emergence of the real Ellie, who proved to be fun-loving, silly at times, but sincere and strong in her beliefs.

"I wanted to tell you again," he said, breaking the silence—he'd rather talk with her than catch fish, anyway. "I had a good time at Merriweather House the other night. Your family thought up a neat idea with those skits, and you were a great actress. You had me going several times."

"You weren't so bad yourself. At times I had to remind myself I hadn't jumped into a time machine and been transported back to the nineteenth century. Then later I remembered you did a year of drama in high school."

He shrugged. "Something Mom talked me into for an elective junior year."

"You miss her, don't you?"

"I'm glad she found another man to marry after Dad died, but yeah, I miss her. Trent's a good man, though. I'm happy for her."

When Ellie had heard of the heart attack that took his father, she'd approached Zak, then a junior in high school, and told him how sorry she was. She'd been one of the few of her clique to do so, and Zak hadn't forgotten. Beth was the only other girl who'd expressed sympathy toward him.

"And you decided to stay in Whiterock with your grandparents after your mother married and moved away?"

"Yeah, it was home, my friends were here, and I was nineteen and able to live on my own." He grew pensive. "It's funny.

When Dad first talked about moving to his hometown years ago, none of the family wanted to come to Whiterock, but once we got here and a better job opportunity arose, no one wanted to leave. Even though I wasn't born here, I feel this is where my roots are."

Ellie looked down at her jeans. "I'm sorry if my mom came across as cold toward you the other night."

Zak had noticed, and since Ellie brought up the subject, he decided to dig further. "I take it you were supposed to mingle with the tourists? I didn't mean to monopolize your time."

"Are you kidding? I wanted to be with you." She glanced away again. "We're not required to mingle. Sometimes I do; sometimes I don't. But that wasn't what was bothering Mother." She grew introspective, staring a long time at the splatters of water on her jeans-clad knee.

"Is it because of where I work?"

She winced, and he felt he'd figured it out.

"Nothing against you, and don't take it personal. She and Daddy both have ideas about what they want for my life."

"What do you want for your life, Ellie?"

Taken aback, she stared at him as if no one had ever asked her the question. He wondered if anyone had.

"What do I want?" she repeated aloud, uncertain. "I suppose what I want is to live my life the way I see fit to live it."

"A reasonable answer. And you can't because. . . ?" He let the words trail off, phrasing them as a question.

She sighed. "It's complicated, but it comes from being the only daughter of a dignitary. My parents gave my brothers more leeway to do as they pleased. Ed married a woman who wasn't Mother's first choice, and of course neither of my parents were a bit happy when Drake left Whiterock to become a race-car driver, so they doubled their efforts in their dreams concerning me. I understand that, and I know that deep down they do want me to be happy."

"Are you?"

His soft question made her pull her brows downward. "I'm tired of trying to live up to expectations I don't want to meet, but at the same time I love them and don't want to disappoint."

He nodded. "I feel the same way about Gramps. I had to draw an imaginary line when my way of living didn't mesh with what he thought I should do. I think sometimes it's hard for a parent or grandparent to realize their offspring has grown up and can make decisions on their own."

"Yes, but it's the fact that they don't think my decisions are worthy of what's right for me. It's not that I don't make decisions period, but that I don't make the ones they feel I should make. Again, it's complicated." She swung her hand out in an agitated, side-sweeping arc, almost hitting Zak in the arm. "Sorry."

He didn't want to push but felt frustrated because he saw how upset she'd become. "Give them time. They'll come around."

"Ha—you don't know my mother!" Her light chuckle didn't veil the somberness clouding her attitude.

"Maybe." He studied her face, and she turned her large brown eyes to his. "But then, you don't know me."

He leaned in to kiss her, a simple, tender kiss, and was surprised at how his heart gave a few quick thuds.

As he pulled back, her eyes opened wider. Afraid he might have moved too fast and embarrassed her, he thought about introducing a new subject, when her lips lifted in a gentle smile.

Encouraged, Zak leaned in close to kiss her again.

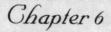

Chapter 6

No doubt about it. Ellie was in love with Zak.

Over the past four weeks, a few sporadic meetings turned into steady dating and phone calls every night, whether they'd just been together or not. In Zak, Ellie felt she'd found her missing half, and though their conversations never evolved into anything serious relationship-wise, she often found herself wondering, *What if?*

At first her mother did nothing when Ellie overcame her nervousness and mentioned she was seeing Zak. The objections Ellie expected didn't surface, but neither did the acceptance she'd hoped for. Then, two nights ago, her mother surprised Ellie by telling her to issue an invitation to Zak for dinner after Sunday's church service.

Ellie's father also said little, though she sensed that he seemed more anxious than upset. As the time came for Zak's arrival, Ellie's nerves grew taut, and her back tensed. When the doorbell rang, she almost jumped out of her skin and hurried to answer it before their housekeeper and cook, Melinda, could.

She opened the door and her heart to Zak's sunny smile, welcoming the gentle touch of his lips on hers. "Are you ready to brave the lions in their den?" she whispered in pretend dread. Ellie had already warned him that she didn't know what to expect. At least her mother wouldn't be able to find fault with Zak's appearance and his crisp white linen shirt and dark slacks, though Ellie loved him in anything he wore.

"That bad?" His brows rose.

"I wish I could reassure you, but the truth is I just don't know. They've barely said a word to me all day."

He squeezed her arm as he moved inside. "As long as I know you're on my side, I think I'll survive," he joked.

"I'm always on your side." Her reply was sincere.

On the surface, the introductions appeared to go well, though she felt tension freeze the air between her parents and Zak. On his part, he acted as affable as ever. Only Ellie recognized the calculating look her mother gave him.

Halfway through dinner, Ellie began to see a pattern and the reason for her mother's invitation—to show the huge disparity between Zak and Larry. Each time her mother mentioned Larry's name in a favorable way, Ellie clamped her teeth together to resist touting a bitter comment.

"So. . .Zak." Her mother said his name as if it were a newly discovered disease. "Do you plan on making your work at Mel's Garage your life's career?"

"Mother!" This time Ellie couldn't resist the quiet-but-appalled objection. The comment seemed polite, even curious, but Ellie sensed the venom trickling through the words.

Her mother blotted her lips with her napkin and replaced the cloth on her lap, paying no heed to Ellie.

"As a matter of fact," Zak said, his manner as easygoing and courteous as ever, "I do enjoy working on cars." He set down his glass of iced tea and leaned back in his chair. "I like any job where I can work with my hands, but I'm saving my money to get a degree in engineering."

"Really?" Disdain dripped from her mother's sugar-coated words. "So you plan on becoming. . .what?"

"To be honest, I'm not sure yet, or even if I'm going to get the chance to attend night school like I want. At this point, my grandfather needs me, so school's out of the question."

"And how is your grandfather?" This time no one could mistake the haughty condemnation of her mother's tone.

"Honey, would you please pass the corn bread?" Ellie's father spoke his first words since dinner had started. Ellie felt he might be exhibiting the peacemaking skills he'd displayed in matters of office and was trying to calm things before her mother ruffled the waters even more.

"He's quite the colorful character," Ellie's mother persisted, handing the corn bread over. "I'll never forget that incident months ago with the fountain in front of Merriweather House. And in the dead of winter, too."

Ellie had never been as embarrassed as at this moment. Her mother's horrid behavior merited no excuse. She scooted her chair away from the table and addressed Zak. "I promised Beth I'd drop by today, and she won't be home later. Will you drive me?"

"Nonsense." Her mother's word was sharp as she lifted a small ceramic hand bell and rang it. "We haven't had dessert."

Melinda shook her head as she retrieved the barely touched dinner plates of fried chicken, corn bread with cheese and onions, black-eyed peas, and collard greens. She brought apple crumb cake, but again Ellie could barely get the few bites she took past the blockage in her throat. Melinda's cooking was top-notch, but today, Ellie thought the crumbs might choke her.

Her mother toned down her attack, but Ellie's irritation at the mistreatment of Zak threatened to make her anger spew. Zak excused himself to go to the washroom. Before she said something she shouldn't, Ellie blotted her mouth and also excused herself, intending to snatch some fresh air and calm down. If Zak returned before she did, Ellie doubted her mother would rip Zak or his family's character apart while she was absent from the table, since Ellie felt the performance had been for her benefit alone.

On the porch, she allowed the sun to warm her head and the exposed skin of her arms and neck, breathing deeply of the balmy, magnolia-scented air. She sensed company and turned. Her father studied her. His hair, starting to silver, caught the sun's rays, but it was the light of concern in his dark eyes that Ellie noticed.

"How could she, Daddy?" Ellie asked, not giving him a chance to speak first.

Her father stepped up beside her, his gaze going past the weeping willows to the paved road in the distance. "She cares about you."

"That's no excuse to hurt Zak! She was downright rude."

"He didn't seem hurt."

"That's because he's too polite to say how he really feels, unlike Mother, who had no compunction whatsoever about showing her true feelings. I still can't believe she would do such a thing. She's never treated a guest so rudely before." Of course, Ellie had always met her parents' expectations and invited guests whom they considered appropriate, so her mother had never had any reason to act in such a manner.

Her father expelled a weary breath. "She could've been nicer, I agree. Sometimes it's hard to know how to respond."

Ellie shook her head in disbelief. "Would you treat your constituents like that? No, you wouldn't," she said, answering her own question. "You were unusually quiet today, but at least you were polite."

"Maybe, but the truth is, Princess, I'm as worried as your mother. The boy barely makes a living. He has no direction—no true course in life. He lives with his *grandfather*." He stressed the word as if that should mean something important.

"Daddy." She kept her voice level. "First off, Zak is a man, not a boy. He does just fine at the garage—maybe not at the level that parallels what you make for a living—but he's consistent, a good worker, and everyone at the garage depends on him. He's with his grandfather for his grandfather's benefit, not because he doesn't have another place to live. He told me he'd been living in an apartment before that."

"Princess." Her father's eyes were kind. "We just want you to have the best of everything. And neither your mother nor

I feel you'll have that with Zak."

"What you mean is you want me to have what *you* believe I should have, not what I myself want to have." She was sounding like a belligerent child and worked to stifle her ire.

"All parents wish the best for their child."

"That's all well and good, Daddy, but there comes a time when the baby bird grows up and must leave the nest."

His expression grew alarmed. "You're not leaving home, are you?"

"No." She laid a gentle hand on his shoulder. "But at times I feel as if my wings are clipped and I'll never fly. Be honest, did Nana and Granddad approve of you at first?"

"They took some convincing."

"Some convincing," Ellie repeated with a wry smile. "Mother once told me they forbade her to date you."

"That's neither here nor there. It was because they thought me a wealthy playboy out to run roughshod over her heart— quite the reverse of this situation." He pinched the bridge of his nose, a sign that he wasn't at all happy with where the conversation had headed. "I suppose all I'm trying to say, Princess, is try not to be so hard on your mother. She has good intentions; she just doesn't always know how to get across what she wants to say in the best manner."

Ellie pondered his words. "And how do you feel, Daddy? Do you really not like Zak?" She didn't see how anyone couldn't like Zak, but her father's opinion mattered. He had always been special to her.

He hesitated. "I wouldn't go so far as to say I dislike him.

He's a nice fellow, but he doesn't seem like what you need."

Ellie focused on the horizon. "You mean because he's not rich like your friends?"

"It has nothing to do with finances, though it would be a plus if he made enough to take care of someone else besides himself."

Before she could argue that he did make enough, her father raised his hand. "No, let me finish, since you asked. Like I said before, he has no direction. Does he have any personal beliefs that he staunchly supports? And if so, what are they?"

"He's a Christian, I know that."

"And what else? Any other beliefs or goals?"

Ellie mentally filled in the blanks. In other words, what cause did he have? How did he compare to Captain Merriweather, who seemed to be the shining example every man Ellie dated must live up to? Not that she'd had many dates in her life, but those boys she'd seen had all been judged by the same internal scoring mechanism of her parents' design. Each time her parents had silently evaluated Ellie's boyfriends, as they had Zak, Ellie could almost see the cogs in their brain revolving while they asked a list of comparison questions.

"Are you serious about him?" Her father asked when she didn't respond.

"We've dated over a month, and I've known him forever, but I really don't know how to answer that question."

"Have you talked about marriage?"

"No." Ellie's face warmed, not because they'd spoken of a future together, but because she'd found herself wishing Zak would.

Relief crossed her father's lined face. "Then I suggest you take it easy; settle back and don't jump into anything."

"Daddy, I'm hardly the type to jump." She laughed. "It takes me an hour to decide between outfits."

"That's why I'm not as concerned as your mother. You're smart, and I know you won't do anything foolish." He looked back at the door. "I suppose we should be returning before they send out a search party." He chuckled, but Ellie wished only to leave with Zak, not return for more of the same. "One more thing, Princess. I'd feel a lot better about the two of you dating if you left your options wide open."

Ellie sighed. "English please, Daddy. I'm not one of your committees."

"Why not go out with Larry once? Invite him to dinner. That would please your mother, and she might be better equipped to handle your spending time with Zak."

Ellie opened her mouth to disagree, then stopped. Actually, that might not be a bad idea. If she invited Larry to a family dinner, their conversation would make it clear they had nothing in common. Going out with Larry might be the catalyst needed to convince her mother once and for all that he wasn't the man for Ellie.

Zak had no idea what had happened.

The previous night with Melinda's help, Zak had found the white plush washroom with its marble sink and gold faucets. He'd let out a quiet whistle after closing the door. Even the first-floor washroom held a stamp of elegance. The two-story home and furnishings bore the imprint of the man who governed Whiterock, and the lavish decor undoubtedly was the work of his stylish wife.

Zak had dealt with parents of former dates before and had been under the proverbial microscope, so this was nothing new to him. He didn't feel as if he'd met their expectations, but that came as no surprise since he'd wondered all along if the mayor and his wife would be in favor of a blue-collar worker dating their only daughter.

Once Zak had returned to the table, Ellie had been quiet, and later when they were alone together as he drove her to Beth's house, she seemed distant, as though something grated on her mind. Which could explain why when he'd just phoned and asked her out Friday night, she told him she had other plans. She hadn't been unfriendly, had even mentioned Nicole and Jason's wedding Saturday and how she looked forward to seeing Zak then.

Andy walked up to the counter where Zak had just hung up the phone.

"I think I'll take my break now." Andy wiped his face with his bandanna. "Can you man the ship while I'm gone?"

Every day, Andy asked the same thing, and every day Zak gave the same answer. "Sure."

Ten minutes later, a blue BMW pulled up beside the self-serve pump. With a glance, Zak recognized Ellie's friends. The four remained inside the car, and for a moment, Zak wondered if they expected him to leave the cash register and pump the gas for them.

—The Princess and the Mechanic—

A girl with long auburn hair tumbled out from the back, obviously not happy to be the one chosen to do the dirty work. While she pumped, the other girls stepped out of the car and walked into the main office.

"Afternoon, ladies," Zak said.

Shelly gave a brief acknowledging motion of her head, while the other two greeted him with a slight smile and nod. Of the four, he knew that Beth and Cassandra were the nicest.

They moved toward a set of nearby shelves under the counter where Andy had candy and snacks available for sale. Tara came into the store and joined them, giving Zak an interested smile. Shelly shot her a dirty look, and Tara dropped her gaze to the snacks.

"I sure hope things work out for your cousin, Cassie," Shelly said to the girl, loudly enough so Zak could hear, too. "He's liked Ellie for some time, hasn't he? I think it's great that she's agreed to date him, and just think, if they do hit it off and get married, you two will be almost sisters."

The petite girl darted an uncomfortable look at Zak. "Well, that's really rushing it, Shelly. Their first date is only Friday night."

"Yes, but they're sooo perfect for each other. Ellie's father is the mayor, and Larry's father is a judge. Not to mention the fact that Ellie's and Larry's mothers have been friends since grade school." The brunette grabbed a sack of onion ring crisps and placed it on the counter.

His mood somber, Zak glanced at her, then rang up the purchases, including the full tank of gas, and told her the amount.

137

He knew exactly what she and her followers were doing—it didn't take a genius to realize they had every intention of letting Zak know Ellie's plans.

Shelly pulled out a twenty and a ten. "Keep the change."

With a haughty smile, she turned on her heel. The other girls followed like obedient rats to the Whiterock Piper and filed into the BMW.

Their immature high school theatrics didn't surprise Zak. He supposed every town contained those people who never grew up. What Zak questioned was how Ellie *really* felt. They'd grown close, and he wondered if she'd agreed to see Larry to get her mother off her back about dating him, since last week Ellie had told Zak her mother had not let up on that wish. He didn't like the idea of anyone dating Ellie but him, but Zak understood if that was Ellie's reasoning. She loved her parents and wanted to please them; at the same time, she wanted to plot her own life road map.

He admired her respect for and loyalty to her parents, but he felt frustrated by her disregard of and lack of commitment to her own personal feelings. Zak hoped she would find a way to reconcile both, because he didn't want to lose Ellie now that he'd found her.

Chapter 7

Dull. Drab. Gray.

Now Ellie understood the expression "as dull as dishwater." Even Larry's monochromatic beige clothes reflected his character. All he could talk about was his stellar position on the staff. Now that he'd passed the bar—on his first attempt, he emphasized more than once—and had become an attorney, it seemed all of Whiterock had been waiting for the day when he would join the law firm and take justice by the horns in his laudable efforts to save the community from the masterminds of crime. Never mind that the sum total of crime in their small town this past spring consisted of a stolen cow and a car full of youths out joyriding—Larry seemed to think he was the man to bring Whiterock's criminals to their knees.

"Ellen, dear." Her mother's voice snapped her from further unflattering thoughts. "Larry asked you a question."

"Oh?" She turned to look at him and noted that his eyes had narrowed. "Sorry, I guess my mind drifted off."

Her mother's eyes shot daggers. Instead of waiting for him

to repeat the question, Mother spoke. "He wondered if you would be free tomorrow."

"Oh, I'm sorry," she replied to Larry, though she felt a twinge at saying she was sorry when she really wasn't. "A friend of mine is getting married tomorrow."

"I don't mind going to a wedding."

"How lovely!" Her mother clapped her hands together with the grace of a well-bred lady. "Then that's settled."

"I. . .What?" Ellie wondered how her life could be manipulated in so few sentences.

"You really don't want to go to Nicole's wedding alone, do you, dear?" Her mother sounded sweet and concerned, but Ellie heard the resonant dongs of unwanted matchmaking.

"Actually, I do." She looked at Larry with an apologetic expression. "I just don't think it would be right to bring a guest at this late date, especially since the invitations were sent RSVP."

"Oh. Sure, I understand."

Yet during the rest of the dinner of sirloin steak, corn on the cob, and fried okra, Larry seemed to sulk. Ellie knew her mother composed the menus and wondered if steak for Larry and chicken for Zak had been another stab at the differences in their status.

Once the "date" was over, Ellie released a sigh of relief, side-stepping Larry's invitation for a future outing with the excuse that she would be busy getting ready for the special Fourth of July event Merriweather House would hold in a month. She spoke the truth but was grateful for the excuse.

"You could have at least tried to get along with him," her

mother said, following Ellie upstairs.

"We have nothing in common."

"You don't know that. You've only really spoken with the man one time."

Ellie spun around on the second-floor landing. "Mother, you heard what he said about my volunteer work. He called it a 'cute little pastime'—as if I were just engaging in a hobby to pass the time, and once bored, I'd drop it and flutter off to the next one. He doesn't see my work as important to me and to the community." But Zak did.

"Oh, phht!" Her mother waved away the words. "Such a small thing to complain about. What's important is that the two of you move in the same circles. With Larry, there would be no unpleasant surprises; you have the same friends, the same ambitions."

"Do we?" Ellie modulated her tone. "Mother, what if I have no desire to move in those circles? The parties and outings can be fun, but after a while, they grow tiresome."

"I cannot believe how selfish you are." Angry tears sparkled in her mother's eyes, shocking Ellie. "Have you forgotten this is an election year? No, of course you don't remember, because you spend all your time volunteering for other people and ignore your father's own campaign."

"That's not fair. I've spent hours upon hours working on mailings and phoning people, and I've always been there for his speeches and the publicity shots with family."

"How will it look for the mayor's daughter to date the local garage mechanic?" her mother persisted.

"Maybe like we're not prejudiced and consider everyone in Whiterock to be an equal?" Ellie countered.

"Not with his grandfather's reputation as the town drunk, it wouldn't! It'd kill any chance your father has of winning a second term."

Ellie felt her mother was exaggerating, but a hint of alarm curbed any comeback. As if seeing that she was gaining ground, her mother changed her tactics, and her expression grew softer.

"If you must see the boy, at least wait until after the election in the fall. Don't ruin your father's chances."

"I'd never do anything like that!"

"I know, dear. That's why I felt it important we talk now. Think about what I've said. He's worked so hard to get where he is, and one day he hopes to run for the state senate."

Ellie did think about it all night and on through Saturday. When she arrived at the Lakeview Rose Inn for Nikki and Jason's wedding, she couldn't force the issue from her mind.

An usher seated her on the bride's side, and a glance to her right showed her that Zak sat in a chair a row in front of her on the groom's side. He looked around and behind him, catching her eye, but before either of them could move or make contact, music pealed from the organ and all eyes turned toward the back.

Looking pretty in a light aqua dress, Shannon, as maid of honor, preceded her mother. Nikki was a vision in a knee-length, sleeveless ivory sheath, with her dark curls piled up in a breezy style atop her head. She wore no veil; only tiny white flowers wreathed her hair, reminding Ellie of springtime.

Ellie held her breath as she watched her friend walk down the elegant stairway and into the Rose Room and take her father's arm. She recalled Nikki's fear that she might fall on her face, stumble, or somehow otherwise embarrass herself. Though the woman was fifteen years her senior, Nikki and Ellie had hit it off upon meeting at Rosie's Diner, and Ellie even offered tips on how to deal with Nikki's daughter, Shannon, since Ellie was closer in age to the teenager. On the phone the day before, Nikki had joked with Ellie that if she did fall, the fashion-conscious "must have everything perfect" Shannon would probably kill her, and Ellie didn't doubt that one bit.

Ellie expelled a relieved breath as, without any mishaps, Nikki joined Jason before the minister. They made a good-looking couple—Jason with his brown hair curling at his nape in a rugged way, Nicole with her mischievous green eyes, as free-spirited as a gypsy.

As if a magnet drew her head around, Ellie looked in Zak's direction. She felt her breath lodge in her throat when she saw him looking over his shoulder at her. They exchanged smiles, but hers was bittersweet. She longed to be with him and knew she couldn't. Inside, her heart felt empty.

The reception took place outside on the deck that stretched across the back of the inn. Below, the lake sparkled silver. Sky blue and white ribbons fluttered in the breeze. Couples danced along the deck, and children played in the grass near the water.

Zak spotted Ellie beside the punch bowl. Beyond her, the happy bride and groom conversed with their guests. Ellie stood in a manner of expectation, and Zak couldn't help but get the impression that she waited for something. When she spotted him walking toward her, her eyes lit up, her shoulders relaxed, and he realized she'd been waiting for him.

"Hello," she whispered when he stood mere inches in front of her.

"Hello." She looked beautiful in a light blue dress with lace at the sleeves and neck. "I've missed you."

The yearning in her expression mirrored his words, though she didn't voice them. "I–I've been busy."

"Getting ready for the big Fourth of July event?"

"Mm-hm." She never broke eye contact. "You look great."

"So do you. Like the best eye candy ever made."

She gave a trembling smile, and Zak sensed something was wrong.

"Ellie?" He drew his brows together in confusion.

"Dance with me."

He chuckled. "I'm not that good."

"I don't care." She took his hand and led him to a corner of the deck that served as a dance floor.

He gathered her in his arms, enjoying her warmth and softness and the vanilla scent of her as she nestled against him. They made several slow turns in a circle to a popular love song. Closing his eyes, he buried his chin and cheek in her hair. "I've missed you so much," he whispered as the song came to an end. He pressed a kiss against her hair.

She tightened her hold around him before she pulled away. "I've enjoyed seeing you, Zak. I'd hoped for stolen moments like this all week—but I've got to go now. I can't stay."

Stolen moments? Can't stay? "Would you like to catch a movie tomorrow night? There's a good comedy at the Palace."

She shook her head, her eyes glistening with what looked like tears. "I can't."

"Some other time, then? I'm off Monday night."

"Oh, Zak. . .I can't see you anymore, at least not yet. Maybe. . ." This time he didn't doubt the tears pooling in her eyes as one escaped to roll down her cheek. "Maybe later. When everything's back to normal."

" 'Back to normal'?" He brushed the tear away. "Ellie, what are you talking about? What's wrong?"

"I can't talk about it, especially not here."

"Then we'll go somewhere else."

"No. Please. I just can't talk about it now. This was a mistake. I need time to think. I'm sorry."

"Ellie. . ."

"No, Zak." She took a step back and almost fell off the raised deck; he grabbed her arm before she could. Once she regained her balance, he continued to hold her.

"Please let me go."

He sensed her trembling words held a double meaning, and though the last thing he wanted was to see Ellie walk away from him, he knew he had no choice. He wouldn't force her to stay when she didn't want to.

He released her, his expression as bleak as his heart. The

message was clear; Ellie was breaking up with him.

She searched his face as if memorizing it and cupped his jaw for a few brief seconds. "Good-bye, Zak."

He watched her walk away, watched her move toward Nicole and Jason to exchange words, watched her hurry to the exit door. Before Ellie left, she gave one last glance toward Zak standing alone at the edge of the crowded floor.

Zak leaned back in his chair against the wall and closed his eyes. In the background he could hear the radio playing a popular song about Alabama. But today he could find nothing sweet or at home about his state. And today, the skies were gray, not blue. . . .

"Didn't your mama ever warn you not to tilt those things if you don't want to wind up with a busted head?" a nervous feminine voice asked in amusement.

His eyes flew open, and he righted the chair on all four legs. Surprised to see Beth, he waited.

She looked around the garage, then back at him as she tugged at the purse strap on her shoulder. "So this is how you spend your time when no one's watching? Catching up on your z's?"

"I'm guessing you've got a reason for being here?" Zak didn't feel like explaining that he was on his break. "So why not tell me and put us both out of our misery?"

Taken aback, Beth widened her eyes. "My, we're in a bad mood today." She shook her head. "You and Ellie both. She hasn't been herself for weeks. Mopes around and snaps at everyone."

Zak was sorry to hear that, but he'd given Ellie what she wanted, so he didn't understand her reason for having a foul temper. After a week of futile attempts to reach her by phone to try to find out what needed patching up between them, he'd given up and taken the hint.

"Mind if I sit down?" She darted an uncertain glance around the cluttered area.

He shrugged. "Sure, pull up a crate." He didn't feel like being courteous and offering her his chair. He hadn't asked for her company.

With a sigh, she grabbed a sturdy plastic box, dragging it closer. "Listen." She sat down. "This whole thing has been one major mistake."

"Ellie's and my relationship?"

"No. Your breakup."

"Excuse me?" Stunned to hear those words coming from one of Ellie's clique, he leaned closer.

"Ellie loves you. She told me so." Beth shook her head. "Every time I call, all she can do is talk about you."

"Which is why she broke up with me." Zak gave a curt nod. "That makes all the sense in the world."

"If you could cut the sarcasm and just listen a minute, please?"

Surprised by the unexpected attack, Zak released a breath and his irritation, realizing he was acting like a jerk. "Sorry."

"That's okay. I'd feel the same if I were in your shoes.

Actually, I have gone through something similar, so I do understand." Her face darkened a shade. "Do you love Ellie?"

"Yes."

Her brows arched. "That was fast. Don't want to think about your answer first?"

"I don't need to. It's all I've been thinking about for weeks."

"Yeah." She nodded as if battling a decision. Seeming to arrive at it, she speared him with her eyes. "I'll admit at first I wasn't in favor of you and Ellie together. I even warned her against it. A lifetime of being told that a certain thing is wrong—like a relationship between two classes of people—can sometimes blind a person to seeing just how right it is."

He lifted his eyebrows in curiosity, and she shook her head.

"What I'm trying to say is, don't let Ellie go. Fight for her. You two are so right for each other. I can see that when you're together. I believe God put you two together, and He doesn't care about status or who makes top dollar or silly things like that."

He remained quiet a moment. "Thanks, Beth. You're a good friend to Ellie, but that doesn't change the fact that she doesn't want to see me. She pretty much ignored me at church these past two Sundays."

"Only because she figures by doing so she's being loyal to her dad. It's election year, and her parents are exerting the pressure. But my dad ran a lot of the campaign, and he told me your dating Ellie shouldn't cause problems for the mayor in the polls.

You're well liked in Whiterock; it's no scandal for her to date you." She blushed again. "Um, I probably shouldn't have said that. Ellie wanted to spare your feelings. She said the breakup was bad enough."

"You talked to your dad about this?" The part about how Ellie's parents felt was no surprise, but Zak was a little staggered that Beth would try to help Ellie and him.

"Yeah, I did. Okay, so maybe I interfered where I had no right, but I don't want Ellie to make the same mistake I made in high school when I was immature and stupid and friends' opinions mattered more to me than what was real. Ellie's not like that; she never has been." Beth stood, preparing to go. "Anyway, I have an appointment. I just wanted to let you know I'm on your side now."

A scuffling of shoes behind a car waiting for repairs made her whip around, and Zak saw that his friend had returned with their lunch.

"Clint," Beth gasped. All color left her face as Zak's friend stepped the rest of the way into view. "How long have you been there?"

"Long enough." He regarded her, his dark eyes steady.

She whirled to face Zak. "You should've told me he was there!" Angry tears glistened in her eyes.

"I didn't hear Clint come back, but would it have made any difference?"

"I might not have spoken so freely." Clearly addled, she pulled her purse off her shoulder, fumbling for her car keys before she slipped it back in place. It slid down her arm and fell.

She snatched it up from the ground.

"Zak didn't know, Beth." Clint took a few steps forward. "It's my fault for eavesdropping."

"Yes, it is." She inhaled through her mouth and darted another look at Zak. "I have to go. I'll do my part with Ellie, but you do your part, too. Don't let her go, Zak. She needs you."

With a swift glance at Clint, she left the garage. Zak didn't see how she could walk so fast in her stiletto heels.

"She still likes you," he said as her little silver sports car roared away down the street.

Clint continued staring at the spot after the car vanished from sight. "Maybe." He turned to his friend. "But this isn't about me. It's about you. And I agree with Beth, though it about kills me to admit it. Ellie's good for you. I know I said to forget her when you first started dating, but it sounds like you both have turned into walking corpses these past weeks."

"Walking corpses?" Zak chuckled humorlessly. "Oh, come on. Give me a break! I haven't been that bad."

"Worse. At least corpses stay quiet and don't moan about girl troubles night and day."

"Not a problem. You won't hear another word from me on the subject."

Clint smiled. "That's what I'm hoping—because, buddy, I'm gonna help you win her back."

✉

Ellie kept the smile on her face only until she left the sunny reading room where she'd read aloud to Mrs. Friedman the continuing woes of Elizabeth Bennett. Ellie could relate to Elizabeth's feelings and longings to see Mr. Darcy, though their situations were reversed. As the book title indicated, pride and prejudice kept the couple from admitting their desire to be with each other. In her own world, loyalty and sacrifice kept Ellie silent regarding her love for Zak.

After a quick trip to the retirement center's cafeteria for a cup of strawberry lemonade to soothe her throat, dry from reading, she rounded a corner just as Zak exited the game room across the hall. She almost dropped the books and her cup. They stared in surprise at each other.

"Zak! What are you doing here?"

"I brought Gramps to his new home."

"His new home?"

He nodded. "Yeah. Last week when we first came to check out the place, he wasn't interested, but after a visit with some of his friends here, he changed his mind."

"Oh." Had Zak forgotten her Tuesday visits? Or was his bringing his grandfather at this time intentional?

"Confound it, woman!" His grandpa's voice sailed from the room Zak had just exited. "Why'd you play a club?"

"Because all I have in my hand are clubs," Mrs. Friedman answered.

"They why in tarnation didn't you *bid* clubs?"

"Don't you raise your voice to me, Charlie Blodgett. If you want me to continue as your bridge partner, you'd best learn to treat me with respect."

His gramps grumbled something indistinguishable, and

Zak grinned at Ellie. "Between those two, life here should be interesting."

Ellie couldn't help the giggle that rose, then realized that even talking to him might be seen as disloyalty.

"I have to go."

He nodded.

She wanted to stay. "How have you been?"

"All right." He shrugged. "I'm enrolling at night school next week."

"That's great. I'm glad you're getting to pursue your dreams."

"Not all of them."

His steady blue eyes conveyed his meaning, and a moment of uneasy silence passed between them. She shifted her books in her arms. "Are you getting an apartment now that your grandfather's moved?"

"Gramps wants me to stay and take care of his place."

"That's good. For both of you." She fidgeted again.

"How's Lacey doing?"

"Her parents took her home from the hospital two weeks ago. She can see well and talks about her 'new eyes' all the time."

"I'm glad it all worked out for her."

Ellie nodded. "So. . .will you be coming to the Fourth of July celebration at Merriweather House?"

"I think the whole town is turning out."

She let out a short laugh. "Probably. Daddy advertised the event far and wide. He even has some important associates visiting from Montgomery that day."

A retirement center employee walked by with a nod of

greeting, which they returned.

"I really should go." Ellie gave Zak a wistful smile. "Take care of yourself."

His grin was just as soft. "You, too."

Ellie forced herself to leave, wishing Zak would call her back, but knowing she couldn't go to him. He'd seemed at ease, while every time she came within view of him, she felt like a jumbled mass of nerves because she had to pretend a distance she didn't feel.

He had the ability to pull her to himself without saying a word, yet she felt abandoned by everyone, including Zak, which made no sense considering that she'd been the one to break up with him. All of her friends except Beth had doubled their efforts to convince her she'd made the right decision. And though it eased her pain to voice her agreement, her heart echoed with the hollow sound of denial.

God's ears seemed deaf, too, and she wondered why she wasn't getting any answers from Him. She had prayed about her dilemma every night. She didn't want to give up Zak, even for five months. Chances were good that during that time, he might find someone else. He was quite a catch in her opinion, and she didn't feel right about asking him to wait in the same limbo she'd put herself into. But neither did she want to cause harm to her father's lifetime career. She felt as if she stood balanced in the middle of a narrow teeter-totter—one party trying to pull her one way, the other a different way—while she tried to keep from tumbling and plummeting to the ground.

That night, Beth called her.

"You don't sound so good," Beth said after Ellie's cheerless hello.

Ellie sighed and stretched out on her bed. "What's to feel good about?"

A pause. "Still missing Zak?"

"I talked to him today, which only made things worse." Ellie smiled sadly at the memory. "It was wonderful to be with him again, even though we weren't really together, but it was terrible at the same time because we can't be together."

"So if you love him so much, why are you doing this?"

Ellie blinked in shock at Beth's unexpected response. "Why am I doing what?"

"Staying away from him. Ellie, if this is just about your dad, my dad told me your dating Zak won't harm the results of the election—just ask your dad if you don't believe me."

Beth was the only person Ellie had confided in. "But Mother said it could."

"No offense, Els. Your mom may be the mayor's wife, but she doesn't know all the ins and outs of politics. So if that's all that's keeping you away from Zak, don't let it."

Ellie tried to assimilate what Beth had just told her. "Why this sudden change of heart? You didn't want me with Zak, remember?"

"Yeah. About that. . ." Beth sounded contrite. "I was wrong, Ellie. You and Zak are obviously so right for each other. My advice is to ditch what Shelly and the others say—don't conform to everyone else's expectations, including your parents'—but instead, listen to your heart. Ask God to put the answer there."

"I have prayed." Ellie blew out a disgruntled breath. "Over and over again."

"But have you listened? By that I mean have you really gotten quiet, not asking for anything, but just listening to what God has to say?"

"And what if He tells me Zak isn't for me?" In that outburst, Ellie finally acknowledged the fear she'd shoved to the back of her mind. Because her parents hadn't approved of her relationship with Zak, she feared God wouldn't, either.

"Well, then it'll be for the best. You and I both know God's way is the only way you'll be happy. You aren't now, and you haven't been since you two broke up. So really, what have you got to lose? At least you'll know for sure."

Ellie knew Beth was right. Since breaking up with Zak, she'd felt that a part of her was missing. And if it wasn't in God's will for them to be together, then she would just have to trust Him to fill the hole, because she couldn't continue in this limbo anymore.

"Thanks, Beth. For the first time in weeks, I don't feel quite so hopeless."

"Great. Make me maid of honor at your wedding, and we'll call it even."

Ellie rolled her eyes and laughed. "You're rushing things a bit. Zak's never proposed. And I need to let God point me in the right direction—isn't that what you just advised?"

"Yeah, but I can't help but feel that'll be His answer."

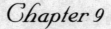

Chapter 9

Warm sunshine and a cool breeze heralded the Fourth of July. Ellie dressed in her costume and ate a quick breakfast of a blueberry muffin and apple juice, nervous and hopeful about what the day might bring. She hoped it would bring Zak.

This past week, she'd become quiet before God, spending quality time in His presence, asking Him to hold her again, as she'd told Lacey she did when worries came, and she felt now that He'd given her an answer. Last night she'd spoken with her father, and while he made it clear Zak wasn't his first choice, he assured her that Beth's father was right and that Ellie's seeing Zak wouldn't affect his chances in the upcoming election.

"You okay?" Beth came up beside where Ellie stood on the lawn. "You look great, by the way."

"Thanks." Ellie finished tying the wide green ribbon of her straw bonnet and dropped a cursory glance to her flouncy, green and white, nineteenth-century day dress. Later she would make a costume change for the interactive ball that would bring the townspeople into the midst of the gaiety, and fireworks would end the evening. Her family had planned the entire day for the town, the activities only partly constructed for publicity. A great deal of the reason for this holiday gala came from her father's love of history and pride in his Merriweather heritage.

No skits were planned—often on commemorative days they took part in reenacting battle scenes at a nearby field—but everyone with any connection to Merriweather House wore period clothing, including her father. All had been instructed to stay in character to add to the fun. Mark had called in with an apology that something had come up and he would arrive shortly before the ball. Ellie explained to anyone who asked that the captain was away on urgent business and should return before nightfall.

The spicy-sweet aroma of barbecued spare ribs carried through the air. Ellie noticed young Billy Reese and his friends sitting at one of the picnic tables and wolfing down as many ribs as they could in a monumental effort not to hurt the cook's feelings. Though she doubted they had to try too hard.

Noon came and went, but Ellie saw no sign of Zak. Discouraged, she strolled with Beth over the expansive green lawn, scanning the crowd of what probably amounted to a few hundred people.

"He'll be here," Beth assured.

"How do you know?" Ellie looked at her, sensing that her friend knew something she didn't.

Beth floundered a moment. "Because the garage is closed today. And since his grandfather came, I feel Zak'll be here, too."

Beth motioned to a shady spot where many of the retirement home residents gathered. Ellie walked over to greet them as her character, Luella Mae. She smiled to herself as she watched Charlie Blodgett hand a full plate and a glass of lemonade to Mrs. Friedman, then sit beside her wheelchair. Obviously, they'd worked out their differences.

"Good afternoon," Ellie said. "I'm delighted all of you could come to our party."

"Have you seen Zak?" Mr. Blodgett asked.

"No, sir, I haven't. I was hoping you could tell me where he is." She spoke before she thought.

Mr. Blodgett assessed her, then smiled. "Any particular reason?"

"No, no reason. I was just telling my friend that it's been awhile since he last visited."

"Hmph. You like my grandson, don't you?"

The sun beaming down through the aspens had nothing to do with the warmth that stole across her face. Ellie stepped out of character again. "Yes, sir, I do."

"Well now, I happen to know he thinks a great deal of you, too." He chuckled. "Yes, ma'am. A great deal."

His words addled her. "Excuse me. I need to see to the other guests. I hope you all enjoy yourselves today."

Ellie searched for Beth, who'd been right behind her. Her eyes widened when she saw her in the distance with Clint, engaged in serious discussion. Beth flipped open her cell phone, punched in a number, and talked to someone. As Ellie walked up, Beth ended the call and snapped her phone closed.

"Hi, Ellie." Beth acted as if she hadn't just talked to Ellie minutes ago.

"What's up?" Ellie drew her brows together and glanced at Clint, then at Beth again.

"Up? Nothing's up." Beth smiled.

"I need to go take care of that little problem." Clint looked at Beth, and Beth nodded. Ellie noticed how their expressions turned almost tender as they stared at each other. "I'll be back." He nodded to Ellie and walked off toward the parking area.

"Well!" Ellie exclaimed. "There's a shocker. So when did you two start seeing each other?"

Beth turned as pink as the roses in her sundress. "It's nothing like that. We're just friends."

"Really?" Ellie hid a satisfied smile, sure after what she'd just witnessed that more than friendship lay ahead for the two. But for herself, she wondered.

"Why so glum all of a sudden?"

"Zak didn't come, and now that I think of it, he never did say he would when I asked him."

"The day's still young." Beth hesitated. "I take it you did what I suggested?"

"You mean listen for God's answer?" At Beth's nod, Ellie went on. "Yes, I did. If it's not too late and if I didn't botch things up between us too badly, I'm going to ask Zak to give me a second chance. I love him so much, Beth. This is different than the idealistic schoolgirl crush I had years ago—this is the real thing."

"Oh, Ellie, I'm so glad." With one arm, Beth drew her close in a hug. "I'm convinced it'll all work out."

But two hours later with still no sign of Zak, doubts hammered at Ellie. She kept the smile on her face, greeting people as Luella Mae, helping to see that everyone was well fed and happy. But her own spirits sank.

She loosened her bonnet, letting it dangle down her back, and turned to seek solace in the house for a few minutes when she heard a horse's hoofbeats in the distance. She turned at the top of the porch stairs. The sun highlighted an approaching rider in a Confederate uniform sitting tall in the saddle. As the newcomer came closer, Ellie's mouth dropped open and her heart skipped. She moved to the edge of the stairs and grasped the white column.

Zak, resplendent in the uniform of a Civil War captain, dismounted with ease. His searching gaze found hers, and his lips lifted in a tender smile, which Ellie returned with one of her own. Instead of joining her, however, he walked to her right. Ellie gasped as Zak stopped in front of her father. Distinguished guests stood to one side, and Ellie's mother to his left. Ellie felt sure her mother's Kodak-moment expression matched her own bewildered one.

Zak smartly saluted. "Sir, with your permission, I've come to state my cause," he said, loudly enough so Ellie could hear.

She felt her stomach drop when she realized he was acting out the part of her ancestor, Captain Merriweather. A sense of unreality teased the euphoria flashing through her. In the constricting corset, she thought she might swoon. She inhaled slowly and released her breath.

"Proceed, Captain." His expression one of baffled curiosity, her father stayed in character.

Ellie darted a look around and realized by the crowd's pleased and expectant expressions that they thought this was just another skit. Swallowing hard, she moved closer on the porch.

"I realize you don't approve of me," Zak began, "and that we don't see eye to eye on various issues. But sir, I love your daughter, and I want to marry her."

Ellie barely heard the collective gasp from the crowd and became vaguely aware that many had turned to look at her. The blood drummed in her ears.

"Oh!" she heard a bystander exclaim. "They're doing the skit with Captain Orville Merriweather asking for Luella Mae's hand in marriage! I love this story!"

Zak removed his gray hat and held it in his white-gloved hands. "I don't have much, but all I have is hers. I can't give her a palace, but I can give her a home. I don't make enough to clothe her in expensive finery, but she'll never be in want, and I vow to you, sir, that I'll do all within my power to make her happy."

Tears of joy clouding her eyes, Ellie brought her fingers to her mouth. Those were not Captain Merriweather's reputed words. Any lingering smidgen of doubt that this might be a surprise skit fled her mind. Zak's words were genuine, as genuine as the answer that swept through her heart.

Feeling weightless, Ellie lifted her skirt and hurried down the porch stairs. The smiling crowd parted for her, still believing it was all an act. Zak turned upon hearing her approach. They shared a look, and in that look, Ellie's dream was realized.

"I love you, Ellie," Zak whispered so only she could hear.

She wrapped her hands around his arm, and he covered her hand with his glove.

She looked at her father. "This is what I want, Daddy."

Love and uncertainty creased his face. "Are you sure, Princess?" He moved closer, lowering his voice so the bystanders couldn't hear. "Have you given strong consideration to this matter and thought about what your future would be like with him? Don't get caught up in the moment."

Her mother moved to stand beside him. "Your father's right, Ellen. You need to think this through."

"Daddy, Mother, I have thought it through. For weeks. And what's more, I've prayed about it, too." She kept her voice low. "I'm prepared to face whatever may lay ahead, because I love Zak." She glanced at him, and he smiled.

"I just want you to be happy." Her mother didn't look pleased, but a quiet acceptance smoothed her features, and Ellie knew that last night her father had relieved her mother of any fears regarding the election.

"I know," Ellie reassured her. "I will be."

Her father nodded in resignation. "Very well, Princess, if this is what you really want." He looked up at Zak. "I was wrong about you. You have more backbone than I gave you credit for, and you do seem to know what you want from life."

"Yes, sir." Zak shifted his gaze to Ellie, and she felt she might swoon from the look in his eyes alone.

"Any man who has the courage to do what you just did,

Captain, is worthy of my daughter." Her father spoke so that everyone could hear, repeating the words Luella Mae's father spoke more than a century ago.

"Thank you. With your permission, sir?"

"What? Oh yes, of course. Proceed, Captain." Her father took her mother's arm and retreated to stand with the dignitaries. Ellie heard one of the men compliment them on the skit and hid a smile.

Zak placed his hat on his head and took Ellie's hands in his. "Ellie, with all that's happened, and when I found out how you really felt about me, I felt I should ask for your parents' consent first. I hope you don't mind."

"I don't mind, but how did you ever do all this?"

"With the help of good friends. They helped me pull it all together." Smiling, he glanced over her shoulder and inclined his head. She turned to see Beth and Clint standing close. Mark, in jeans and a T-shirt, stood behind them. All three of them waved.

"But now I want to make it official." Zak slipped his hand inside his pocket and withdrew a ring. Still holding her hand in his, he dropped to one knee. For her ears alone, he said the words she'd been waiting a lifetime to hear. "Ellen Sue Merriweather, will you do me the honor of becoming my wife?"

She felt as if she might float away. "Oh yes, Zak. Of course I will."

He slid the solitaire onto her finger. The diamond glistened in the sun, and Ellie loved the sweet simplicity of it. He stood, and she looked up into his deep blue eyes.

"Great show!" someone in the audience called out. "The best yet!" Applause and cheers filled the grounds.

Not looking away from each other, Zak and Ellie smiled. "Should we tell them?" he asked as the clapping continued.

"Not yet." She wrapped her arms around his neck. "Daddy can announce our engagement at the ball later. For now, let's just you and I indulge in the wonder that our story *will* become a happily ever after."

He chuckled. "Just think. I might've never asked you out if not for your visit to the garage months ago."

"Then I guess we have my bad driving skills to thank for us getting together."

He grinned. "That. . .and other things."

Other things?

Before she could ask what he meant, Zak lowered his head to hers, and the crowd went wild. Soon lost in the warmth of their kiss, Ellie forgot all else existed but him.

PAMELA GRIFFIN

Pamela juggles her time between writing, homeschooling her two sons, and engaging in all the activities that make a house a home. She fully gave her life to Christ in 1988, after a rebellious young adulthood, and owes the fact that she's still alive today to an all-loving and forgiving God and to a mother who steadfastly prayed and had faith that God could bring her wayward daughter 'home.' Pamela's main goal in writing Christian romance is to help and encourage those who do know the Lord and to plant a seed of hope in those who don't.

Matchmaker, Matchmaker

by Lisa Harris

Dedication

To my wonderful hubby and kids,
who encouraged me to follow my dreams,
and to my incredible crit buds.
I couldn't do it without you!

Trust in the LORD with all your heart
and lean not on your own understanding;
in all your ways acknowledge him,
and he will make your paths straight.
PROVERBS 3:5–6

Chapter 1

Samantha Kinsley jammed the toe of her boot against the rough shingles in an attempt to stop gravity from pulling her down the steep slope of the roof. But the last-ditch effort failed to end her fall; her legs buckled beneath her as she plunged over the edge of the ranch-style house.

Scrambling to find something to grab on to, Sam grasped the top of the gutter. Her feet swung toward the house, almost hitting the brick exterior with the tips of her heavy shoes. She could hear the popping sound of metal screws being yanked out of their holes.

This wasn't a good sign.

She'd been the one who had repaired the gutter last winter, and considering the quality of her fix-it skills, she was certain it would be only a matter of seconds before the entire gutter plummeted off the side of the house. Give her a yard to landscape any day over roof repairs. She could handle that. This situation was simply an unfortunate sign of where her refusal to hire a professional had left her—hanging in midair with nothing to break her fall but a patch of green grass and the ornate potted plant her father had given her last Christmas.

"Sam?"

"Garrett?"

Her high-pitched response sounded more like her younger sister, Mandy, but with her body practically airborne, what did one expect? She glanced down at the familiar face and tried to ignore the fact that she must look like a complete idiot. Here she was, hanging off the roof in her faded blue jeans—with holes in both knees, no less—her father's over-sized shirt, and not an ounce of makeup on her face. Even worse, she'd been so busy, she wasn't sure she'd remembered deodorant this morning. Of course, it wasn't as if Garrett would notice what she looked like. They'd been friends for-ever, and surely he'd seen her in just about every situation possible. Except this one.

He stood below, his fists on his hips. "What in the world are you doing up there?"

"What does it look like?" The slipping metal screws sounded like nails on a chalkboard as the gutter separated from the eaves. Did he actually think she was swinging from the roof for her own amusement?

Garrett reached to steady her legs. "Let go. I've got you."

"It's still too far down." She wasn't afraid of heights, but falling was a whole other phobia.

"I'll catch you, Sam. Trust me."

She did trust him. Didn't she? Before she could decide, she heard the chilling screech of grinding metal as the gutter let loose, and she landed in a heap on top of him.

"Ouch!" She rolled onto the grass and held her head, not sure if she'd bumped into him or hit it on the ceramic pot.

"Ouch is right." Garrett grabbed her wrists and helped to pull her into a sitting position before running the tips of his fingers across her forehead. "Are you okay?"

"I think so."

"You're probably going to have a goose egg, but other than that, it doesn't look too serious." He shoved the fallen gutter out of the way. "I never knew you had such a hard head."

"That's what my father always tells me." She rested her arms against her knees and tried to catch her breath. "Are you all right?"

He stared at her with a twinkle of amusement in his sky blue eyes. "I'd say the worst-case scenario would be a possible concussion—"

"Please." She punched him playfully in the arm, then struggled to stand, but her legs felt about as steady as a barometer in a thunderstorm.

"Slow down." He jumped up and grabbed her waist, not letting go until she'd found her equilibrium.

"I'm okay, really." She took a step back and leaned against the brick wall of the house, still feeling a bit breathless. "Thanks for breaking my fall."

"My pleasure." His familiar smile, the one that showed off identical dimples on each side of his face, suddenly evaporated into a solemn frown. "I do have one question to ask, though. What do you think you were doing up there on the roof?"

She brushed a patch of dirt off the front of her pants. "Loose shingles."

"Loose shingles? You risked your life for a loose shingle?"

" 'Risking my life' seems a bit. . .melodramatic, don't you think?"

He folded his arms across his chest, regarding her as if she were one of his delinquent parolees, and he was about to read her her rights. "Samantha, I've known you for, I don't know, my entire life, I suppose, but I have to tell you this has got to be the most stupid—"

"Stupid?" Her eyes widened in disbelief. She couldn't believe he'd actually used that word.

"Yes, stupid."

She could feel the edges of her temper begin to flare. "And as a man, if you'd been up there and happened to slip, what would that have been? An unfortunate accident? An—"

"Don't try to change the subject." He shoved his hands in his pockets. "I'm not trying to be chauvinistic here, but if you need help, then ask. Just because your dad's sick doesn't mean you have to do everything yourself."

Despite her irritation at him, she couldn't help but flash him a smile. "Why, Deputy Young, I do believe you have a heart, after all."

"Call me next time, okay?"

"Okay."

"Promise?"

She didn't really need his help, but if it would make him happy. . . "All right, I promise."

"And one more thing." He reached out and pulled a dried leaf from her hair. "The least you can do after my saving your life is to offer me a glass of milk and a couple of your double chocolate fudge brownies. I could smell them a mile away."

"With icing?"

"You bet."

"Then you're lucky. I just frosted a batch about twenty minutes ago." She laughed and started for the kitchen, wondering all the way there why she still felt so breathless.

Mandy sat on the padded window seat in her bedroom, recalling Sam's face as Garrett helped her up off the ground. Sam had been blushing, and she'd never seen her sister blush before. In fact, for as long as she could remember, she'd never seen Sam react in any romantic way toward the opposite sex. And to think that Garrett had been right under their noses all along.

The facts were simple. At twenty-five years old, Sam should get married. Between Sam running the family business, taking care of their dad, and helping her with school, Mandy had no doubt that her sister could use a husband. But in order for her to actually snag herself a man, she was going to need some help. And that's where Mandy would come in. Hadn't she been the leading factor in the recent romance and marriage of her uncle Riker to Chloe Simpson? She may have been only sixteen years old, but it was apparent God had chosen to gift her with the subtle skills of matchmaking.

A plan was already forming in her mind that would be the

perfect first step in transforming her sister's nonexistent love life. Mandy pulled a red envelope from her school backpack. Billy Reese and his delinquent friends had left the envelope sitting on the school lunch table after passing it around and laughing. It hadn't taken Mandy long to figure out that it was the poem Shannon had written, then tossed aside because she didn't like her handwriting. The love poem might not have been penned by the hand of Shakespeare, but that's what made it perfect. It would seem genuine. Nothing made a girl swoon more quickly than a gift from a secret admirer. And if Sam just happened to think that the poem was from Garrett. . .well, where was the harm in that?

Mandy smiled. Tomorrow she'd put step one into action, and from there, with a few discreet suggestions from her end, Cupid's arrow would do the rest.

Chapter 2

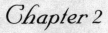

Sam finished wiping down the kitchen counter and decided she'd have to make another batch of brownies tomorrow. She'd planned to take some to Mr. Winters, whose wife had recently passed away. Instead, she'd sent Garrett home with a paper plate piled high with the rich dessert, positive they'd end up at the precinct. Nothing like supporting your local sheriff.

Garrett always seemed to manage to drop by on the days she found time to bake. It was as if he had a sixth sense that let him know the exact moment she pulled the hot pan out of the oven.

She wrung out the sponge in the sink, then went to collect the day's mail off the kitchen bar. Besides her brownies, she'd never considered herself to be a good cook. Quite the opposite, in fact. She just happened to have one recipe she'd managed to perfect. Beyond that, she found every excuse she could to order takeout and buy ready-made meals. Especially now that her dad, who normally did the cooking, was facing another two months of chemotherapy.

Snatching one of the last of the brownies off the plate, she spotted a red envelope on the dining room table where Garrett had been sitting. Strange. She didn't remember him having anything in his hands.

She picked up the envelope and slid out a folded piece of paper. Taking a big bite of the gooey chocolate, she started reading the enclosed poem:

> *If I could gather my dreams, one by one, and hold them inside my heart, they would reflect you.*
> *Bright as the stars on a midsummer's night, your smile chases the clouds away.*

"Your smile chases the clouds away"? Licking the frosting off her lips, Sam flipped the envelope over to see who the note was addressed to. It was blank. Strange.

> *Gentle as the rain that falls at midday, your voice reaches into my soul.*
> *Sweet as the wildflowers that sweep through the valley, your laugh sends quivers through my heart.*
> *In your eyes, I see my future.*

Sam stifled a laugh. Some Shakespearean wannabe had obviously missed the mark. Sam had majored in accounting in school, not English, but even she could tell that the poem had a bit of a juvenile ring to it. It must be from someone who had a crush on Mandy.

"What's that, sis?"

Sam started as Mandy entered the room and pressed the letter against her chest. "You scared me."

"Sorry. It was just an innocent question."

This was ridiculous. Why should she feel as if she'd been caught holding up the local five-and-dime? All she'd done was read the poem.

Sam handed it to her sister. "I think this is yours. You didn't tell me you had a secret admirer."

"A secret admirer?" Mandy took a look at the letter, chuckled, then promptly handed it back. "No way. It's not mine."

Sam lowered her brow. "Then who's it for? I suppose we can count out Dad. I can't see any of the older women at church writing something so. . .so lame."

Of course, stranger things had happened. Last week at church, Charlie Blodgett, Zak's grandfather, announced his engagement to Mrs. Friedman. And it wasn't as if Sam was opposed to love the second time around, but the man was eighty-three years old.

"You think this is lame?" Mandy clasped her hands together and pretended to swoon. "Having a secret admirer could never be lame, Sam. It's too romantic. Whoever wrote it obviously has a difficult time expressing himself, but give the guy a break. Maybe it's for you."

"For me?" Sam choked on the last of her brownie, barely avoiding spewing a glob of chocolate icing down the front of her shirt. "Right. You seem to have forgotten that I'm not in junior high where kids send dorky love notes to each other. Besides, the only person who's been here all day is Garrett. . . ."

Garrett?

The very thought was ludicrous. As if Garrett, the most handsome deputy sheriff in the whole county, would ever write a love poem and give it to her.

Sam cleared her throat. "As I said, the only person who's been here all day is Garrett, and while I've known Garrett my entire life, there's no way possible that he sees me as anything other than a good friend. Changing that would—I don't know—ruin everything."

She let out a sigh of relief. Of course that was true. It must be a childish prank of one of the neighbors. Besides, it wasn't as if it had her name on it. Thinking that Garrett had written the letter, even for a second, was preposterous. Simply impossible.

Mandy grabbed the last brownie off the plate and popped a bite into her mouth. "I've always thought Garrett was perfect for you."

"You what?" Sam saw the innocent look her sister gave her but didn't fall for it.

"Who knows?" Mandy said, taking another morsel. "What if he harbors feelings for you, but has, for whatever reason, never found a way to tell you?"

Sam tapped the letter against the palm of her hand. "And you think this is the way he would tell me?"

"Why not? Stranger things have happened. You remember the way Zak and Ellie finally got together, don't you?"

Sam laughed at the memory. "Zak dressed as Captain Orville Merriweather in a Civil War uniform. If that's possible, I suppose Garrett could. . ."

Garrett could what? Leave some childish letter on her dining room table for her to find, expressing his undying love for her? No. The entire conversation had gone too far.

"This discussion ends right here, Mandy." Sam slapped the envelope onto the table and headed upstairs to her room. "I'll call and order takeout from Rosie's Diner in an hour. We'll eat at six."

Sam didn't hear her sister's response. She was too focused on the letter she'd left on the dining room table. The whole situation stunk of foul play. By whom, though, she wasn't sure. If the letter wasn't for Mandy, then what other options were there?

She hurried up the wooden stairs to her room. Romance wasn't exactly her winning category in the game of life. Besides watching a romantic comedy at the theater once or twice a year, anything that had to do with two people speaking to each other like starry-eyed fools sounded like a foreign language to her.

One day she wanted a husband, kids, and a white picket fence, but somehow, life had gotten in the way. Her mother had died eight years ago, leaving Sam in charge of running the household, and with her father sick, he needed her help to run the family landscaping business.

Dating and falling in love had gotten lost between taking her dad to chemotherapy sessions, helping Mandy with her chemistry, and mulching Mrs. Sanders's garden. Marriage might make her life easier in some ways, and it would be nice to share her responsibilities with someone she loved, but was that the right motivation to marry?

Sam sat down cross-legged on the creamy thick carpet in her room and pulled out one of the dozen or so scrapbooks that lined the bottom shelf of her bookcase. The one she grabbed was from her sophomore year in high school. Page one featured a close-up of her and Garrett smiling at the camera. She cringed at the puffy hairdo she'd sported, but he looked just as handsome. Funny. She'd never thought before just how good looking he really was or how entwined her life had always been with Garrett's.

She flipped through pages of band practice, church camp, and football games. She'd been five the year they first met. From day one, when Michael Ramsey tried to steal her pimiento cheese sandwich, Garrett had been the one to defend her. And he'd been there for her ever since. She'd just never considered him to be marriage material. She ran her finger down the picture of the two of them holding the trophy after winning the state band competition. He played the drums, and she'd played the flute until she got braces.

Sam slammed the scrapbook closed with a thud. Garrett had always been. . .well. . .Garrett. Good friend, buddy, and pal.

And she didn't have any intention of changing things.

Garrett chewed the last bite of his brownie, then licked a glob of the icing off his finger. He'd known that Sam's brownies would be a hit at the Whiterock sheriff's department. Within five minutes, the staff had managed to wipe out the entire plate of goodies. He'd barely managed to snatch one for himself.

Even his boss had grabbed an extra-thick piece before saun-tering off to his glass-enclosed office with a smile on his face. Maybe Garrett should try hiring Sam on the side to keep them supplied with every chocolate lover's Achilles' heel. When the sheriff was happy, life was easier on all of them.

Carl Mann, Garrett's partner for the past two years, leaned back in his chair and propped his feet up on the desk. "Boy, that girl knows how to cook."

Garrett chuckled at the balding deputy's exuberance as he wolfed down his second piece. "Sam might make the best dou-ble chocolate brownies with icing south of the Mason-Dixon Line, but don't ask her to cook anything else."

"You're telling me that the creator of these can't cook?"

"Let's just say I've been friends with Sam since kindergarten and still avoid her contributions to the church potlucks unless they come in a fast-food bucket."

Carl reared back his head and let out a belly laugh. "So the brownies are just a fluke?"

"An unexplained scientific phenomenon." Garrett nodded slowly. "You're not interested, are you?"

"In Sam Kinsley?" Carl shrugged a shoulder. "She's a nice enough girl and all, but I've got to find myself a woman who can cook me up a blackened catfish and sweet potato pie for dinner every night like my grandmother did for my grandfather."

Garrett shook his head. "Then don't even go there, brother. You'd be eating from Rosie's Diner more often than not."

"Ouch." Carl took off his glasses and started cleaning them with the hem of his shirt. "Nothing against Rosie's Diner, of course, but a man just can't live on burgers and french fries. This man, anyway, needs regular, home-cooked fare. What about you?"

"What do I like to eat?"

"No. Sam Kinsley." Carl slid his glasses back on. "She's nice and single and—"

"A good friend." It was time to put a stop to this conversation right now. Garrett knew where Carl was going, and the last thing he wanted was ribbing from the guys over a misinterpreted conversation. "My friendship with Sam is something I don't plan to ruin by trying to make it into something more."

"Just remember that you're not getting any younger, man."

The whole idea was nuts. While he and Sam spent a lot of time together, he'd never thought of her as someone he would date. She was more like one of the guys. A last-minute bowling partner when Carl was sick. Someone to talk to when he had to handle a difficult case. Sam was just. . .well. . .Sam.

And he didn't have any intention of changing things.

Mandy sat on her pink bedspread across from her two best friends, Shannon and Poppy, and pulled out her notebook. After school today, she'd called an emergency meeting of the Whiterock Girls' Club. It was time to move on to step two of her latest matchmaking scheme, and she needed the girls' help if she was going to accomplish her objective. Quickly, she filled the girls in on the results of the planted love letter.

"That's so romantic," Poppy said.

"Totally," agreed Shannon.

Mandy held out her hand, knowing there was little time for small talk. "You both know we have our work cut out for us. We're going to have to convince Sam to turn in her blue jeans and oversize shirts for dresses and lipstick."

"The proper shade of lipstick, of course." Poppy was a fanatic when it came to wearing makeup properly. Her aunt sold Kerrie Jay cosmetics and had taught her niece everything she knew about the correct way to apply makeup.

"We have a lot of things to do, girls. So, Poppy, you'll be in charge of updating Sam's makeup. Shannon, you'll be in charge of her wardrobe."

"Check." Shannon took her assignments very seriously. She also was one of the best-dressed girls in the school and planned to go to design school after graduation.

Mandy scrawled a few official notes for the minutes. "I'll be in charge of hair. I'm thinking washable blond highlights will be perfect for Sam's fair complexion. Maybe a tint of strawberry would look nice, too."

Poppy and Shannon nodded in unison.

"Good. We'll each need to plan out our strategies. Step two will officially commence tomorrow after school." Mandy flipped the notebook shut, then held up the red envelope. "This poem has already played a role in Sam's life. It wouldn't hurt for Troy to find out how you feel about him, and this would definitely get his attention."

A blush crept up Poppy's face. "I'll think about it, but for now, let's stick to your sister."

Chapter 3

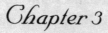

D o you need anything else, Dad?" Sam sat back down on the edge of her dad's bed and took his worn hand in hers. He'd shared this room with her mother for twenty years, and now, eight years after her death, it was still filled with the furniture, books, photos, and knickknacks from their marriage.

He gave his daughter a weak smile. "A new bill of health would be nice."

"With the doctor giving you a 95 percent chance of a complete recovery, I'd say you're about to get one." Sam reached out to fluff his pillows. "But I know you're bored to death. Have you enjoyed the laptop I borrowed from Garrett last week?"

Her father nodded. "It's been wonderful. I feel connected with the world again."

"The bronchitis is just a minor setback." She touched the edges of his gray hair, and she was struck by how much he'd aged in the past few weeks. He looked a full ten years older than his actual age of fifty-five.

"I'm just so tired," he told her. "I never meant to dump everything on you."

"Of course you didn't, but don't sound so defeated. We're going to beat this thing."

"I know, but the business—"

"You've forgotten that you trained me well. Everything's going fine. I promise."

"You'd tell me if that weren't the case."

Sam squeezed his hand. "Have I ever lied to you?"

Despite his pain, her father's eyes twinkled with a familiar mischievousness she rarely saw anymore. "You once told me that a gremlin had messed up your room so you didn't have to clean it."

"I was four." Sam chuckled and stood to leave. "You need to take a nap, but if you're nice, I'll bring you a brownie when you wake up."

"I'll be waiting." Her father stifled a yawn. "And Sam?"

Sam turned around in the doorway. "Yeah, Dad?"

"Thanks."

In the kitchen, Sam checked the timer on the oven, then sat down at the built-in desk to go over the week's receipts. Dad would be asleep soon, the brownies were in the oven, and Mandy would be home from school in a few minutes. While she knew she could never replace their mother, Sam was usually able to be here when her teenaged sister arrived home from school. She hoped it gave Mandy a feeling of stability.

Stability, though, was not something she was feeling today. Sam tapped the pen in the ledger and glanced down at the row of tiny hearts. She blinked her eyes twice. Surely she hadn't been the one to decorate the top of the ledger sheet with romantic artwork. She buried her head in her arms. If she wasn't careful, she'd be writing out things like "Garrett loves Samantha" and "Mrs. Garrett Young" in red ink. The whole thing was ludicrous.

She went to the half-empty fridge and rummaged through the shelves, coming up with nothing more than a handful of wilted grapes. She popped one into her mouth, frowned, then dumped the rest into the garbage. She should have time to go grocery shopping in the morning before the landscape shop opened at ten. Of course, probably the best thing would be to start shopping online as Garrett had suggested. She'd obviously come up short balancing the landscaping business, Mandy's schooling, and her father's illness.

Running her fingers through her hair, she tried to figure out what else had her feeling like a caged bird wanting escape. Surely it was something besides dreams of Garrett's pale blue eyes and bright smile that had kept her tossing and turning half the night.

She dug through the pantry and came up with a dozen stale crackers. If she was honest with herself, she had, at one point in her life, imagined what would happen if something beyond friendship developed between her and Garrett. It was the same summer her best friend, Joanna, dumped her longtime boy-friend. Joanna and Greg never spoke to each other again after the nasty breakup, and Sam decided it wasn't worth losing what she had with Garrett to change their relationship.

Sam munched on another cracker. Maybe it was the business. Taking over for her father had been stressful, but she had four competent workers who had been with them for the past ten years. They were like part of the family. She herself had worked for her father for almost that long and knew everything there was to know about landscaping, plants, and garden decor.

So what had her feeling so fidgety today?

Mandy entered the room with Shannon and Poppy in tow.

"Hi, girls. Do you want something to eat?" Sam paused at the refrigerator, remembering that she'd just thrown out or eaten the last of anything resembling a snack. "I can offer you a brownie in about ten minutes."

"Thanks, but we're not hungry." A gleam sparkled in Mandy's eyes.

It made Sam nervous.

She studied the three girls carefully, certain something was up. "So what's going on, girls? Lots of homework this afternoon?"

Poppy shook her head. "It's Friday."

"Big plans tonight, then?"

"You could say that." Mandy glanced at the other girls. "What about you, sis? Any big plans yourself?"

Sam laughed. "Let's see. I need to give my employees their paychecks, pop a frozen lasagna in the oven for dinner, and then I plan to take a bubble bath and finish reading P. T. Riley's latest mystery novel. . . ."

That's when Sam noticed the red envelope in Mandy's

hand. Poppy had a Kerrie Jay cosmetics bag, and Shannon had a stack of books. Sam craned her neck to read the cover of the one on top.

"*A Woman and Her Wardrobe?*" Sam frowned. "Sounds. . . interesting."

It was the red envelope that had her worried. Mandy had connected the envelope to Garrett, which gave her the sinking feeling that the girls were up to something. Something she wanted no part of.

Mandy cleared her throat. "Tonight you're ours, sis."

"Excuse me?" Sam's eyes widened in question.

"If Garrett is interested, you can't let him get away."

"I knew this had something to do with the poem!" Sam grabbed the envelope out of Mandy's hands and waved it in front of her face. "I told you this is not from Garrett."

"So?" Mandy snatched the envelope back and folded her arms across her chest. "Even if it's not, what do you have to lose?"

"She's right, Samantha." Shannon took a step forward, while Sam debated what kind of medieval torture she should inflict on the three girls if they came any closer.

Mandy tugged on the sleeve of Sam's shirt. "Look at what you're wearing, sis."

Sam forced herself to look down. Baggy yellow T-shirt. . . blue jeans. . .worn tennis shoes. . .

"Okay, girls, besides the fact that what I wear is comfortable, I happen to run a landscaping business. I can't exactly go tromping across the work site in high heels and a white two-piece suit."

The girls looked at each other, then back to her.

"Well, I can't!" Sam tried to sound forceful, but instead her voice cracked.

Mandy shook her head. "We know how hard you work, and we just want to help. Isn't it time you did something for yourself?"

Great. Now they were trying the "you're worth being beautiful" approach. It wasn't enough to say that she looked sloppy and tired and would never catch a man. . . .

Was that what they were saying?

"What did you have in mind?" Sam kept her voice as casual as possible on the off chance that they were right. It was a sad state when three teenagers had more of a social life than she did.

"A total and complete makeover." Mandy drew out her words like an announcer on television.

"A total makeover?" Sam didn't know if she should feel offended or grateful. At least they hadn't turned in her name to be featured on some reality show. . .or had they?

She glanced around the kitchen for the hidden cameras. Thankfully, nothing in the rooster decor seemed out of place.

Mandy laid a reassuring hand on Sam's shoulder. "I know it sounds drastic, but we're talking wardrobe, hair, and makeup."

"All of that?"

The girls drew in closer around her, and Sam struggled to take in another breath.

Poppy fingered a strand of Sam's long hair and nodded. "Like Mandy said, total and complete."

Sam wanted to escape, wondering if there was a way out of this. She was too busy with work and her father to worry about putting on makeup in the morning and donning the trendiest styles.

Mandy held up the red envelope and fluttered it in front of Sam's face.

She swallowed hard. If it were true, shouldn't she at least consider their suggestions?

Sam didn't remember actually agreeing to the girls' preposterous idea, but twenty minutes later, she sat in front of her mirror with a tube of Kerrie Jay's Rose Passion lipstick in her hand.

"Sam, you have some beautiful clothes." Shannon held up a vintage-looking skirt. "And I thought we'd have to go shopping."

Mandy nudged Shannon with her elbow. "We can still do that."

Shannon pulled out a lavender sundress. "Perfect."

Sam's stomach clenched. "Perfect for what?"

"Step three." Mandy just smiled.

Saturday morning, Garrett parked his 4x4 in the front lot of Kinsley Landscape Service, then stepped out into the warm fall air. He hoped Sam would be here today. He loved the suggestions she'd given him for his yard and hoped to talk to her about several other ideas he had if she wasn't too busy. A couple of his friends thought he was crazy to buy a house, but just because he hadn't found Ms. Right yet didn't mean he had to wait. Buying a house was an investment. If he ever did marry and his future wife hated the three-bedroom country house he'd bought, they could always sell it.

Stepping inside the store, he took in a deep breath of fresh-cut flowers. The family business had done especially well the past five years, and Garrett had no doubt that it was because of Sam's artistic touch. She'd helped to expand the business from a simple landscaping service to a nursery, garden center, and design corner.

Moving past a display of miniature gnomes, he left the air-conditioned shop for the outdoor nursery. These aisles were filled with a variety of fall flowers, and he was tempted to buy several more of the garden mums for his wraparound front porch. Sam had brought him a pot filled with the fall flowers as a housewarming gift, and it had become the first bright spot outside.

Gardening had never been his thing, but Sam's suggestions had made him excited about what he could do to his yard. Next thing he knew, he'd have a picket fence, a golden retriever, and two-point-five kids. He chuckled at the thought. He'd wait on the kids, but Carl's ridiculous comment yesterday regarding his age had gotten him thinking once again about dating, love. . . and marriage.

Still, twenty-five wasn't old, and until God showed him the right woman, he was content to stay in his comfort zone of singledom.

Wasn't he?

Rounding one of the aisles, he caught a whiff of jasmine

perfume and almost bumped into another customer.

"Excuse me."

Garrett glanced down and nodded briefly at the pretty blond wearing a sundress and high-heeled white sandals. He never could understand how women could walk in those man-made stilts.

Garrett shook his head and headed for the counter. With no sign of Sam around, he went up to the nearest salesperson to place an order for a truckload of topsoil.

Sam took a step backward and teetered on her heels. Placing a hand on the rim of a large terra-cotta pot, she recovered her balance but not her pride. She couldn't believe that Garrett had walked right by her and not even recognized her. Tears sprang up in her eyes. Why had she allowed Mandy to talk her into this? She glanced down at the lavender sundress she wore and her matching painted nails. It was a good thing Garrett hadn't noticed her. She would have been the laughingstock of the entire town if this had gotten out. She could see the head-line: LOCAL GARDENING GIRL TRIES TO SNAG MAN WITH A COMPLETE MAKEOVER AND FALLS FLAT ON HER FACE.

"I'd like to place an order for a truckload of dirt to be delivered this afternoon if possible. . . ."

Garrett's smooth voice played in the background as he talked to one of the salespersons. Garrett had bought a new house two months ago and was ready to landscape. He'd discussed with her the possibilities for the yard one Sunday afternoon, and she'd offered him her advice on where to place the trees and flower beds that he wanted.

She couldn't help but wonder if he had someone in mind to share the three-bedroom house with. She'd seen Garrett talking to Shelly in the singles' class at church last week. The problem with Shelly was that, though she dressed like a fashion model, she couldn't tell north from south. Knowing Garrett, a girl like Shelly would end up driving him crazy.

Garrett needed someone who would challenge him intellectually and make him laugh.

Like me?

Sam shook her head and pushed away the unwanted thought. She wasn't jealous of girls like Shelly. Far from it. She just wanted Garrett to be happy. Maybe Connie Masters. . .

Sam tried to take a step forward, but the heel of her left shoe was wedged in a crack in the pavement.

Great.

Bending down, she slid her foot out of the stuck sandal and tried to balance on one foot. But she wasn't used to the three-inch heel. She stood and grabbed for a nearby trellis, but it was already too late. Sam stifled a scream as she tumbled backward and landed inside a huge terra-cotta pot.

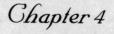

Chapter 4

I fell into a huge terra-cotta pot, girls." Sam had thrown her sandals across the kitchen floor and now sat rubbing her aching feet at the dining room table.

The only good thing about the entire situation was that no one had seen her in the embarrassing predicament as she'd struggled to hoist herself out of the pot. There was no doubt about it. It was time to put an end to this ridiculous charade. She and heels were like oil and water. They just weren't meant to be together.

Mandy set a plate of sandwiches and some potato chips on the table and sat down between Shannon and Poppy.

"I do appreciate your good intentions, but this isn't going to work." Sam grabbed a sandwich and took a bite of the tangy tuna fish. "When I go back to work in an hour, I'll be wearing my usual wardrobe of jeans and—"

"No!" The three girls' voices rang out in chorus.

Sam buried her face in her hands. At least she'd gone grocery shopping and had a pint of peanut brittle ice cream

194

waiting for her in the freezer that she could down for dessert.

"There's no way you're going back to jeans and Dad's oversize shirts." Mandy reached out and squeezed her hand. "You had a rough start, but that's no reason to throw away all the work we've put into you. You look beautiful today."

Pushing a strand of curled hair behind her ears, Sam frowned, still not convinced.

"She's right." Poppy nodded. "You do look beautiful."

Sam munched on a handful of chips. Besides a scuffed shoe and the need for a new coat of lipstick, she'd managed to survive the embarrassing situation, but that was beside the point. She couldn't run a landscaping business in heels and fancy clothes.

She shook her head resolutely. "I don't know. Even if Garrett managed to see me dressed like this, what if I fall on my face again—but in front of him this time?"

The phone rang, interrupting the conversation. Sam reached behind her to pick it up off the counter.

"Hello?"

"Hey, Sam, it's Garrett."

"Hi." Her voice squeaked, and Sam inwardly groaned. Without a doubt, Mandy's matchmaking scheme had gone way too far.

"Who is it?" Mandy tugged on her arm, and Sam got up from the table, trying to push her away.

Sam cleared her throat and spoke into the phone. "So what's up?"

"It's Garrett," Mandy said, leaning forward toward her friends. "You can tell by her voice."

A pair of giggles ensued.

"You cannot." Sam glared at the girls as she walked away, trying not to rip the phone off the wall.

"I can't what?" Garrett asked.

"Just a minute." Why hadn't she taken the time to update to a cordless? She covered the mouthpiece with her hand. "You can't tell who I'm talking to by my voice. Now be quiet for a minute."

She pulled her hand away. "Sorry about that. I'm just serving lunch to Mandy and some of her friends, and they're all a bit. . .exuberant today. You know how teenagers are."

Sam ignored the three amigas' piercing stares.

"No problem." Had Garrett's voice always been so smooth and deep? "I was at the shop today. Guess I missed you."

"Oh?" What could she say? The truth that he *had* seen her but thankfully had missed the ten o'clock show where she dove into a garden pot while wearing heels?

"Anyway, I'm sorry I missed you," he continued.

"Yeah. Me, too."

She mouthed, *He's sorry he missed me*, before she thought about what she was doing. Mandy and her friends leaned forward in unison.

Sam sat back down in her chair. Was he really sorry he missed her? And what did that mean exactly? Was it simply a conversation filler, or was there more meaning behind his words? On any other day, she wouldn't have given such a statement a second thought. But that was before the red envelope had arrived.

"So. . .did you need something?" She twirled the cord between her fingers.

"I just had a question."

Her eyes widened as she covered the mouthpiece. "He wants to ask me a question."

The girls all covered their mouths with their hands in an effort not to break the sound barrier with their screams.

Sam lifted the phone back to her ear.

"What was that noise?" Garrett asked.

"Nothing." Sam worked to sound casual.

Was he going to ask if she'd found his letter? Or maybe he was going straight for the punch and was going to invite her out on a date. Her stomach churned. She'd always felt completely natural and comfortable around Garrett. What if she'd been correct all those years ago and a date ruined the relationship they had? Maybe she should say no.

"So. . .what's the question?"

"It's about that small oak tree I bought."

The oak tree?

Sam forced herself to breathe. He hadn't called for a date, just a tree.

"What about it?"

The girls motioned for her to tell them what he asked, but she just shook her head.

"I'm not sure if the backyard is the best place for it," he began. "I'm thinking of the future, and it's going to grow to be a large part of the landscape. There's already a big tree to the left of the drive. What would you think about in the front yard, but on the other side of the house?"

"The front yard." Sam tapped her nails against the table. "Of course. That would be perfect."

Sam tried to swallow her disappointment. Had she really expected Garrett to ask her out on a date? Of course he wasn't going to. This was Garrett—her childhood friend and buddy, her bowling partner when Carl was sick, and the guy who always called her for free landscaping advice. Why ruin all of that?

"Sam? Are you still there?"

"Yeah, sorry. I just. . ." She blinked back a tear. "You definitely need to put it in the front. That will give the living room shade in the summer, as well."

"Well, thanks so much for the advice. I'll see you at church tomorrow."

"Great. At church tomorrow. Bye."

Sam hung up the phone with a loud clang.

"No date?" Mandy asked.

Sam shook her head and worked to swallow her disappointment. "Is that really what you all thought? Come on."

Poppy leaned her chair back on two legs. "That was a chicken call."

Shannon nodded. "I think you're absolutely right!"

"Do you really think so?" Mandy asked, munching on a chip.

"Without a doubt." Poppy's chair hit the ground with a thud. "Think of Ted."

"Ted." Mandy and Shannon spoke in unison and nodded in agreement.

"Who in the world is Ted, and what's a chicken call?" Sam asked.

Mandy grabbed another chip. "Last week, Ted Bunner called Poppy's older sister for a date, but he chickened out. Instead, he asked her if he could see her homework notes."

"And how do you know he ever intended to ask her out?" Sam rubbed her temples. This entire conversation was beginning to give her a headache.

"Two calls later," Poppy informed her, "Ted finally got up the nerve to ask her out."

"This happens a lot," said Mandy.

Sam waved her arms in front of her, wanting to put a stop to the entire line of conversation. "There is one thing you all seem to have forgotten. Garrett and I aren't in high school. Just like we don't pass notes in church anymore, we also don't make chicken calls."

Had she actually spoken that phrase aloud?

She gripped the edge of the round table between her fingers. "Garrett called because he had a landscaping question, not because he wanted to ask me out for ice cream. The letter is obviously not from him. I wouldn't be surprised at all if one of the boys in your class intended that letter to be for one of you."

She slapped the table for emphasis.

"How can you be sure?" Mandy asked.

"Because. . .because. . ." Could she be sure? Of course she could. But what if she was wrong? "I do admit I'm not completely sure it's not from Garrett, but—"

"Then we're not done here, are we?"

Sam sighed. She had to get back to work. There was the month-end inventory to finish, and she needed to make a list of what she had for this year's Christmas displays. . . .

"Promise us one week," Mandy said.

The other girls nodded in agreement.

"One week?" She folded her arms across her chest, wanting to put up a fight but feeling rather defeated. "I don't know."

"One week, Sam." Mandy's gaze held steady. "Remember, you have nothing to lose."

They'd obviously forgotten her dignity.

She mulled over the proposition. Surely one week wouldn't be that bad. She'd already landed in a flowerpot and managed to escape with her self-respect intact for the most part. Besides, in one short week, what else could go wrong?

Three hours later, Sam found out.

"You're going to have to make the delivery yourself, Ms. Kinsley."

Sam stared at Mary Jane, former employee of the month, and tried to imagine herself wearing a similar nose ring. She shook her head to erase the image. "Excuse me?"

"I know it's an inconvenience, but it's the last delivery of the day, and we're running behind. We close at five, you know."

No doubt, Mary Jane and the rest of her valued employees were anxious to go home. "You're telling me that Simon lost his glasses, and now he can't drive the delivery truck?"

"Yes, ma'am, and unfortunately, besides yourself, he's the only one licensed to drive the truck. He'll go with you, though, and unload the dirt."

Something smelled rotten.

She was afraid to ask the next question. "Where's the delivery going?"

Mary Jane checked her ledger. "It's to be delivered to a Mr. . . .a Mr. Garrett Young."

With Simon sitting beside her in the passenger seat, Sam fumed all the way down Azalea Street, toward the town center, and past the park. By the time she got to the road that led to Garrett's neighborhood, she was mad enough to spit nails. The truck rattled beneath her, and she had no doubt that she'd be numb by the time she arrived at 121 Sweet Gum Street.

Why hadn't she simply gone home and changed clothes? None of the employees had said anything about her drastic change in attire beyond the cashier's comment, "I didn't recognize you." Saying she had to change would have brought unwanted attention to herself, and she was determined to avoid any unnecessary explanations.

Now she'd have to face Garrett.

She pushed in the clutch to shift gears, and the truck jerked forward. The shoes made the job a nightmare. At least Simon was the silent type. If he did notice her bumbling attempts at being a lady while driving a dirt truck, he wasn't saying anything.

She took the last curve too fast.

Easing off the gas, she managed to turn the corner by just barely clipping the curb. One more block and she'd be there.

Even from this distance, she could see the newly planted flower beds in front of the house where Garrett now worked. He had a knack for landscaping. The splash of color in front of his long porch gave the house a feeling of home. A large oak tree grew beside the garage, its tall branches looking proud and majestic. The second one would add the needed balance.

Her heel caught in the floorboard.

"Garrett!"

She was still moving too fast. He couldn't hear her, and she couldn't stop.

"Brace yourself, Simon."

The truck jumped the curb. Sam yanked back her foot to free herself from the confining shoe, then slammed on the brake, while at the same time swerving to avoid Garrett and the house.

Instead, she hit the tree.

Chapter 5

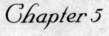

Garrett looked up in horror as the dump truck from Kinsley Landscape rammed into the tree at the side of his house. He jumped over the pile of dirt that slid out of the truck and onto his newly planted flower beds, then pulled open the truck door to make sure the driver was all right.

The door creaked open and a high-heeled shoe tumbled to the ground. Familiar blue eyes stared down at him.

"Sam?"

"Garrett." Sam shot him a half smile.

"Are you all right?"

"I think so." She turned to the passenger. "What about you, Simon?"

"I'm fine, Ms. Kinsley. I'll hop out and check on the damage to the truck."

Garrett reached up to help her out of the truck. She smelled like jasmine. Jasmine? Hadn't he caught a whiff of the same scent recently? He shook his head as his hands encircled her waist, and he lifted her to the ground. She felt so soft. . .and feminine. He must be imagining things. But there was no doubt about it. Samantha Kinsley was wearing a dress and high heels.

Once she was down on the ground, he waited until she seemed to have her equilibrium back before he let go. "What in the world are you doing driving a dump truck in high heels? You could have killed yourself."

Sam avoided his gaze. "I. . ."

"Well?" When she still didn't answer, he raised his arms in frustration. "Are you sure you're okay?"

"I think so." She pushed her hair out of her eyes and took a deep breath. "I'm just feeling a bit shook up."

Garrett brushed a smudge of dirt off her cheek. He'd never realized what beautiful blue eyes she had, or that there were subtle curves under her oversize shirts. Why hadn't he ever noticed before? Wide eyes. . .pink lips. . .curly blond hair. . .

He took a step back.

"You look. . ." For a moment he was speechless. "You look beautiful."

There was no other word to describe her. How could he have never noticed that Samantha, his old buddy and friend, was stunning?

"I know." Sam tugged on her dress. "I look ridiculous."

She must not have heard him. "Not at all. I said you look—"

"Don't think the truck suffered much damage," Simon said as he rounded the corner, interrupting them as he brushed off his jeans with his hands. "The back gate broke open with the impact, though, and dumped dirt on part of your flower garden."

"I noticed," Garrett mumbled, not taking his eyes off Sam.

Simon headed for the back of the truck. "Won't take me long to get things cleaned up and unloaded."

"Kinsley Landscape will take care of everything." Sam's voice was barely above a whisper.

Of that, he had no doubt, but at the moment he was more concerned for Sam's well-being. "Maybe I should take you to the hospital—"

"No, really. I'm fine." Still seemingly unsteady on her feet, she reached out and rested her hand on his arm for balance.

Was that his heart pounding?

Garrett cleared his throat. "Why don't you come inside, and I'll get you something to drink while Simon unloads the dirt."

Sam sat down on the brown leather couch, wishing she could hide behind it. Completely disappearing would be even better. Like taking a step through C. S. Lewis's magic wardrobe, she could vanish into another dimension. She'd rather be anywhere but in the same room with Garrett. Maybe it was just the shock of the accident, but she'd known from the beginning when Mandy talked her into this harebrained scheme that it more than likely would backfire on her. And sure enough, it had done just that.

While Garrett fetched her a drink from the kitchen, she glanced around the living area and tried to relax. Garrett had added a few touches since the singles' barbecue he had hosted a couple of weeks ago. A winter landscape hung behind the couch, and he'd bought two additional end tables, as well. While decorating wasn't really his thing, he'd done a good job

SWEET HOME *Alabama*

of making the home comfortable without making it look like a typical, sterile bachelor's pad.

The place needed a woman's touch. A colorful rug in the center of the room. . .burgundy curtains over the wooden blinds. . .a bowl of flowers on the back of the piano. . .a few candles. . .

Great.

Here she was, doing it again. Letting all of Mandy's and her friends' words of nonsense—and that crazy love poem—get her into trouble. She had no right imagining herself as such an intimate part of Garrett's life. No right remembering how handsome he'd been when he'd helped her down from the truck and put his arms around her. Thinking this way would ruin everything between them. She was his friend, not his wife.

Garrett's wife?

The thought sent a pleasant shiver of goose bumps down her arms. She'd never wanted their relationship to change, but suddenly she knew she wanted it to. Her fingers clutched the smooth edge of the couch. If only she wasn't afraid she might lose his friendship if she opened up her heart.

Her head jerked up at the sound of Garrett's boots as he crossed the parquet floor. He handed her a tall glass of strawberry lemonade, letting the tips of their fingers brush.

Her pulse skipped a beat.

"Thanks." She avoided his warm gaze. "You remembered my favorite."

"Of course I remembered. After twenty-odd years, I should know all your favorites. Strawberry lemonade, sloppy joes, and brownies with extra-thick chocolate frosting. . ."

She couldn't respond. She hoped he couldn't tell that her heart was about to explode at his presence. Touching her lips with the back of her hand, she hoped her lipstick hadn't smeared in the accident. She already knew she'd busted the heel of the shoe, which wasn't too great of a loss.

No. This was crazy.

She'd never thought twice about lipstick and shoes. And she'd never felt uncomfortable in front of Garrett. She shoved aside all of her ridiculous thoughts of marriage, wishing everything could go back to the way it had been. That she could tap her heels— okay, her feet—together and she'd end up at home in her tennis shoes and jeans with everything back to normal. But she knew things were never going to be the same between them again.

He sat down across from her in his recliner, then took a sip of his drink. "So, you seem to have been staying busy lately."

Sam gulped. "Why would you say that?"

"Well, first of all, you look sensational."

He thought she looked sensational? "I do?"

"Not that you didn't look good before, but you've always been, you know, Sam."

He held out his hand as if he knew he'd backpedaled right into a hole. "I mean. . . That didn't come out the way I intended. Being Sam is a good thing. A very good thing—"

"Forget it." She squeezed the glass between her fingers until she was certain it was going to crack under the pressure. "I'm just glad you like the new me. At least, I think I am."

She wasn't so sure the new her was going to be around much longer. Not if it continued to get her into so much trouble.

Garrett leaned back in his recliner and took a sip of his drink. "How's your father doing?"

"Better, I suppose." Sam twirled the ice in her glass. "The doctors say he's slowly improving, though the bronchitis has made his recovery much more difficult."

"You're good to him, Sam. Both to him and your sister." Sam could feel the heat rising in her cheeks as he continued. "You've been the force that has kept not only the business running, but your family together. I'm proud of you."

Personal compliments always made her uncomfortable, so she decided to shift the conversation away from herself. "You've been a great help yourself. He's been so bored, and the laptop you let him use has really been a blessing."

"Good." His broad smile tugged at her heart like a magnet. "I'm glad I could be of assistance."

Sam struggled to breathe. "I've been telling him for the past few years that we need a Web site. He's finally decided to listen to me and has started working on one."

"That should boost your business considerably."

"This is Whiterock." She managed a slight grin. "It's not like we have a lot of competition, but we'll see."

Neither of them spoke for the next few minutes. It was simply too awkward. How could a bit of makeup and heels suddenly seem to put such a huge barrier between them?

Sam stood up. "I need to use the. . .uh. . .the ladies' room."

He stood as she left the room, her bare feet sliding noiselessly against the floor. It was like a scene from one of Jane Austen's novels. As if they were both bowing to the stiff formalities of

Regency society, but neither of them knew exactly what the rules were anymore.

In the bathroom, she placed her hands on the counter and drew in a deep breath. *Breathe, Sam. It's just Garrett out there.*

If it was only Garrett out there, why did she feel like an awkward teenager hoping he would ask her to the prom? She looked into the mirror but wasn't sure whose face stared back at her. Reflected in the glass was someone she wanted to both keep and reject. She didn't want Garrett—or anyone else, for that matter—to change how he treated her simply because she'd changed her outward appearance.

I think I made a big mistake, Lord. All of a sudden, I don't know who I am anymore.

She heard voices coming from the living room. Simon must be finished. At least she wouldn't have to sit around anymore and pretend that things hadn't changed between her and Garrett.

Garrett watched as Sam, shoeless this time, backed out of the drive. He'd offered to run the truck back to the shop for her, but Sam had insisted she was fine. Something was different between them, though he wasn't sure exactly what. Sam had always been like a best friend to him. The sister he never had.

Today, though, he wasn't thinking of her as a sister.

He went back inside, trying to shake the feelings of confusion that had come over him. Sam wasn't the only one who had changed lately. The changes in him were just subtler. Buying a house. . .Carl constantly reminding him that he wasn't getting any younger. . .strong feelings of wanting to settle down and have a family, a wife.

Sam's image flashed before him.

He combed his fingers through his hair. He'd never really thought about Sam in that way. She was the one he'd always gone to for advice, and she'd never seemed to mind it when he asked her about another girl he was interested in. Maybe subconsciously, he'd always been afraid that if he pursued her romantically and things didn't work out between them, he'd lose her friendship. That was something he couldn't let happen—ever.

With the sun beginning to set, Garrett pulled a frozen dinner out of the freezer and popped it into the microwave. He was tired of the quiet. Night after night, he came home to an empty house. He'd thought about getting a dog, but Sam had cautioned him because of his workload. And she was right. He knew it wouldn't be fair to leave an active puppy locked up while he was gone much of the time.

Garrett walked back to the refrigerator and pulled off a picture of the two of them laughing into the camera. She'd taken it on his birthday and had given him a copy. She was pretty—even without makeup—and lipstick or not, her smile always lit up his world. The way she looked today only emphasized what she already had.

The microwave dinged, and the smell of roasted chicken filled the room. Only he wasn't hungry anymore. Running his finger across the picture, he knew suddenly that he'd never be able to look at Sam in the same way. Maybe it was finally time to risk taking things one step further.

We're going to be late for church if we don't hurry, Mandy." Sam picked up her brush off the bathroom counter and pulled it through her hair.

"Why are you in such a rush? We've got plenty of time." Mandy slammed the door to her room, then stepped into the bathroom. "Let me help you with your hair. You need a few more curls in the back."

Sam frowned. "I'm the one who should be helping you."

Obediently, Sam sat down on the padded stool at the vanity. Wasn't it only yesterday when Sam had fought Mandy to pull her hair into a ponytail for school each morning? Today her long black skirt and red sweater showed that she was no longer a little girl but a young woman.

Mandy sectioned off a strand of hair and clamped it in the curling iron. "You've spent your entire life helping others. Mom, Dad, me. . . It's time you start thinking about yourself for a change."

Sam couldn't help but chuckle. "Sounds a bit selfish as we're getting ready to head off to church."

"Which reminds me." Mandy opened the curling iron and let a curl fall out. "You never told me why you're in such a hurry to get there this morning."

"Ouch!" Sam winced as Mandy started brushing out a section in the back. "I'm making an announcement today about our service project, and I'm a bit nervous."

"You've never been nervous speaking in front of people."

"Today I am." Did she have to explain everything to her sister?

"It's Garrett, isn't it?"

Sam let out a long sigh. Talking to her sixteen-year-old sister about relationships seemed strange, but Mandy had always seemed more grown up than other kids her age—with the exception of coming up with this entire makeover idea.

She gnawed on the edge of her lip. "Why would you bring up Garrett?"

Mandy set the curling iron on the counter. "You can talk to me, sis. I'm not a kid. Face it: You're in love with him."

"I don't want to talk about it." Sam shook her head. "Everything's changed between us, and it's because of that dumb love poem and this crazy makeover idea."

"Are you sure?"

Sam wanted to scream. No, she wasn't sure. She wasn't sure about anything anymore. That was the problem. Part of her loved what she saw in the mirror, but the other part of her wanted to run away. It was the same part of her who wanted to run when she thought about what might be happening between her and Garrett.

He loves me, he loves me not. . . .

She didn't know what she wanted anymore.

She bit her nail, then quickly pulled the manicured finger away from her mouth. "I just don't know if this makeover was a good idea. Looks aren't everything."

"Of course they're not, but what's wrong with wrapping the gift in something beautiful?"

Sam spun around on the stool to face her sister. "So now I'm a package ready to be set out on display?"

"You know what I mean." Mandy twirled Sam back around and continued working. "You and Garrett have been friends forever, but he's always seen you as just that—a friend. He already knows everything there is to know about you, more or less. This makeover is like throwing a glass of cold water in his face. Something to get his attention so he realizes that he wants more to your relationship than a last-minute Friday night bowling partner. Get it?"

Do I?

"I suppose. . .but—"

"Absolutely no buts." Mandy put her arms around Sam and squeezed. "Come on. We're going to be late for church."

Garrett sat back in his seat and listened to Marvin Gillespie, the town mortician, make the announcements for the church's singles' class. After a lesson on how they should all find ways to connect as a part of God's family, he knew he shouldn't be so critical, but he couldn't help it.

Especially when he caught the man's toothy smile aimed at Sam.

Something boiled inside him. There was no way Sam would ever be interested in Marvin. First of all, the man had no inflection in his voice. It was totally monotone. Second, he dressed as if he were on his way to a funeral. Maybe it had to do with the fact that he spent most of his time with dead bodies. The whole idea gave him the creeps. Greased-back hair, a suit from the eighties, and a tie to match, no less. No wonder the man was thirty-six and still single.

Garrett pressed his head against the back wall. *I'm sorry, Lord. I know my thoughts haven't been pleasing to You this morning. I'm just having a hard time handling these new feelings toward Sam.*

Marvin sat down, and Sam took the podium to talk about this year's upcoming Christmas project. She smiled before addressing the crowd, and Garrett felt his knees tremble. She looked gorgeous today. Her hair fell against her shoulders in soft waves, and he loved the pink dress she wore.

"As most of you know," Sam began, "last year's toy drive was a huge success, so we've decided to do it again. This year, though, we feel as if we need to take things a step further. The committee believes that it isn't enough to simply write out a check for a new toy to give a child. We would like to see our class get involved in these children's lives so we can in turn show them Christ. The latest statistics I found show that unemployment for a rural town like Whiterock is over 6 percent. And instead of getting lower, the poverty rate has been climbing the past few years."

She paused briefly, making eye contact with a few people. "We'd like to host a Christmas-themed fun night and invite local families, especially those without a church home. We'll serve food and have plenty of activities for the kids. It will be up to each of us, then, to follow up individually with these families and try not only to get them connected to the church, but most importantly to help them find a better future in a relationship with Christ Jesus."

Beth Archer, sitting next to her boyfriend, Clint, raised her hand. "What specifically can we do to help out?"

"I'm glad you asked." Sam's smile broadened. "This week I've planted the idea in your heads. Next week we'll pass around a sign-up sheet. Just make note that if you don't sign up, the committee will be calling you personally."

Laughter broke out across the room. Garrett had forgotten how well Sam could handle a crowd.

"We'll have a number of ways to participate, from food preparation, to decorations, to follow-up visits with the families who come."

Darryl Meester, principal of Whiterock Christian School, raised his hand. "What about trying to get different businesses to sponsor the night financially?"

Sam nodded in agreement. "An excellent suggestion, Darryl. Anyone else?"

Garrett watched as Sam fielded a few more questions, then

took her seat across the room from him. Several people clapped and nodded. Her passion for God had been evident in her voice and challenged his own spiritual stance. Last year he'd bought several toys for the donation basket, then never thought of it again. Never once had he prayed for the children living in his own community who not only lacked gifts at Christmas, but also lacked many of the essentials year-round. This year he knew he wanted to get personally involved.

Once again, Sam had managed to touch his life in an unexpected way. Wasn't it what she'd always done? Managed to find ways to bring out the best in him in her own quiet and unassuming manner?

When the class was dismissed, he made his way across the room to speak to Sam, but Marvin beat him to it. Garrett stopped along the back wall of the room. He hadn't thought about having to deal with competition.

By now, most of the class had filed out of the room toward the auditorium. He didn't want to interrupt her conversation with Marvin, but he did want to talk to Sam about her announcement. Okay, so it was more than that. Her passion for God and others, her sense of business savvy, even her smile were things he'd spent his life taking for granted. And, he realized, he'd been taking their relationship for granted, too. He wanted to invite her out for coffee after he got off work tonight and discuss what was happening. Ask her if there was a chance something might develop between them.

Garrett's jaw tensed as Marvin took Sam's elbow and ushered her out of the room, deep in conversation with her. Garrett had missed his opportunity. She hadn't even noticed him waiting for her. He tried to swallow his disappointment. He had to be at work directly after services, and no doubt Marvin had plans to sit by her during the service. He'd try calling her later this evening, because it would be over his own dead body that he let Sam slip away from him.

✉

While she didn't like the thought that it was the new way she looked that was attracting attention her way, Sam couldn't deny the added confidence she felt. Throughout the morning she'd received compliments from both men and women on how nice she looked. She had to admit that she felt like a princess in the pink chiffon dress she wore with its slight flare at the hem. She'd been saving it for a special occasion, but Shannon had found it in the back of the closet and declared that the perfect occasion was church today.

Only one thing had dampened her day. The one person she wanted to talk to had been Garrett, and she never even had the chance to tell him good morning. Worship had been extra special, though, and for a while, she'd been able to push aside her heart's confusion over Garrett and focus only on her Savior.

After the service ended, Marvin stayed at her side as she made her way outside, chatting with different people on her way out.

"There's something I wanted to talk to you about," Marvin said once they were alone.

"Of course. What is it?"

Marvin clasped his hands behind him and leaned forward. "In private. I wondered if I could take you out for a quick bite to eat. It won't take long."

Sam hesitated, glancing around the parking lot that had begun to clear out. She had nothing against Marvin except that he was rather. . .well. . .dull. Typically, conversations with the man revolved around topics that had to do with the latest techniques of embalming or new funeral services he was now offering. Not exactly your normal dinner discussion.

Still, there wasn't really any reason to say no. Mandy had plans to spend the afternoon with her friends. Even their dad was expecting company. One of the men from church had volunteered to bring lunch and play a bit of chess with her father, an offer Sam had gratefully accepted.

She glanced back at Marvin and his toothy grin. It wasn't as if he was interested in her. He just needed some advice.

Mandy watched her sister cross the church parking lot and get into an older-model red sports car with Marvin Gillespie and cringed. Surely she hadn't gone to all this trouble for her sister to fall for the local mortician. Mandy rubbed her temples and willed her growing headache to go away. She scanned the thinning crowd for signs of Garrett, but he must have slipped out early. She'd noticed him sitting on the far side of the auditorium during worship but hadn't seen him since.

Maybe something had gone wrong yesterday. Sam had acted strange when she returned home from work last night and really hadn't told Mandy anything more this morning. A quick call to Mary Jane had confirmed that Sam had driven the truck out to Garrett's to make the delivery, though as hard as Mandy had tried, her sister had refused to tell her the details. Maybe she'd gone about things all wrong. Who said it had to be Garrett who fell for her sister? Mandy had seen several of the single men eyeing her sister after the service. If only it wasn't Marvin who'd seemingly won her attentions today.

No matter what the reason behind Sam's leaving with Marvin, one thing made Mandy refuse to give up. She had no doubt that Sam was in love with Garrett and was just as certain that Garrett was in love with Sam. They just obviously didn't know it yet. Pulling her sweater around her shoulders to block the wind, Mandy reentered the lobby in search of Poppy and Shannon. She wasn't sure what had managed to sidetrack her plans, but one thing was sure. It was time for another emergency meeting of the Whiterock Girls' Club.

Chapter 7

Garrett dialed Sam's number for the umpteenth time on his cell phone and waited for an answer. Pacing across his living room floor, he let it ring until the answering machine clicked on, then he flipped the phone shut. He'd already left a message on her cell phone, two at Kinsley Landscape, and one at her house.

Where was she?

He stopped in front of the fireplace and pressed his palm against the cold stone. He was being ridiculous. Sam was a grown woman, and he certainly had no say in what she did. That was the problem. He wanted to be a part of her life. He knew that now. He'd spent the past twenty-four hours working overtime and thinking about the one person he'd known his entire life. And he realized that she was the one person he wanted to spend the rest of his life with.

He tried Sam's home number again. This time it was busy. At least someone was home. Maybe she was talking on the phone. He knew that she kept in close touch with Joanna, her friend from high school, and no doubt their conversations ran long.

Garrett jumped into his car and headed for Sam's. Switching on his headlights, he drove past their old high school. The park where they'd celebrated birthdays and played baseball in the summer. The supermarket where they'd both worked the summer before their senior year. Why did everything remind him of her?

As an only child, he'd always enjoyed interaction with Sam's family. His parents divorced when he was nine, and the Kinsley family had always seemed so. . .normal. Sam's mother had been a fantastic cook, and he'd stayed for dinner every time he could manage to finagle an invitation. After Mrs. Kinsley's death, things began to change. Sam rarely had time to hang out, and even her involvement with the youth group dropped. Still, Sam had always been there for him whenever he needed a good laugh or someone to talk to.

How had he managed to miss love when it had been standing right in front of him?

Five minutes later, he pulled into their drive. Mandy answered the door, looking as if she'd been crying.

His protective instincts kicked in. "What's wrong, Mandy?"

Her head rested against the door frame. "It's Sam. I don't know what she's gone and done—"

"What do you mean?" Garrett ushered Mandy into the living room and sat her down on the floral couch.

"She—she went off with Marvin earlier this afternoon. I didn't really get to talk to her, but—" Mandy hiccupped, and the tears started flowing again. "I think—I think I matched her up with the wrong man."

Garrett leaned forward. "What do you mean you matched her up with the wrong man?"

She started sobbing again, and all Garrett knew to do was pull her close and wait for her to settle down. After a minute had passed, he tried talking to her again.

"Mandy, I want you to take a deep breath and count to five. You've got to get control of yourself."

"I—I can't." She wiped away the tears with the back of her hand.

"Yes, you can." Garrett took her by her shoulders and looked her in the eye. "I want you to count to five, then tell me what happened."

"Okay. I–I'll try." Mandy took a deep breath and hiccupped again. "One. . .two. . .three. . .four. . .five. . . I think Sam's run off to elope with Marvin!"

Marvin and Sam? He blinked his eyes. Surely he hadn't heard her correctly. "What did you say?"

"Sam and Marvin. I think they've gone to Montgomery to elope."

He'd heard the same words twice and still couldn't believe what Mandy was saying. He resisted the urge to hurl his cell phone across the room. The very idea of Sam falling for Marvin was impossible. And Sam would never agree to marry that man.

Garrett worked to control his temper. "Why do you think Sam's gone off to elope? I need to know exactly what has happened."

She took another deep breath and seemed to get better control of her emotions. "Yesterday after church, Sam went out with Marvin for lunch. I was surprised that she'd agreed to go. I never thought I'd have to worry about her falling for a mortician."

"I'm sure there are plenty of happily married morticians in this country." Garrett stopped. What was he doing defending the man? "What happened next?"

"When I got home from school today, Sam was dressed up in her best white suit and acting really weird."

"Weird how?"

She shrugged a shoulder. "I don't know. Nervous and excited at the same time. Like she'd made some sort of big decision."

"A decision that had to do with Marvin?"

"Maybe." Mandy played with the fringes of a green throw pillow while she spoke.

"Did she say anything specific about her plans with him?"

Mandy shook her head. "She just asked me if I minded taking care of Dad tonight. I said of course not. She does so much for him. Sam even had dinner in the oven for us but told me not to wait up for her. Now I'm afraid she's not coming home—"

"Wait a minute." Garrett worked to put the facts together. "Sam and Marvin went out on a date to dinner tonight or to a show. That still doesn't explain the hysterics and why you think they plan to elope."

"This is the number she left." Mandy pulled a business card out of her back pocket and handed it to him.

Garrett felt the veins in his neck bulge. "This is for a hotel in Montgomery."

"I know. I went onto the Internet, and there's no waiting

period for a marriage license in Alabama. They could have gotten one today."

He took a deep breath, reminding himself that Mandy was a sixteen-year-old with an active imagination. Sam wasn't the kind of person who did something without thinking it through. She'd always had her head on straight. Running off and eloping simply wasn't something Sam would do. Especially with Marvin.

Garrett shook his head. "Sam would never run off and elope with Marvin. That's impossible."

"Not really. Think about it." Mandy wiped her cheeks with the back of her hand. "I know Sam puts up a good front, but she's under a lot of stress. Between caring for Dad, running the business, and me. . .well, maybe she thought that marrying Marvin would help. You know. She'd have someone else to help her run Kinsley Landscape."

Surely Sam wasn't that desperate. If anything, marrying Marvin would complicate life for Sam, not make it easier. Knowing Marvin and his lack of people skills, Sam would end up being forced to help run both businesses. And there was another important issue. Garrett loved Sam. Marvin could never love her the way he did.

"There's something else I need to tell you." Mandy lowered her head. "And it's all my fault."

Garrett didn't like where the conversation was going. "What do you mean?"

"If I hadn't tricked her into thinking you'd sent her that stupid love poem—"

"Wait." Garrett combed his fingers through his hair, more confused than ever. "What are you talking about, Mandy?"

Mandy pulled hard on the pillow tassel. "I found a love poem at school that one of my friends wrote for an assignment, and it gave me an idea. I'd seen the way Sam looked at you and even the way you looked at her and figured the two of you just needed a push in the right direction. Instead, I pushed her straight into Marvin's arms."

Mandy started crying again. "All I wanted to do was—was something nice for her. She takes care of Dad, and me, and the business, but she never takes time for herself. I got her thinking about love and marriage, and how she needed someone. . ."

Garrett leaned forward. "Mandy, I'm going to ask you something, and I expect the truth. Is what you're telling me right now just another part of this—this matchmaking scheme of yours?"

"It's not. I promise." This time she looked him straight in the eye. "You're the one she loves, Garrett. She's just confused. You've got to stop them. She loves you."

"And I love her, too." The words came out before Garrett could stop them. He stood up to leave but stopped when he saw Sam's dad resting against the door frame that led from the hallway.

Mandy rushed to his side. "What are you doing out of bed, Dad?"

Garrett helped Mr. Kinsley to the couch, where he struggled to sit down. "I may be old and sick, but I'm not deaf."

Garrett took a seat across from him. "I'm sorry if we upset you, Mr. Kinsley—"

"I'll only be upset if you're too late."

"Too late?"

Mr. Kinsley's hand shook as he set it in his lap. "I'm sure that Marvin Gillespie is a decent man, but I know my daughter, and he's not the man for her."

Mandy reached out and squeezed her father's hand. "Garrett loves Sam, Dad."

"I know. I heard him." Mr. Kinsley reached into his pocket and pulled out a small cardboard box. "Garrett, I've known your family since you were younger than Mandy. It's a shame I didn't have the courage to do what Mandy's done and put a fire under the two of you. I've watched you and Sam together these past years, wondering when your friendship would finally take a turn and blossom into love. I suppose you've been afraid that falling in love might change what the two of you have, but there's nothing wrong about a married couple being best friends. I reckon that's the way the good Lord intended things."

Garrett sat in silence while Mr. Kinsley caught his breath before continuing and wondered how the older man could have pegged the situation so precisely.

The older man's eyes reflected the pain in his body, but his voice was still strong. "I was married to Sam and Mandy's mother nearly twenty years before she passed away, and she was the best friend I ever had. Do you truly love my daughter, Garrett?"

Garrett had no doubts anymore. "Yes, I do, Mr. Kinsley. I'm just sorry I didn't realize how much until now."

Mr. Kinsley chuckled softly. "I might not get around the

way I used to, but I have a feeling she feels the same way about you. She just might not know it yet."

"I hope you're right, sir."

"I want you to have something." Mr. Kinsley opened the small box and held up a solitaire diamond ring. "This was my wife's engagement ring. I always wanted it to be a family heirloom, and I can't think of a more worthy young man to give it to my daughter when the time is right."

Garrett had friends who had asked their future fathers-in-law for permission to marry their daughters, but he'd never heard of a situation in which the father said something to his daughter's suitor first.

All he could do now was pray that Mandy was wrong and that he wasn't too late.

✉

Sam stood in the entrance of the hotel, wondering what she'd done. She'd never been one to make rash decisions. In fact, decision making had never been her strong suit. Yet here she stood with Marvin Gillespie at her side. Something she'd never imagined until yesterday, but something in Marvin's voice and the way he'd looked at her had persuaded her.

The truth was, she hadn't found Marvin's company nearly as dull as she'd expected. Once she managed to sway the conversation away from embalming fluid safety and other such topics, she'd actually found him to be fairly pleasant. No doubt, he'd gotten used to people seeing him as a bit of an odd duck, considering his occupation but, in her opinion, a mortician fulfilled a need that everyone would have someday, including herself.

But now wasn't the time to think about death—or Garrett.

While she was having a hard time not thinking about him, she'd come to the conclusion that romance between her and Garrett would never work. She was better off simply guarding their friendship. Look what had happened when she'd tried to get Garrett to fall for her. The results had been disastrous. All she'd ended up doing was making a fool of herself, and she was lucky she hadn't done anything to the truck besides damage the bumper—not to mention Garrett and his property. No. Hurting their friendship was something she would never do.

Marvin offered her his arm, and for a moment, she stared at the dizzying pattern of the hotel carpet. "You're not having second thoughts, are you, Sam?"

"Of course I'm not." Sam turned to Marvin and smiled. "Let's go."

Chapter 8

Garrett checked the speedometer on the dashboard and pushed his foot against the accelerator. It was already past five. If Mandy was right, he didn't have any time to lose.

The radio played "Lovin' You," and he punched the OFF button. A sappy love song was the last thing he wanted to hear right now. If Sam really had tied the knot. . .

The thought made him nauseous. The diamond engagement ring felt as if it were burning a hole in his front pocket. He still couldn't believe that Mr. Kinsley had given him the ring, but Garrett's fear was that it was too late. And if it was too late, he didn't know if he'd ever be able to forgive himself.

Red lights flashed in his rearview mirror. Great. With his luck, it would be someone he knew from the department.

Sure enough, Carl tapped on the window seconds later.

"Now this is interesting." Carl rested his arm against the roof. "What's the problem, Garrett? Late for your own wedding?"

On any other day, Garrett would have had a quick comeback,

but this wasn't any other day. This might be his last chance to tell Sam he loved her. "Actually, I'm trying to stop a wedding."

"You're kidding, right?"

"Not at all. It's Sam—"

Carl's face lit up with surprise. "Sam's getting married?"

"It's a long story. But I've finally realized that I have feelings for Sam—"

"I knew it!"

Garrett didn't have time to spell out the entire situation. Nor did he really want to. "I'm in a hurry, Carl. Can I go?"

"You were going sixty-five in a fifty-five-mile-an-hour zone. Just because you're one of the good guys doesn't mean I can ignore—"

"Marvin and Sam are on their way to Montgomery to elope." Garrett had had enough. "I've got to stop them."

"Marvin Gillespie? You've got to be kidding." Carl leaned into the driver's seat. "You've been drinking, haven't you?"

Garrett held up his hands. "Don't be ridiculous."

"Step out of the car, Garrett."

"What?"

"You heard me. Step out of the car."

Garrett complied, slamming the door. Their boss would hear about this.

"Now you listen to me." Carl pointed his finger in Garrett's face. "I know you've been under a lot of pressure at work. We all are. But speeding across the state trying to catch some runaway bride isn't the answer. You'll only get yourself killed."

"It's Sam."

Carl took a step back. "Are you in love with her?"

"That's what I've been trying to tell you." Garrett's hands balled into fists at his sides. If he knew it wouldn't land him in a cell, he'd take a swing at his partner.

Garrett pulled the ring out of his pocket and showed it to Carl. The pear-shaped diamond caught the light.

"Sam's father gave this to me. I'm going to ask her to marry me—if she hasn't already tied the knot with Marvin."

"Being in love isn't an excuse to break the law." Carl seemed to be considering Garrett's admission. "And you'll definitely lose your chances with her if you end up dead somewhere on the side of the highway."

"I need to go, Carl."

"Promise to stay under the speed limit, and I might cut you a break." Carl tapped the roof of the vehicle. "Be smart, man, and go get her."

Garrett merged back onto the highway, this time making sure he didn't exceed the speed limit. Carl was right. Taking foolish risks would never accomplish anything.

Gripping the steering wheel, he tried to make sense of everything that Mandy had told him. Something was wrong with the entire situation. He just couldn't see Sam eloping with anyone, let alone Marvin. On the other hand, Mandy had been right. Sam was under a lot of stress. He tried to stop by as often as he could and help with anything that needed to be fixed or replaced, but part of the problem was that Sam was stubborn and didn't want to be a burden on anyone.

Had she decided she couldn't do it alone anymore? What

had Marvin promised her? Financial help? Emotional support? Love?

He slammed his fist against the steering wheel, setting off the horn. He was the one who loved Sam. While part of him still searched for another explanation, he knew he couldn't do anything until he got to the hotel.

The sun had begun to dip beneath the horizon. He was losing time. A sign for the hotel flashed by. Three miles. He could be there in less than five minutes. But would five minutes be too late?

Four minutes later, he pulled into the hotel parking lot. His eyes scanned the parking lot for Marvin's car until he found a red sports car on the east side of the lot.

Painted on the back window in shaving cream were the words *Just Married*.

Mandy paced across the living room again before finally plopping down beside her father on the couch. "I need to call Poppy and Shannon. If ever there was a need for an emergency meeting of the Whiterock Girls' Club, it's now."

She reached for the phone, but her father laid a gentle hand across her fingers. "Don't you think you've spent enough time trying to work things out by yourself?"

Mandy set the receiver down. "What do you mean?"

He pushed back a strand of hair that had fallen across her eyes. "It's been rough for you, hasn't it? Your mother dying and now my illness. . ."

232

He coughed, and Mandy handed him a glass of water from the end table. He took a sip, then wiped his lips with the back of his hand before continuing.

"I know you care about your sister," he said, "but sometimes we have to rely on God's strength and not our own. Did you pray about this before planting that love letter for Sam to find?"

Mandy felt a tug of guilt pull at her heart. "Well. . .no."

"I've learned that often when life looks the darkest, that's when God's love shines the brightest. But you've got to let go sometimes."

Letting go of control wasn't easy. She'd already been forced to let go of her mother and now her father. . . . She'd needed to be in control of something.

Mandy drew a throw pillow tight against her chest. "I guess I haven't done that lately, have I?"

As her father spoke, his eyes seemed to light up with a new-found joy. "Remember what the book of Proverbs says: 'Trust in the Lord with all your heart and lean not on your own understanding; in all your ways acknowledge him, and he will—' "

" 'Make your paths straight.' " Mandy lowered her head. Somehow she'd got so caught up in doing things herself that she'd failed to let God be her true source of strength and wisdom.

"If I could only teach you one thing, Mandy, it would be to trust in the Lord with all your being. Don't take things into your own hands. Let Him lead the way."

"What if I messed everything up by trying to do things on my own?"

Her father squeezed her hand. "I think it's time we started praying for Sam and Garrett."

Garrett barely remembered crossing the parking lot and shoving open the glass door of the hotel lobby. For a few seconds, he stood paralyzed in the entranceway of the crowded room. Everything blurred before him. Tiled flooring. Clusters of couches and chairs. Businessmen working on laptops. Families trying to keep their kids in tow. . .

He had his heart focused on only one thing: finding Sam.

What do I do, Lord? What if I'm too late?

The answer came immediately. *"Trust in the Lord with all your heart and lean not on your own understanding."*

The reminder from Proverbs filled his mind. He had memorized the scripture verse as a child, but suddenly he was struck by how far he'd moved away from those words. When was the last time he'd prayed for God to direct his path? Sure, he went to church, tried to be a good, moral person, and tithed his income. But when it came to one of the most important decisions in his life, he'd tried to work things out on his own.

And had failed miserably.

"Can I help you?"

Garrett turned and stared at the bellboy, who was dressed in a red and black uniform. *I can't do this alone anymore, Lord. Show me what to do.*

Garrett pushed his shoulders back and nodded. "I'm looking for someone."

"It's crowded right now, but they can help you at the front desk."

Waiting five minutes to talk to the desk clerk in the crowded lobby seemed more like five hours. He approached the short brunette when it was finally his turn.

"I need to find a—" Garrett stopped.

How would they have checked in? Mr. and Mrs. Gillespie? Garrett wasn't sure he could say *Sam* and *Gillespie* in the same sentence.

Trust in Me.

Garrett swallowed hard. "I'm looking for a Mr. Gillespie."

"Is he staying at the hotel?"

"I believe he's just checked in with. . ." He couldn't say the word wife aloud either. "Yes, I think so."

He tapped his fingers on the counter while the woman pecked the computer keys with her long red nails.

"I'm sorry." She looked up at him and smiled. "I don't have anyone by that name staying here tonight."

Garrett wanted to jump across the counter and look at the computer screen himself, but he managed to rein in his temper. This time, he was going to do things God's way. He'd seen Marvin's car, but maybe they'd gone to dinner before checking in.

"I'm sorry I can't help you," the clerk said. "Perhaps Mr. Gillespie is taking part in one of the conferences going on tonight? Two of our ballrooms are full."

"I don't think so. He's here on his. . .on his honeymoon."

Garrett scanned the crowded lobby. *What do I do now, Lord?*

None of this was making any sense. He had the business card Sam had left with Mandy. He'd seen Marvin's car. They had to be here somewhere.

". . .funeral directors' conference."

Garrett's head shot up as he turned back to the clerk. "What did you just say?"

"About the ballrooms?"

"No, after that." He leaned across the marble counter. "The funeral directors' conference."

"Their annual awards dinner is currently in progress."

Garrett smiled. He had no idea that morticians had conferences, let alone awards dinners. Did he dare hope that this was all some horrible mistake, and Sam really was here on a date as he'd first suggested to Mandy?

"How do I find out who's on the guest list?"

"The group has a table set up down the first hallway to your left."

"Thanks."

Garrett felt himself relax. Surely not even Marvin would be cheap enough to combine a morticians' conference with his honeymoon.

He found a sign that marked where the group was meeting. Ignoring the aging gentleman standing beside the entrance and no doubt guarding the awards dinner from party crashers like himself, Garrett opened the ballroom door and stepped inside. The room was crowded with people sitting at round tables, finishing their dinner.

A thin man wearing a tuxedo took the podium. "And now,

for the highlight of our evening, it is my pleasure to announce this year's annual director's award."

Garrett leaned against the back wall and scanned the tables one by one for Sam. No doubt his casual attire stood out, but he didn't care. Sam had to be somewhere in this room.

"Tonight's winner is. . ." The crowed remained silent as the man pulled a slip of paper out of an envelope.

This awards dinner must be competing for popularity against the Oscars.

"Our winner is Marvin Gillespie."

Garrett saw Marvin first. The man stood up at his table near the back of the room, then made his way up to the front. Garrett couldn't remember Marvin displaying so much expression on his face before.

He saw Sam next. She was sitting at Marvin's table, clapping with the rest of the audience. Garrett made his way across the back of the room until Sam was only one table away. Marvin made a speech from the front podium. Garrett didn't want to interrupt the man's moment of fame, but he had to know from Sam if she had come tonight as Marvin's date. . .or as his wife.

Chapter 9

Sam clapped her hands, wondering at the same time how much longer the evening would last. She stretched her neck to relieve some of the kinks, moving it gently from side to side. Something caught her eye in the back of the room.

Garrett?

She stifled a yawn, certain she must be imagining things. Marvin's speech dragged on. She turned toward the back of the room again to double check. This time she knew she hadn't made a mistake. It was Garrett. He'd obviously just seen her as well and made a subtle hand signal for her to join him.

What in the world was Garrett doing at a morticians' awards dinner?

Not wanting to cause a scene, she waited until Marvin had returned to his seat.

"Congratulations." She shot him her best smile and nodded at his inscribed crystal award.

He held it up proudly. "Thanks. I can't tell you how long

I've dreamed of this moment."

"It's quite an honor, I'm sure." Sam leaned a bit closer to Marvin so she wouldn't disturb the other guests, who were listening to the emcee tell another joke. "Would you mind if I step outside for a moment? I could use a bit of fresh air."

"Of course not." He reached out and squeezed her hand. "These evenings do tend to run long, and unless you enjoy mortician jokes. . ." Marvin's laugh came out more like a snort.

Sam slipped out of her seat and hurried toward the back of the ballroom where she'd seen Garrett step outside. He was waiting for her in the middle of the hallway, where a row of windows overlooked the pool.

"I'm sorry to interrupt," he began.

"No problem." Sam straightened her skirt. "I'm just happy to see someone who doesn't want to talk about the latest casket designs—"

"Is that all?"

Sam cocked her head. "Is that all what?"

"Is that all you feel at seeing me?"

"I don't understand. You haven't even told me why you're here."

"I need to ask you something."

Something was not right. Garrett's jurisdiction didn't go this far, so he wasn't here for work. Besides, he wasn't wearing his uniform. So if work wasn't what had brought him here, why had he needed to track her down? Surely Garrett hadn't driven all the way to Montgomery to ask her a question. "What's going on?"

"I need to know the truth about you and Marvin. Did you elope with him?"

"Excuse me?" At first she thought he was joking, but she could tell by the expression on his face that he was dead serious.

"You and Marvin—"

"Did we elope? Have you been drinking?"

"That's the second time I've been asked that today, and I'm starting to get offended." Garrett's voice rose a notch. "What happened to male chivalry, and the fact that it's honorable for a man to go after the woman he loves?"

Sam grabbed Garrett's hand and pulled him out of the center of the hallway so they could sit down and not cause a scene. Her pulse quickened as she plopped down in the chair across from him. "The woman you love? What are you talking about?"

"Mandy thinks. . . She told me she thought you and Marvin were coming to Montgomery to elope."

"My sister told you I was going to marry Marvin?" Sam tried not to laugh, but she couldn't stop herself. "And you believed her?"

"Mandy's pretty convincing, and there was the issue of the love poem."

Sam wasn't smiling anymore. "What are you talking about now?"

"She confessed that she gave you some love poem and convinced you it was from me."

Sam covered her mouth with her hand. Surely this wasn't happening. If the love poem had been nothing more than a matchmaking scheme on Mandy's part, it meant that everything she'd done to get Garrett's attention had been for nothing.

And it meant that Garrett didn't really love her.

Sam stood to go. She couldn't stand the fact that she'd made such a fool out of herself.

"Wait." Garrett grabbed her hand and pulled her back down onto the chair.

Sam shook her head. "Please let me go. You just don't understand."

"Maybe not, but there is one thing I do understand."

"Garrett, please. . ." This was like falling into the potted plant, only worse. Worse because Garrett was sitting here beside her making her heart race. And now she knew he didn't love her the way she loved him.

He didn't let go of her hand. "I told you I came to Montgomery to ask you something. I can't leave until I do."

"Fine." The sooner he said whatever it was he had to say, the sooner she could escape his presence.

"Samantha Gwen Kinsley, I followed you to Montgomery because I'm in love with you. Finding out you're not married has made me the happiest man alive."

"What?" Sam's breath caught in her throat as Garrett slipped to one knee in front of her.

Garrett loved her?

Her surroundings began to spin. Garrett looked up at her. She forced her eyes to focus on his familiar face. His bright blue eyes. His dimples. Surely she hadn't heard him right. He pulled something out of his pocket and held it up to her. It was a ring.

Her mother's diamond engagement ring.

"Where did you get that?"

"Your father gave it to me. He gives us his blessing in what I'm about to ask you."

Sam's heart felt as if it was about to burst, and for the first time ever, she was speechless. All she could do was smile.

"Sam, I've known you my entire life, and after all these years, I can't believe I never realized my feelings for you run much deeper than simple friendship. I've always known you were beautiful, but when I helped you climb out of that dump truck, you woke something within me. I knew you were the one."

Sam couldn't stop the tears that slid down her face. She wanted to pinch herself to make sure it wasn't all a dream. But she knew it wasn't. Garrett loved her.

"Samantha, will you marry me?"

"Tell him yes!" Someone started clapping.

Sam looked up to see that a crowd had gathered around them. She felt the heat in her cheeks and knew she was blushing. She heard whistles and cheers in the background, but she only cared about one thing.

"You've always been there for me, Garrett." Sam struggled for a moment to get ahold of her emotions. "I think I was afraid that love would ruin what we had, but now I know that's not true. I believe God had plans for us; it just took us both awhile to see them."

"So will you marry me and spend the rest of your life with me?"

Sam laughed and let him pull her into his arms as he stood

up. "Of course I'll marry you."

Their first kiss was sweeter than she'd ever imagined it could be. The cheering of the crowd faded, and she was lost in his embrace.

The group of people finally decided to give them a bit of privacy and started to disperse. Marvin stood in the middle of the hall, looking at her and Garrett.

"Marvin." No matter how happy she was, what she'd done to Marvin was wrong. Sam took a step forward. "I'm so sorry, Marvin. I shouldn't have left; it's just that—"

"I can see. Congratulations." His face remained deadpan.

Garrett rested his arm around her waist. "I'm the one who needs to apologize. I came here with the wrong intentions and haven't shown any respect to the fact that you were here with Sam."

"Actually, I'm relieved." A smile appeared on Marvin's normally expressionless face.

"You are?" Sam asked.

"We both know that you were bored to death in there. I appreciate your agreeing to come with me, Sam. You were one of the most beautiful women in the room, and you saved my honor by escorting me so I wouldn't have to come alone. There's something else, though. Or someone else, I suppose I should say."

"Marvin?"

A short blond woman stepped up behind Marvin.

Marvin took the woman's hand. "Sam, I want you to meet Georgia Philips. She works in the family business over in the next county. We've met a time or two, but until tonight I didn't realize just how much we have in common. We chatted over the cheese platters, but it was awkward since I came with you, and I didn't want to hurt your feelings."

The woman patted Marvin's hand. "He's such a dear, and the award he received tonight is such an honor."

"It's nice to meet you, Georgia, but you don't have to worry about hurting my feelings." Sam leaned back against Garrett and held out her left hand. "I wasn't sure how to tell Marvin my news. Garrett's just proposed."

"Congratulations." The woman smiled and admired the ring.

Garrett squeezed her hand possessively. "So I guess you won't mind if I drive Sam back to Whiterock, Marvin?"

"Not at all."

After saying good-bye, Sam followed Garrett to the car, relishing the feel of his arm tight around her waist.

"So you came with Marvin on a date."

They stepped off the sidewalk into the parking lot. "Do I detect a hint of jealousy?"

Garrett laughed. "Much more than a hint."

"Well, I almost backed out, but yes. Just a date to help out a friend."

Garrett stopped under a streetlight and caught her gaze. "I've got to ask you one thing. What about the JUST MARRIED sign on the back of Marvin's car?"

"Just married?" Sam shook her head. "You must have seen the wrong car."

He pulled her close and brushed his lips against hers. "Then I don't care. As long as I got the right girl."

With his arm around her, they continued to his car. She couldn't remember ever feeling so content and happy. "We need to come up with a way to teach Mandy a lesson about meddling in other people's affairs."

"Don't be too harsh on the girl; her plan did work." He pulled her closer. "Besides, God's taught me something through all of this. It's time I start trusting in Him instead of in my own agenda. I'm listening to Him from now on."

Sam laughed and leaned her head against his shoulder. "So when should we plan the wedding?"

"Soon. I'm not waiting another twenty years before you're totally mine."

LISA HARRIS

Lisa is the author of five novels and three novellas. She lives with her husband and their three children in South Africa, where they work as missionaries.

Ready or Not

by Pamela Kaye Tracy

Dedication

To Doris Bowman and Elizabeth Weed,
two leaders who inspired others to want to follow,
two teachers who made a difference
in the lives of countless children,
two friends who know God and live His Word.
Thank you for all you've given me.

*"Do not love the world or anything in the world.
If anyone loves the world, the love of the Father is not in him.
For everything in the world—the cravings of sinful man,
the lust of his eyes and the boasting of what he has and does—
comes not from the Father but from the world.
The world and its desires pass away,
but the man who does the will of God lives forever."*
1 JOHN 2:15–17

Chapter 1

To Callie Lincoln's way of thinking, there were two kinds of true New Yorkers. The first kind were loud, brassy, bigger than life, with voices that could echo through Manhattan. The second kind were reserved, elegance personified, with impeccable presence, able to still a crowd with a mere look.

She was neither, but she desperately wanted to be the second kind.

"Maybe," said the brassy woman sitting across from Callie in Dr. Jonas T. Falk's waiting room, "this guy ain't worth the money. I mean, he can't even afford to decorate."

Callie winced. Dr. Falk's lack of clutter was exactly what had appealed to her, although she could just imagine what the other woman thought a child psychologist's waiting room *should* look like. Ms. Brassy would have bunny posters on the wall suggesting "Hoppy Days." Plastic toys fraught with germs would spill across the floor.

"My little boy's a bed wetter," the other woman confided.

"Doesn't bother me a bit, but my husband, a firefighter, just can't stand it."

Just when Callie feared the other woman might ask what was wrong with Callie's son, the door to Dr. Falk's office opened and Micah peeked out. "You can come in now, Mom."

Saved! Callie resisted the urge to check her watch. Micah was at the age where he didn't miss a thing. He needed to know that he was more important than her job. It was just that leaving work early felt so foreign. Grabbing her Kate Spade purse, she followed her son into an inner office she'd only seen one other time: four months ago when Micah started counseling.

Dr. Falk touched a button on his phone and said to his assistant, "Micah's going to spend some time with you."

Micah, who'd obviously spent time with the secretary before, sailed into an office that would have made Ms. Brassy happy.

"It's not time for our six-month consultation," Callie said. For the first time, an inkling of fear suggested that maybe this session was more about *her* than about Micah. Why else would Micah be sent from the room?

Dr. Falk pushed aside a file with Micah's name on it. He leaned back in his chair and studied Callie. "Mrs. Lincoln, you have a wonderful young man."

Callie smiled. This wasn't so bad. She loved hearing compliments about her son. She relaxed. Maybe, just maybe, things were settling down. Since Bill's death, both she and Micah had been ships passing in the night: both needing direction and neither knowing where to put to port.

"You're wasting your money sending him to me."

"Fabulous," Callie said, standing up and reaching over to shake the doctor's hand. She'd had to halt Micah's piano lessons in order to fit in Dr. Falk's sessions. "You've done a great job, Dr. Falk. I truly see improvement. I'll be sure to recommend—"

"Sit down, Mrs. Lincoln. I've done what I could. Now it's your turn."

"My turn?" Callie slowly sat back down, careful not to wrinkle her gray skirt. She tucked one graceful ankle under the other and struggled to regain control. She was the boss. She paid this man money—not the other way around. The vulnerable, lost feeling that had stalked her since Bill's death returned full force.

"My turn?" she repeated.

"Micah doesn't need counseling. He needs mothering."

✉

Guilt was a tangible entity that followed Callie from the doctor's office and into the first cab that pulled over for her and Micah. She barely remembered her mumbled response, although she was pretty sure it hadn't been what the doctor hoped for.

Traffic was at a crawl. Her son chattered about some school play he'd been in, a play she'd missed because she hadn't taken the time off work. School had only been in session three weeks. How could there have been a play already? Guilt knew when to push the knife in deeper: *Micah doesn't need counseling; he needs mothering.*

The last time Callie Lincoln had enjoyed time off work had

been seven years ago when Micah was born.

Enjoyed being the key word.

Back then, she'd thought life was perfect. Bill had acted like the husband she'd dreamed of. Micah had snuggled into the crook of her arm with his downy hair brushing against her cheek. And Callie had spent six blissful weeks taking care of home, husband, and baby. Then she'd returned to Wall Street, high heels, and six-dollar cups of coffee. She'd, of course, chosen to return to work. She'd mistakenly thought she was cementing the family's future. What she'd really cemented was a "we need two paychecks to maintain this type of lifestyle" way of life.

Now that Bill was dead, she could no longer afford to live in Manhattan. Not that she'd acknowledged the fact. Instead, during the year since Bill's death, she'd made time for extra work but hadn't made time for Micah.

Micah doesn't need counseling; he needs mothering.

Oh, she told herself it was necessary. Micah needed piano lessons and then counseling sessions. He needed karate lessons. He needed after-school care. She'd needed to pour herself into her work in order *not* to miss Bill.

She hadn't even realized that by making sure she didn't miss Bill—his humor, his wisdom, his help with their son—she was missing Micah. Yet in all honesty, even as she wrote the checks to pay for all the activities she made sure Micah was involved in, she'd known something was missing. She'd just paid a child psychologist more than five hundred dollars to tell her something she should have known, something she didn't know if she could fix, and something she definitely couldn't provide with one paycheck. At least not in Manhattan.

The cab made two frantic lefts and one wobbly right, then pulled over to let them off in front of the high-rise they called home. It was a far cry from Callie's upbringing. She'd grown up on a farm in Whiterock, Alabama. Her childhood consisted of no cable television, no unending streets of shopping possibilities, and no end in sight to chores to be done before catching the school bus.

Micah greeted the doorman and scrambled into the lobby. Callie followed at the speed her high heels allowed. The elevator delivered them to the sixth floor, and Callie barely had time to open the door to their apartment before Micah headed for his bedroom and his PlayStation.

Callie used the time to make a phone call. She'd been dating Bill's boss, Richard Fletcher. He was a bit older and a bit set in his ways, but he was also available and liked having people see her holding on to his arm. She didn't love him, but not everyone married for love. Some married for survival. If Callie were to survive—make that stay—in Manhattan, she couldn't do it on one paycheck.

Cars already sat in the school parking lot when Darryl Meester pulled in. He hated that, especially on Mondays. He liked being the first to arrive. He wanted to make a pot of coffee, check the doors to make sure all was safe and secure, and then sit at his desk and look over his agenda before being overtaken by the wants and needs of an elementary school with just over a hundred students, fifteen employees, and ten volunteers.

Just two years ago, he would have been the first to arrive, but now that Troy was in high school, life was much more complicated. Take this morning, for instance. Troy wanted—*needed*, he insisted—to drive to school. In just two days, the boy would turn sixteen and own that all-important driver's license. Darryl admitted Troy needed all the practice he could get, but why did the weekend promise "You can drive to school on Monday" have to turn into such a challenge of wills? Troy still turned corners too fast, still waited too long to slow down before a red light, and still tended to show off when he saw a buddy. When Darryl pointed out the error of Troy's ways, his son certainly didn't appreciate hearing it.

By the time they arrived at Whiterock High School, Troy was mad, Darryl was mad, and the car probably wondered at the human who seemed to prefer the gas pedal to the brake.

Only forty-eight hours remained before Troy would be making these mistakes without Darryl alongside. It would be a mixed blessing. Darryl would no longer be forced to wait in the morning as his son searched for homework, his football jersey, and any excuse to hold off leaving for school. But the driver's license also assured hours of unprecedented worry. The only positive outcome the quest for a driver's license had encouraged, at least in Troy's case, was an amazing increase in academic standing.

After all, what kind of example would Darryl be if he didn't hold his son to the standards he recommended over and over to other parents? "If you want your driver's license," Darryl had harped since Troy turned fifteen, "then you'd better keep your grades up."

"Morning, Mr. Meester." Alberta Williams, who'd been Whiterock Christian School's secretary for the entire twenty years of its existence, handed him a cup of coffee—he knew it would be weak—and a stack of messages.

"Morning, Alberta." He took the messages into his office and scanned them while he drank the coffee. The sooner the pot emptied, the sooner he could be in charge of making a new pot. Most of the messages remained stacked. They'd be returned to Alberta. Why she thought he needed to see everything was beyond him. Alberta looked like Aunt Bea and knew she was the *real* head of the school. For one thing, she knew where all the bodies were buried. For another, she was loved by all: parents, students, and staff. She did things her way, and that's the way they'd always been done. Such as giving Darryl *all* messages. Truthfully, Darryl wanted to know everything important that was going on, but that didn't include the fact that little Roxanne Timberlake would be staying home today because she had the sniffles, that Mrs. Smith thought charging a quarter for a little carton of milk was outrageous, and that Mr. Wannamaker thought the open house should be moved to a Friday night instead of a Thursday. When Darryl finished with the stack, Alberta got back all but two messages.

One: Make sure to catch the single mother of Emma Watkins and tell her today might be Emma's last day of private school. The check used to register little Emma back in August had bounced, plus September's bill had not been paid. The school had made every attempt to reach Ms. Watkins, but she'd mastered Avoidance 101 until today.

Two: Another parent had called to complain that the second grade teacher, Ms. Cavanaugh, gave too much homework.

Walking around the school, he unlocked the classroom doors of the teachers who hadn't yet arrived and checked on the ones who had. Ms. Cavanaugh was busy putting papers on her students' desks. Darryl stepped in, praised the cheerful decor of the room, and mentioned the complaint. Laurie Cavanaugh nodded. She received the same complaints every year, yet her class was full. Her test scores were high, her class the most hands-on he'd ever seen, and the drama programs she put on were recorded on family home videos the town over. Darryl wished he had ten more Lauries.

After leaving Laurie's classroom, he found Wanda Thomas already at her chalkboard writing the morning poem for students to copy. Margie Agate was already laying out hamburgers for lunch—good. The bathroom stalls all had toilet paper—good. Darryl checked his watch and headed for the front door. Emma Watkins was usually the first to arrive for before-school care.

This was one of the most unpleasant tasks a private school principal had to perform. But in order for teacher salaries to be paid, for more playground equipment to be bought, for more nutritious lunches to be planned. . . The list went on and on as to how to spend a student's tuition.

The old blue Volkswagen slowed well before the front door. Darryl knew Ms. Watkins saw him. She inched forward and then gunned the rest of the way. He went to her side of the car before Emma could exit, knowing that most errant parents were quite willing to leave the principal coughing in exhaust fumes in order to put off today what couldn't be handled tomorrow and what should have been addressed yesterday.

"Do we have to do this now, in front of Emma?" Ms. Watkins whispered.

"Emma, why don't you go inside?" It was an order more than a question.

"But Mommy's supposed to check me in and—"

"I'll take care of that later," Darryl said.

Emma nodded. She hadn't really been arguing with Darryl, more asserting that a change in routine was uncomfortable. Smart kid.

Darryl, too, hated changes in routine. Maybe he could convince Troy to wait a month before getting his driver's license. Yeah, right. And maybe Ms. Watkins would hand over, in cash, the amount she owed to date.

"Ms. Watkins, you know why I'm stopping you."

She nodded. "I'll write a check and drop it off when I pick Emma up from school."

"Emma may stay today," Darryl agreed. "But what needs to be dropped off when you pick her up is a cashier's check for the full amount. If you do not have a cashier's check, she will be dismissed from school. I'll have her transfer papers ready."

Ms. Watkins became a dripping faucet of sorrow, and Darryl stepped back and watched while trying to keep his expression neutral. Inside, Darryl prayed. Prayed for this little family he knew too much about. Prayed that he could blend compassion with common sense and fair play. The previous principal of Whiterock Christian School had been a very compassionate man, as proven by a high turnover of teachers, who expected to get paid, and a high turnover of bookkeepers, who took exception to an excessive amount of late fees and penalties. When the school board hired Darryl, it had been with the agreement that both common sense and business sense would be at the forefront of school dealings and that things would change. Fair play meant that some students didn't come to school for free while others sacrificed.

He finally gained the support of parents, teachers, and staff when purchasing classroom materials as well as updating the playground equipment were put first on the agenda of change. Even Alberta begrudgingly admitted that playing hardball was necessary sometimes. She just refused to help.

"I can't put her in the public elementary school," Ms. Watkins said.

"It's a good school."

"Please. My ex-husband's new wife has children attending there. They tease Emma. I need her to be here. I need her to be safe and happy."

"Then you have to pay tuition like everyone else."

"I'm not like everyone else," Ms. Watson moaned. "They probably *have* money."

Watching her pull out of the parking lot while a few other parents drove in, Darryl had to agree that in most cases, she was right. More than 80 percent of the students at Whiterock Christian School came from families for which the tuition was no hardship. The other 20 percent sacrificed to send their children to a church-based school. If only Ms. Watkins had answered the first late notice and come in and spoken with him. Kicking a child out of school was not the first choice of any administrator. He'd worked out satisfactory arrangements with ten other families, which is why ten volunteers were spending their time at Whiterock Christian School.

"Mr. Meester!"

Turning, Darryl watched as Margie, the lunch lady, barreled his way. He'd never seen her run before. The color of her face didn't look too good, either.

"Mr. Meester, come quick! Alberta's collapsed!"

Chapter 2

The bathroom mirror at the all-night truck stop showed a downtrodden woman with no money, no job, and no apartment. She finished the coffee and threw the cup away before splashing cold water on her face one last time. The water didn't improve her looks or her disposition. Yeah, this was how she wanted to return home. Her golden brown hair, usually styled and stunning, hung straight and drab. She was in public with no lipstick. Whiterock's one-time homecoming queen was coming home.

This was all Richard Fletcher's fault. When she had called with the news that she needed to either quit her job or cut back her hours in order to spend more time with Micah, her late husband's boss hadn't gotten the hint. When she mentioned moving back to Whiterock, he didn't hesitate before telling her good-bye and saying he would be sorry to see her go. Hanging up the phone a mere two weeks ago, she'd known the truth. To meet the needs of her son, she had to make a huge change, and once she'd uttered the words, "I'll probably move back to

Alabama," her fate was sealed.

She tried not to cry as she followed Micah back to the U-Haul. They were twenty minutes from Batesville on Highway 82 and then another forty minutes from Whiterock. Micah could hardly wait to see his grandparents. She'd heard "Are we there yet?" a hundred times, "I need to go to the bathroom" about fifty times, "I'm hungry" at least twenty-five times, and "Do you think I can have a dog?" no fewer than ten times.

They'd left New York yesterday afternoon. She'd planned, of course, to leave early in the morning, but Micah's last-minute shenanigans, her own tendency to double-check everything, and the flat tire on the U-Haul truck hindered all efforts to follow a sensible schedule and arrive at a decent hour. Now Whiterock and a Sunday morning sunrise waited just ahead. Taking out her cell phone, she called her mother. Both of her parents were up and pacing the carpet. They were thrilled she was coming home. They had room for both her and Micah indefinitely. They wondered why she'd stayed in New York—alone—so long.

She'd been in New York ten short years. She'd lived her dream, lost her dream.

The lights of the town warned her before she saw the sign: WELCOME TO WHITEROCK, POPULATION 8,400. There were probably more hardy souls now if the new restaurant and motel on the outskirts of town were any indication. Callie wondered if progress was affecting business at Big Al's. Probably not. Her parents thought a fast-food hamburger was a waste of money. Too expensive, claimed her dad. Bland, claimed her mother.

She drove through town, past the Kinsley Landscape

business—*It sure has grown—two buildings now*—and past Big Al's—*It hasn't changed a bit.* Then Grant Street turned into a dirt road. The minute her tires left pavement, the surreal feeling of home settled in. Of course, the feeling might well be extreme fatigue, but Callie doubted it. She'd traveled this stretch of road countless times, especially during the school year when their farm had been the starting point of the rural bus route. Every morning she gazed out the bus's window at first the Munchkin Farm, owned by the McKenzies, who raised miniature horses; then the Golden Goose Farm, owned by the Tuckers, who raised beef cattle and kept geese as more of a tourist attraction than a trade; and finally the Tracy Farm. The Tracys didn't care about silly names. They specialized in turkeys.

Her family's farm, the Barrets' Beef Farm, was the oldest and at one time the biggest. When Callie was little, she couldn't count the number of grass-fed cattle that roamed the land. Her mom kept pastured chickens and free-range hens. Her great-great-great-great-grandfather had settled the land after the Piqua Shawnee Indians were forced to move. He'd helped decide the street names of Whiterock back when it had been a two-street town. Her great-great-great-grandfather had sold land to the Tracys. Her great-great-grandfather had sold land to the Tuckers. Her great-grandfather had sold land to the McKenzies. Her grandfather didn't believe in selling and had told his son, Callie's father, that nothing was more valuable than land.

It was good advice, except that Callie's older brother left when he turned eighteen and so did Callie. Their father, Tom

Barret, was getting up in years, and the farm had to be a bit more than he could handle. Hiring help became expensive. For the past two years, letters from Callie's mother had outlined how much leasing of land her father was doing.

The U-Haul seemed to know right where to go. Callie parked next to her father's old Ford truck. Stepping from the cab, she felt good old Alabama soil beneath her feet. A crisp Whiterock breeze mussed her hair. She didn't bother to pat it back into place. Crickets made their presence known with their cacophonous racket, and the light on the porch glowed a welcome. The door opened, and the two people who loved her most stepped onto the porch.

Seeing their faces, realizing just how glad they were that she'd returned, Callie suddenly knew that she'd failed at being a daughter just as much as she'd failed at being a mother.

Darryl would never forget to appreciate Alberta again. In the days since his secretary had fallen and broken her hip, he'd been working double-time and felt ready to collapse himself. Today he'd been handed the news that Alberta would not return to work this school year. Since school had been in session only five weeks, this was not good news.

Already he'd had to send out announcements moving the open house back a few weeks. Alberta had been the writer, producer, and director of the night for years. Finding a replacement who could handle everything was not going to be easy. Everyone agreed it had to be done, and now. Alberta had been wheeled out of the school on Monday, and if all went well, this coming Monday someone else would be sitting behind her desk. How quickly things changed.

All ten volunteers wanted the full-time position that brought with it not only a paycheck but the benefit of having immediate family members—namely children—attend school for free. Two of the volunteers had no computer skills. They didn't see this as a problem, since Alberta never used the computer on her desk, either. She preferred her old IBM typewriter. Three of the volunteers had no social skills. The other five volunteers were all qualified, yet Darryl didn't want to hire any of them. He didn't trust them to understand the privacy issues a school secretary must hold sacred.

Issues such as little Emma Watkins, who was still attending school and who still hadn't paid a dime. Darryl's meeting with Ms. Watkins had been postponed until he could find both time and a secretary. Issues such as which students were failing, be it because they were struggling or because they'd given up. Issues such as which parents were facing marital strife or a faith crisis. Darryl knew Alberta sometimes found herself privy to family information she didn't want or need to know. She likened it to knowing who were the wise families who built their houses on the rock and who were the foolish families who built their houses on the sand.

A secretary with a loose tongue could easily bring the walls of the foolish families' houses tumbling down—and the reputation of the school along with them.

What Darryl needed was another Alberta, only with

computer skills. To Darryl's way of thinking, the only good to come from her collapse was the lack of time Darryl had to worry about Troy. For two days, Troy had been behind the wheel of a used Toyota—not the car he wanted, but the car he needed—and Darryl had barely noticed.

"Mr. Meester, who's going to collect lunch tickets today?" Margie stepped into the hallway and wiped her hands on a towel. She really wasn't asking him a question; she was issuing a gentle reminder that he'd be collecting tickets.

"I'll be right there." Darryl had been on his way to deliver the lunch a mother had dropped off for her second grader and had been distracted by the need to stop fourth graders from running down the hall. Getting busted by the principal had not made their day.

Darryl took his place behind the ticket table. Kindergarten through third grade ate between 11:30 and noon. Fourth grade through sixth grade ate between 12:15 and 12:45. Fifteen minutes wasn't much time for cleanup, but it had to do. While the older kids ate, the younger kids went outside. After the tickets were collected, it was his job to make sure no child skipped a meal. Darryl also made sure students with allergies were taken care of. His third job was to make sure no one got a hot lunch who hadn't paid for it. In truth, Margie had a sixth sense concerning students without lunches, and she'd give them a free lunch even if Alberta, who usually took tickets, or Darryl happened to catch them. His final job was to act as the cafeteria monitor.

"Help me, Mr. Mister." Roxanne Timberlake handed him

her juice box. The tiny straw was bent from her effort to insert it into the tiny hole.

Darryl easily remedied the situation.

"My big sister has a crush on Mr. Mister's son," Roxanne announced to her first-grade table while taking a drink. Juice dribbled down her chin.

This was not news to Darryl. Poppy Timberlake called at least three times a week, and lately, Troy not only had started calling her back but also was instigating calls. A first love *and* a first driver's license. Darryl wasn't sure he was ready for all this.

Roxanne took another drink and said, "Tank you," before sneezing on his hand.

"And thank you," Darryl replied.

After both lunches were over—at least for the second lunch there were no juice boxes—Darryl met with the school's bookkeeper. It was a productive meeting with Darryl agreeing to convince the school board to purchase an updated accounting program for Alberta's dusty computer. Darryl doubted the purchase would be a problem. The school board was very aware of the archaic way Alberta dealt with money issues.

The board members would have an emergency meeting Saturday afternoon. All of them were members of the Whiterock Community Church. All were concerned with Alberta's health. And either they were married to a teacher who worked at the school or they had family attending. Until the accountant's request, they'd had only one item on the agenda: replacing Alberta, who couldn't be replaced.

"Excuse me."

Darryl looked up from the note he was making about Saturday's meeting.

A woman stood at his office door. A boy who appeared to be a first or second grader stood by her side. Darryl glanced at his calendar, sadly incomplete, and asked, "May I help you?"

"I'd like to look around the school. I'm considering placing my son here."

"Do you have an appointment?"

"No, is that a problem?"

Not a chance, Darryl thought. The last two females he'd had a conversation with had been Margie Agate and Roxanne Timberlake. Margie had left a smudge of spaghetti sauce on his white sleeve. Roxanne had sneezed on him.

The woman standing in his doorway was as put together as a wannabe June Cleaver. And prettier. Her golden brown hair hung in waves to her shoulders. Her peach jacket and knee-length skirt reminded him how long it had been since he'd seen a woman, except at church, in anything but casual clothes. The women in his life were teachers and mothers. They dressed to accommodate chasing children. The woman in the doorway was wearing heels, and she knew how to look comfortable in them—something his late wife had never mastered. She'd wobbled and stumbled and had laughed before kicking them off and replacing them with her well-worn brown flats.

He'd been thinking about Susan a lot lately now that Troy was growing up. *Growing up without a mother.*

Darryl stood and held out his hand. "No, now is a good time. I apologize that no one was at the front desk to greet you.

We lost our secretary due to a fall. We haven't had a chance to replace her yet. Things are a bit chaotic. She's a twenty-year employee."

The woman nodded and returned his handshake. "I'm sure that's causing hardship," she said.

The boy pushed his way into the room and looked around. "This is sure a small office," he announced.

Darryl looked around, too. He'd had it now for almost four years. When he'd first arrived, he, too, thought it was ridiculously small. His principal's office in Birmingham had been three times the size. But there was a huge difference between a small-town school and a big-city school. Here, he didn't need a big office. Here, he didn't spend his days cooped inside. Why, here, if a teacher took sick at the last minute, Darryl might actually fill in as the substitute.

Seeing the office with fresh eyes and thinking about the boy's comment, Darryl realized he needed to thank God more often for this current position, a position that allowed him more time to know his staff, his students, his community, and most of all, his son.

"It's just the right size for me," Darryl said.

"So's my new bedroom at the farm," the boy agreed.

They certainly didn't look like farmers to Darryl. He motioned for them to sit in the chairs in front of his desk. He hurried to Alberta's desk, opened a file drawer, and took out a folder labeled NEW STUDENTS. Returning to his office, he sat down, opened the folder, and removed the papers from inside. "Here's the application. We'll need transcripts, birth certificate, medical records. . . Well, everything is listed there." Turning to the boy, he asked, "What is your name, and what grade are you in?"

"I'm Micah Lincoln, and I'm in first grade."

Ah, another potential student for Mrs. Thomas.

"After you furnish this information, we can start testing—"

Before he could finish his sentence, she placed a notebook on his desk. "Everything is here. I'll fill out the registration form. Let's go ahead and schedule his testing."

Most parents scrambled for documentation. Some even had to wait for weeks after sending away for copies of the originals they should have had on file. He opened the folder and took out Micah's birth certificate. He moved on to past report cards. Micah's grades were outstanding. No surprise, Darryl thought after noting the prestigious Manhattan school the boy had attended. Micah's medical records were up to date. Turning a page, Darryl drew a breath. A few notes from a child psychologist documented the boy's reaction to his father's death.

"I'm sorry," Darryl said.

"Sorry?" the Widow Gorgeous repeated.

"About your husband."

She didn't even blink, but Darryl saw the shadow that passed over her face.

"It does get easier," he said. "I lost my wife six years ago. My own son was just ten."

She visibly relaxed, and that was when Darryl saw her true beauty. *Boy, if she wasn't so uptight, she'd really be something.*

"We're just staying a year."

Darryl stood. "Let me go down and see if Mrs. Thomas can

test Micah after school today. Is that okay with you, Micah?"

"Sure."

When Darryl returned to the office after obtaining permission from Mrs. Thomas for after-school testing, both the Widow Gorgeous and her son were in the outer room.

"Your phone rang twice," Micah said. "Nobody answered it."

Darryl shook his head and smiled down at the boy. "I'm glad you told me. I'll check my messages. The school board's going to decide on a secretary on Saturday."

The Widow Gorgeous drew a deep breath as if steadying herself and said, "I've completed Micah's school application. I'd like to fill out an application for the secretary's job, too."

He said the words before he realized how foolish they were: "Do you know how to work a computer?"

She raised an eyebrow. "Of course."

He handed her an application and watched as she settled down at Alberta's desk. She carefully moved paperwork, pens, two boxes of red pens, and a stapler aside.

The notebook with Micah's records in it listed his mother as one Callie Lynn Lincoln. She didn't look like a Callie. She should have been named Cassandra or Calista—some sophisticated, exotic name.

Well, one thing was for sure: If she became his secretary, life around Whiterock Christian School would be anything but dull.

Chapter 3

allie walked the hallways of Whiterock Christian School, looking at colorful "Welcome to School" bulletin boards, similarly decorated classroom doors, and coatracks with an occasional jacket or even lunch box still hanging. She'd attended the Christian school during its first two years of existence. There'd been only sixty or so students back then. Her dad had been on the school board, and she could still remember how proud everyone at the church had been when they'd opened the school.

When her dad suggested she look into the school for Micah, she'd said no. Surely her parents remembered how she'd hated those two years. She'd left her best friends behind at the public school. She'd been in a class with only five other students, because while parents seemed more than willing to fill the lower grades, the fifth and sixth grades had been pitifully small. Public junior high had been such a relief.

"But," her dad urged, "give the Christian school a chance."

She'd stopped at her old public elementary school and

taken a tour. It was much as she remembered it. Micah had been impressed with the playground. It seemed to go on for miles. Her only complaint was class size. The first-grade classes had almost thirty students enrolled! The population increase of Whiterock had necessitated a second elementary school, but it was on the other side of town, and since she didn't have a car—hadn't needed one in New York—the drive would be a problem.

She hated to admit how impressed she was with the new, improved Whiterock Christian School. According to the student names plastered to each grade's bulletin board, most classes had twenty students. She liked that number.

The playground equipment was top-notch, too. A long-buried sense of fun almost inspired her to kick off her heels and run through the sand.

Even the lunchroom gleamed. There hadn't been a lunchroom eighteen years ago. They'd had to bring their lunches. She'd eaten a sandwich, an apple, and a bag of chips every day.

Peeking into classrooms where teachers either sat at their desks grading papers or worked with students, Callie had to admit this was exactly what she was looking for and what she had had back in Manhattan. Everyone was friendly, too.

Especially Mr. Darryl Meester. Wow, if the principal had looked like him during her sixth-grade year, maybe she'd have enjoyed the school a bit more. He'd mentioned a sixteen-year-old son. That meant he was probably in his thirties, possibly close to forty. He still had a head full of chocolate brown hair, cut so it stood up in a loose military style. Her husband, Bill, had mastered the going-bald-man's flip, and he'd cracked jokes about only so many perfect heads.

Callie wouldn't call Darryl Meester's head perfect, but it sure came close. Mr. Meester was a tall man, one her dad would have described as a tall drink of water. He seemed to be in control, especially with Alberta missing in action, and Alberta had been a driving force at the school even way back when Callie had attended. Which made Callie wonder at the wisdom of applying for the job. Being the driving force of an underpaying Christian school could in no way, shape, or form equal the hustle and bustle at the stockbroker's firm she'd left just two weeks ago. Back there, she'd grown the customer base, adding new clients weekly. Here, with a school enrollment of about one hundred, her customer service skills wouldn't be so needed.

But the secretary's position was tailor made. In a year, she'd have recouped her relationship with Micah, number one on her list of things to do; repaid the rest of her debt, higher than she wanted it to be, but not so high that a year of living frugally wouldn't put her back on her feet; and regained some of her self-esteem, if possible.

This morning at breakfast, her parents had discussed Alberta, Ellie and Zak's upcoming wedding, her brother's new job, the new calf born just two weeks ago, and the fact that the McKenzies were paying beaucoup bucks for satellite television. Micah ate his breakfast in wide-eyed wonder. When Bill was alive, they'd had a nanny who took care of breakfast. After Bill died, Callie had made breakfast while Micah talked. Now she wished she'd done more than just answer.

Micah would probably love the Christian school just as much as Callie had hated it. Just as he loved the way her parents bantered at the breakfast table.

Just five days in Whiterock and already Micah felt more at home than Callie ever had.

"Mrs. Lincoln?" Mrs. Thomas, who had taught Callie many, many times in Sunday school and who now obviously didn't recognize her, beckoned and pointed to a chair that was much too small for an adult.

It wasn't easy, it wasn't fun, it probably wasn't pretty, but Callie sat. The skirt was a bit too tight for a graceful descent, and Callie felt her nylons twist in a very uncomfortable manner. Smiling as if everything was absolutely perfect, Callie waited. It seemed as though lately all she did was wait for someone to tell her something she didn't know about her little boy, her life.

"You have a very bright little boy, but I bet you know that." Callie nodded.

"His tests show him above average in reading and writing, but his math skills were a bit low. Were you aware of any problems at his old school?"

"No. His teacher never said anything to me."

Across the room, Micah sat at a small table and started working on a puzzle. Math? He was having trouble in math? Bill used to play a game with raisins. When Micah gave a correct answer, they'd eat the raisins used. After Bill died, Callie had never even thought to help.

She'd thought everything was fine. His report cards didn't

suggest any problems except in behavior, which was why they'd gone to Dr. Falk.

"What can I do?" Callie asked. "Should I buy some books or tapes or hire a tutor?"

"Oh," Mrs. Thomas pooh-poohed, "you just need a box of raisins."

Saturday afternoon, the school board met in the elders' and deacons' office and started their meeting with a prayer, which Darryl led. The applications were passed around—fifteen in all. The position didn't pay much, and everybody knew that it would only be for a year. Once Alberta regained her health, she'd be back. They hadn't advertised the position: Word of mouth had brought in the applications they had, which in Darryl's opinion were too many.

Ten of the applications were discarded immediately—no real discussion needed. Two of the women threatened to pull their kids out of the school if they didn't get the job—enough of a reason to make sure they weren't hired. At least three others would mope for a month. Not an environment Darryl wanted at his school, but one they'd certainly experienced before. Most of the others would grin and bear it.

The school board debated the remaining five. Darryl would have the final say, but he intended to let the board do most of the work. He had his opinion, but he wasn't honest enough to admit that his feelings were slanted in the favor of a golden-haired stranger. One he was entirely too interested in.

Her application had certainly intrigued him. She'd actually attended Whiterock Christian during its early years back when the teachers were volunteers and the entire fifth and sixth grades could fit into Alberta's van to go on a field trip. Her parents were Tom and Helen Barret. Tom had, at one time, served on this very school board. He'd resigned after his son moved away and the farm required even more of his time. Currently he served as a deacon of the church. Helen headed up the church's ladies' Bible class every Thursday morning.

While the school board discussed potential secretaries, Darryl listened as they carefully debated the merits of each applicant. He trusted this school board. They were godly men, firm and fair.

Firm and fair. Two attributes he strove for but didn't always achieve. Troy had taken Poppy on a date last night. They'd gone to Rosie's Diner and then to a movie. Darryl had sat in front of the television all evening, trying to lose himself in hour after hour of reruns. Most were of shows he'd never seen and hadn't been aware existed.

Troy's curfew was ten. At five minutes after, Darryl had gone to the living room window. At ten minutes after, Troy pulled in, and suddenly Darryl could breathe again.

"How was your date?" Darryl asked.

And for the first time in, oh, about three months, he and his boy actually carried on a conversation. Troy was nervous, which Darryl found odd, but maybe his nervousness was due more to the date than to the verbal exchange with his father. There was hope for the boy.

"What do you think, Darryl?" Clarence Dowdy asked. The man was referred to as Pop-Pop by half the town, was older than dirt, and had five grandchildren attending the school.

"Tell me again who you've narrowed it down to."

"Diane Matthews and Callie Barret, I mean, Callie Lincoln."

"Both choices work for me."

"Do you have a preference of the two?"

"No, not a bit. I just want both of them to be clear that the position is only for a year."

"I believe we've made that clear."

Tom Tracy cleared his throat. Darryl almost winced. Of all the school board members, Tom usually took the ultra-conservative stand. One a little narrower than the majority of members were comfortable with.

"I've been praying on this all day," he said. "But we need to consider something. If we hire Callie, we're going to require her to sign a contract that states she's an active churchgoer."

Darryl could guess what was coming next.

"She's not," Tom said. "Her father's had the elders and deacons pray concerning her faith more than once."

"Now that she's home, I'm sure her situation will change," Pop-Pop said. "She's still reeling from her husband's death. This position might be just what she needs."

"Are you sure?" Tom said.

"What I'm sure of," Pop-Pop said, "is that this is a situation where God is putting one of his children in our laps and saying, 'Here's an opportunity.'"

"Why don't we call both of them today," Darryl said before

Tom could offer any more insights, "and set up interviews for Monday morning? Perhaps three of us can arrange a time to meet, and we'll see which of the two is better suited for the job."

The five men nodded. Pop-Pop volunteered his time, as did Mac Kinsley, who, since his recent bout of chemotherapy, was working only part-time at Kinsley Landscape and now let his daughter Sam handle the reins.

The closest phone was in the minister's office. Pop-Pop slowly walked from the room. While he was gone, Darryl filled the other members in on the accountant's request and on little Emma Watkins's situation.

"Well," said Pop-Pop, entering the room, "looks like you have your secretary."

"What?" Darryl asked.

"Diane Matthews is pleased as punch with her new job at the Lakeview Rose Inn."

"I didn't know there was a job opening at the Lakeview Rose," said Mac.

"Seems yesterday," Pop-Pop announced, a proud expression on his face, "Nicole Roth found out she's expecting twins. Doctor's ordered her to slow down. Jason's making sure she does."

"So," Darryl said slowly, "Callie Lincoln's going to be my new secretary?"

"It 'pears so," Pop-Pop replied.

As the men gathered their paperwork, Darryl felt a bit euphoric. It was the first time in his history that he wondered if the new secretary would show up for work wearing outlandish heels.

Chapter 4

Callie took a breath and climbed into her dad's old Ford. On the passenger side, Micah pulled himself up and strapped on the seat belt. This was her first day on the new job. She was as nervous as she could remember. On Saturday after Callie had received the call, her mother had fussed about memories and full circles. Out came Callie's baby book, her elementary school report cards—which Micah thoroughly enjoyed looking at—and her high school yearbook, which listed her as the one most likely to go places.

She just hadn't counted on one of the places being her old elementary school.

But even as she combated a bad case of disappointment, she also felt the beginnings of accomplishment. Working at his school would keep her close to Micah. It would also help her remember what it was like to be a child: how to play, how to laugh, and maybe how to cry. Seeing the other mothers, many of whom she'd gone to school with, would ground her in motherhood, help her get over the rut she was in, maybe keep her focused on what she had instead of what she'd lost.

Oh, Bill, I'm back in Alabama. I'm on the farm.

Her goal was a year. With hardly any expenditures and a real effort to pay off bills and then save money, she should be able to return to New York—

Oh, who was she kidding? It had been just over a week, and she'd called Richard Fletcher last night. If she were to return to the Big Apple, it would have to be as his wife.

Did she really want that?

One thing she didn't want was a hassle over her church attendance. And she knew she'd get it from the people at the school.

She wasn't ready; maybe she'd never be ready.

God had forgotten about her, her dreams.

No, this was not the way she wanted to start the day. Reflection on the past could smother the future. Reaching over, she tousled her son's hair. "You really enjoyed this morning, following Gramma around, didn't you?"

"Yup, I like them chickens. Gramma said I can name the next batch she keeps."

"I used to name her chickens."

"Really? You never told me that."

No, she'd neglected to tell him much about her childhood. Instead, she'd encouraged Bill to tell about his. Bill had been to seven countries by the time he was ten. He'd gone to prep school, and all of his school pictures showed him dressed in blue blazers with gold crests on the pockets. Callie's first venture out of Alabama had been to Disney World when she was twelve.

They stayed four days.

It looked as though only Micah's kindergarten picture would show a uniform.

Micah looked much happier in his jeans and T-shirt this morning. Maybe it was time to realize that what she needed was exactly the opposite of what Micah needed, wanted. Micah already loved the farm; he loved the dirt! Their apartment in Manhattan wasn't so kid-friendly. She'd always thought it was, but watching Micah dig through her dad's tool box and build a paperweight made out of wood and duct tape had been ten times more enjoyable than watching him play with his Game Boy.

Some things just plain felt right at the farm. Callie headed for the dirt road and the civilization that Whiterock offered. "When I was your age, we had this old steer, and he was friendly. I called him Blue. I don't know why; he wasn't blue. My favorite thing was to go out and put hats on Blue. My grandma, your great-grandma Rose, was alive then. She had a whole drawer of old hats. I guess Blue wore them all, one time or another. Somewhere around the house there's a picture of Grandma Rose and Blue, both wearing identical hats."

"Where? I wanna see it."

"We can look for it today after school."

"Yippee!"

Yippee? In her dad's company for a week and already Micah was saying "yippee."

They left the dirt road and wound up on Grant Street. The school was two more left turns and one right. The old Ford knew the way. It had been Dad's main vehicle for more than ten years. Now it was Callie's main vehicle. The school's parking lot was empty. Well, that made sense. She was a good two hours early. She wanted to explore the office and get started without the prying eyes of a too-good-looking principal.

Alberta had called Saturday night, barely five minutes after Callie had received the official phone call from Pop-Pop informing her she'd gotten the job.

"Welcome aboard," Pop-Pop had said. She knew "Welcome home" was what he'd really meant. He'd been the giver of peppermints during her childhood days at church. He'd led the Boy Scout troop her brother had belonged to.

"Here's whatcha do. . . ," Alberta had said. Callie knew "Do it my way" was what she'd really meant. The secretary had called again last night with a few more last-minute directions.

Dad had given her two keys: one for the front door and one for the office. Micah took off down the hall to see if his name had been added to the bulletin board—obviously an important part of a first grader's first day at a new school. Sitting at Alberta's desk, Callie took a moment to get comfortable by adjusting the chair, repositioning the phone, and carefully removing all of the personal photos and mementos that belonged to Alberta. She put them in the bottom drawer of the file cabinet. Then she took out the list she'd created the night before.

First, make a pot of coffee. Her boss should be here any minute and, according to Alberta, he liked his coffee to be ready and weak. Mr. Meester would have to compromise on this issue. Weak coffee had no place in a busy office. Once the Folgers was brewing, she went back to the desk.

"My name's up!" Micah glowed.

"Good." Callie cleared off a chair and made room for Micah. In the week since Alberta had been gone, things had piled up. Mail lay unopened, Lost and Found had found a new home, and anything and everything that needed a place had found a new place in the front office.

Micah settled down with his Game Boy and left her alone while she cleaned the office. No way could she work in the clutter. She threw away what was obviously trash, put away what was obviously necessary, and made a neat pile of what was questionable. Surely after being both secretary and principal for a week, Mr. Meester wouldn't mind spending some time today going through her important-or-not-important pile.

Micah deserted his Game Boy and happily sorted stickers. Alberta had a whole drawer full. Callie would divide them up among the primary grade teachers. Watching as her son worked alongside her, Callie felt her breath catch. He worked with his tongue sticking slightly out and to the side—just as she did when she was really concentrating.

Love swelled. That's the only way Callie could describe what she was feeling. He was such a good boy. And for the last year, she'd missed so many milestones.

No more, she promised herself. Micah was all that mattered.

She plugged in the code that allowed her access to the messages and listened to all fifteen. Most were parents calling in with sick children. Two messages were from unidentified callers who thought Callie was a poor choice for school secretary— "Why, she hasn't even been to church since she's been here."

One was a parent complaining about how much homework Ms. Cavanaugh gave. Only a couple of messages looked important enough for Mr. Meester's attention.

Callie carried them into his office, noting how neat the room was. She'd noticed that during their meeting. Alberta's clutter and haphazard ways probably drove him nuts.

After returning to her desk, Callie started sorting the mail into piles. She'd just finished when Margie Agate arrived, came into the office, and took a card out of a gray holder on the wall. She signed in at 6:45 a.m. Callie had gone to school with Margie's sons. They'd both left for the big city, and the Agates had sold their farm and moved to town. Margie's husband now worked at Kinsley Landscape, and Margie had taken a job at the school. From 7:00 to 8:30, she did before-school care and recess duty; from 9:00 until 2:00, she was in charge of hot lunch and cleanup. Then, starting at 3:00, she did after-school care.

"Howdy, Callie," she said. "It's sure good to see you."

Callie remembered going to the Agates' farm for a Teen Day. Margie had organized a scavenger hunt for the girls. There had been six of them. Callie had been teamed up with Mona Gillespie. They'd come in first. They'd found an apron in the chicken coop, a Betty Crocker cookbook in the haystack, a feather duster in a top chain of the front porch swing, and a prayer book in the machine shed lean-to. The prayer book was their reward for finding all of the hidden items, and Margie had purchased two so that both girls received one. Callie no longer remembered where the prayer book was. She did remember Margie's home. It was a one-hundred-year-old farmhouse that smelled like cinnamon and bore the marks of generations of boys and girls who knew the meaning of home. Margie's old home looked like Callie's parents' home, and Margie looked every bit the farmer's wife, still.

"The cat seldom had your tongue, young lady. You a bit nervous about your first day?" Margie looked around the office. "Well, that was a silly question. You're not nervous. You've already put your stamp on the office. Darryl will approve. My, my, you look nice. I've always liked that color."

Callie didn't know why she'd stood up, but since she had, she made her way over to Margie and gave her a hug. The woman still smelled like cinnamon, while Callie smelled like a too-expensive perfume that she wouldn't be able to replace once the bottle was empty. She'd dressed carefully this morning, wanting to impress, and knew her teal jacket over a white silk shell and black dress pants looked impressive. Black heels completed the outfit. "Thanks, Margie. I needed that."

"Not sure it's what I'd wear." The front door buzzer sounded, and Margie turned. "There's the little Watkins girl. She's a sweetie. I'd like to take my husband's old tractor and run over that father of hers."

It was the first time Callie had heard anything negative come from Margie's mouth.

"Just kidding, of course. I just get so mad at the injustice of it all." Margie waved at the little girl and headed for the front entrance. "Oh, by the way, the teachers meet for prayer at eight sharp. We only take about five minutes, and it's a great way to start the day. We'd love for you to join us."

Before Callie could question what the injustice was or even turn down the invitation to the prayer session, another harried mom and three children crowded around the Watkins girl. Soon more than ten children ran wild in the gym. Micah joined them, covered with stickers, his Game Boy forgotten. Callie stowed it in her purse. Maybe he'd forget he even owned it. Maybe he'd learn to climb trees. Maybe she could actually relax in Whiterock for a while.

A year—she'd give it a year. Even if Richard called, she'd stay a year.

The door opened, this time without the buzzer, and Mr. Meester walked in. He wore gray pants, a white shirt, and a gray-and-black-striped tie. He'd look right at home on Wall Street.

"Wow," he said, looking around at the office. A slow grin filled his face. He turned. "Wow," he said, looking at her.

To think he'd almost been annoyed. Here it was another Monday when he wasn't the first to arrive. He'd been running late, thanks to his son. Darryl had traded pushing, nagging, and coercing his son into a dad-chauffeured car with pushing, nagging, and coercing his son into a son-chauffeured car. Troy had missed the "getting places on time" gene that Darryl considered so important. Cleanliness and timeliness were both next to godliness to Darryl's way of thinking. It looked as though Callie Lincoln understood the concept. Troy didn't know the concept existed.

He'd recognized the Ford truck in the parking lot as belonging to Tom Barret. Personally, he liked the vision that immediately came to mind of a teal suit sitting on the cracked seat and high heels pressing down on the gas pedal, and Callie was short enough that she probably had to jump down instead of step down. Maybe someday he'd be around to offer her a hand.

For a moment, he wondered how she'd gotten in. For the office to be this clean, she had to have beaten Margie. Then he remembered her father probably had a key to the school. All of the deacons did.

"Morning, Mrs. Lincoln," he managed. *Wow* wasn't quite the greeting he wanted to give to a new employee, especially when *wow* had more to do with her than with her fantastic cleanup job. "Welcome to your first day on the job. Let me start a pot of coffee, and I'll get you started."

"Coffee's already made."

He nodded, walked to the kitchen, poured a cup, and took a drink. If a chair had been nearby, he'd have fallen into it. Life just didn't get any better. She could make coffee, too.

"Perfect," he said, coming back into the front office.

She followed him to his personal office. She didn't chatter the whole way like Alberta did. He rather missed the banter, but maybe the camaraderie would come later.

"I've listened to the messages. The ones that need your attention are on your desk, as is your personal mail." She turned a faint shade of pink and pulled a yellow happy face sticker off the top of her shoe. "I hope you don't mind Micah sitting in the outer office with me until day care starts."

"Not a bit. My son used to sit in here before school. I miss those days."

287

She didn't thank him, merely nodded.

"How were you able to retrieve the messages?" he asked.

"Alberta had me on the phone for three hours Saturday night."

That certainly made his job easier. "Do you have any questions so far?"

"Alberta said I needed to get with you and look over the plans for next week's open house."

"There should be a file somewhere in the cabinet. Why don't you find it, and then we'll schedule a time later in the day to discuss what Alberta planned and how we're going to pull it off. I also need to go over your job contract." Taking a seat at his desk, he opened a drawer and took out his calendar. "I should have some time around ten. Does that work for you?"

Judging from her expression, she knew what was in the contract and how it could affect her job. She also probably knew that the open house, the first real event that got the parents in the door, was an important function and one she was already behind on.

"Perfect," she said.

And *perfect* could have described the rest of his morning. No one called in sick, no one got hurt on the playground, and Callie Lincoln proved to be the efficient secretary he'd dreamed of. At ten, she came into his office carrying a clipboard with a paper titled "To Do," and she'd written down his suggestions quickly and precisely. After reading the school's employee contract, she'd signed it without complaint.

Maybe Tom Tracy was incorrect about her church attendance.

She had, after all, only been in town a week. And parents always worried about their chicks when they were out of sight. With the help of Margie, Callie had handled the morning rush like a pro. Margie took care of the day-to-day routine questions that Callie couldn't know yet, while Callie took payments and issued receipts. After Margie went into the lunchroom, Callie booted up the computer and recorded cash flow in a manner that would make the accountant swoon with joy. Intermittently, she answered the phone. If she didn't know the answer, she'd either ask him or run down to Margie. She found the file of past open house schedules and put together a tentative schedule for the open house next Thursday. Best of all, she relieved him from lunch duty.

At the end of the day, Emma Watkins's mother came in and handed him a cashier's check in the full amount she owed. It seemed the judge was not as impressed with the ex-husband's lawyer as the ex-husband had thought. Seeing the smile of relief on Ms. Watkins's face was the icing on the cake of a day that had been truly perfect.

When the last after-care student signed out and Margie's car disappeared from the parking lot, he joined Callie and Micah in the office. She was locking the file cabinet.

He opened his mouth to tell her just how perfect the day had been. That's when the buzzer sounded and he turned to see Deputy Garrett Young waiting. All thoughts of *perfect* left. It wasn't time to schedule Stranger Danger Day, and the only reason Darryl could think of for Garrett to stop by was that a student was hurt, or possibly Troy.

"Do you want me to stay?" Callie asked.

"Yes," Darryl said. "If a student has been hurt, you can comfort the family."

After telling Micah to stay put, Callie followed Darryl to the front door.

The police cruiser was double-parked. Garrett didn't look happy. It took only a moment for Darryl to realize why. Two people sat in the back of Garrett's police cruiser.

Next to him, he heard Callie's soft "Oh no."

Oh no wasn't a strong enough exclamation.

Oh no didn't begin to describe what Troy would be feeling after Darryl found out just what trouble his son was in.

Chapter 5

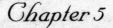

Troy Meester, for all his sullen looks and one-syllable responses, wasn't a bad kid or worker. He carefully folded notifications, put them in envelopes, slapped on a label and a stamp, and handed them to Micah to lick. Callie picked up the rest of the open house announcements, divided them up, and put them in the teachers' boxes. For the last two days, she hadn't been the first to arrive. Each morning Darryl had been there first, son in tow, and the weight of the world balanced so firmly on his shoulders that Callie figured soon he'd be a much shorter man.

So this was what she had to look forward to, raising Micah without Bill.

Thanks to Margie, Callie had the complete history. A drunk driver had crossed the median and slammed head-on into Susan Meester's van. The drunk survived. Susan didn't. That the man responsible had attended Darryl's church and that Darryl had forgiven him was almost impossible for Callie to comprehend.

Darryl had someone to be mad at: a human.

For Bill's death, Callie could only be mad at God—a God who would take a man still in his prime. Bill had only just turned forty. He was careful because of his asthma and didn't take chances. He'd stepped from their master bathroom one morning. He'd called for her.

"Honey."

Then she heard a thud and rushed to find him on the floor, already dead. She hadn't heard him gasp, cough, anything. It made no sense. No sense at all. And the one thing that carried Callie through the burial, her work, and now this new life in Whiterock was a deep anger that burned just under the surface.

Yet Darryl had publicly forgiven the driver, had stood up at his church and announced his forgiveness, and then he'd packed up his son and his life and moved away from his memories.

In many ways, Callie had moved away from her memories, too, but unlike Darryl, she hadn't mastered forgiveness and only wanted a temporary relocation.

"What can I do next?" Troy asked.

By the time he and Micah finished taping open-house posters, handmade by Ms. Cavanaugh's class, all over the school—and yes, they were crooked—it was time for before-school care to begin. Part of Troy's community service was to help Margie corral the students.

"Mom, it's time for before-school care. Can I go?" Micah handed her the two open-house posters they hadn't gotten to and looked longingly at the gym.

"Go." She shooed him out the door, first pulling him back for a quick kiss on the top of his head. Funny how the last few days she'd noticed again the feel of his hair, the way his hand was always a little damp when he placed it in hers, the scent that meant "little boy."

Her little boy.

Thirty minutes later, she watched as Troy and Darryl, not talking, got into Darryl's Taurus. Troy was rigidness combined with cockiness with a whole lot of teenage angst thrown in. Darryl was staidness combined with sternness with a whole lot of "I'm doing this because I love you" thrown in.

Her respect for Darryl Meester increased every day. He treated all of his staff with equal respect. He made sure they had what they needed when they needed it and didn't ask why for every little thing. It was all so different than her cubicle on Wall Street. There, she'd existed in a bevy of noise, movement, and constant stimulation. Almost every decision she made felt like life or death. Here, sometimes the biggest decision of the day was whether to give a sobbing child a Snoopy Band-Aid or a Winnie the Pooh.

Maybe in some ways, she liked it here better. She certainly liked watching a competent and caring boss handle the day-to-day crises. She'd seen him deal with the Watkinses and with the mother who seemed intent on making Ms. Cavanaugh's life miserable. With the exception of his son, he seemed unflappable when it came to life's daily problems.

But then, what parent would know how to act when a police officer showed up at the door, teenager in tow, and reported a hit-and-run accident? Darryl had been rocked off his feet. Callie knew the look: utter devastation. They'd both stood there while Garrett told the story.

Troy had hit Mayor Merriweather's car. He'd just won his second term of office and in celebration had purchased a new car. It was Troy's misfortune that Marvin Gillespie had witnessed Troy backing into the mayor's car and then speeding away. Troy's biggest sin had been leaving the scene. He hadn't stopped to leave a note, hadn't gone home and told his dad, basically hadn't done the responsible thing. And Poppy Timberlake, on what she considered to be a dream date, wasn't about to tell what had happened. Because the accident occurred on private property, theoretically, Troy could pretend nothing had happened because the cops had no jurisdiction.

Troy, according to Garrett, watched too much cop TV. And Darryl had fatherly jurisdiction. Which meant the beloved, coveted driver's license was now destined to be locked in a safe for six months. And community service was also up to Darryl. Callie figured Troy would rather be on a chain gang in Alcatraz than serving under his father. Luckily for him, Darryl figured the same thing, and both Margie and Callie found themselves in charge of a new assistant.

Micah was in heaven. He hadn't spent much time around teenagers and thought Troy was far better than his Game Boy—a Game Boy, Callie was more than relieved to note, that had been sorely neglected lately. What had also been neglected lately was Callie's routine. Now that Darryl arrived first, Callie couldn't do her work in peace. For some reason, Darryl's presence distracted her from performing her morning duties. Luckily, by the time the a.m. rush occurred, Darryl would be on his way to the high school with Troy in tow. Callie took in funds, scheduled appointments, and answered mundane questions: *Yes, the open house is next Thursday. Yes, notices were sent home—three times. No, if a parent misses this open house, another one isn't scheduled.* She kept track of attendance, recorded tardies, and soothed the parents who'd forgotten to pack their child's lunch, forgotten to pack their child's gym uniform, and forgotten to sign the field trip permission form that enabled their child to attend the field trip that day.

Today, by the time Darryl returned, everything was quiet and under control.

At ten—their "special time"—Callie caught Darryl up on what had happened and what needed to happen. Together, the two of them worked on schedules, problems, and upcoming events. When they were finished, Callie locked the office and made her way to the lunchroom and her least favorite duty, lunch. At one time, the teachers had shared the duty. Callie wished they still did. With Ms. Cavanaugh spearheading the movement, the teachers convinced Darryl and the school board that they needed downtime during the lunch period. Now the teachers ate in the kitchen while Callie and a mother volunteer staffed the lunchroom. Callie had just broken a nail attempting to open a hot soup canister—one that didn't wish to be opened—when she heard a distressed sound behind her.

"Mrs. Lincoln, I don't feel good." Roxanne Timberlake tugged on Callie's skirt. That really wasn't unusual. Roxanne loved the feel of soft clothes and visited the office at least twice a day to touch Callie's outfit, pat Callie's hair, or stroke Callie's nylons.

What was different today was the look on Roxanne's face.

She looked much the way Darryl had when he realized his son was in the backseat of the police cruiser.

The only difference was that Roxanne really did throw up.

He was back to doing lunch duty but, truthfully, Callie did need to change her clothes. He had to admit, Callie had acted admirably. She'd turned white, but she'd quickly grabbed a couple of napkins from the table—never mind they were dirty—and cleaned Roxanne even as they both hustled down the hall to the ladies' room. Laurie Cavanaugh had called Roxanne's mom, who soon joined them in the restroom. A moment later, Callie borrowed Laurie's oversized and seldom-been-washed art shirt and took off without permission. Where to was a guess. The Barret Beef Farm was a good hour-long round trip, but none of the shops in town sold designer labels. It might be interesting to see what Callie returned wearing. The first lunch crowd hit the playground, and Margie along with two volunteers began wiping off tables and sweeping.

Margie obviously thought the whole thing was funny. "I shoulda warned her instead of complimenting her."

"What do you mean?"

"That first day, she showed up in clothes more appropriate for a law office than a school office, and all I could tell her was she looked nice."

"She did, does look nice."

Margie raised an eyebrow.

"Margie, I'm not blind."

"No, I can see you're not."

Standing there trying to convince Margie he'd simply made an innocent remark would accomplish nothing. Margie would think what she wanted, and he only had fifteen minutes before the next lunch crowd entered.

"Callie will be all right," Margie finally said. "You do realize that?"

"What do you mean?"

"You think she's a fish out of water. She's not. Underneath the veneer, she's farm girl through and through."

Of all the things Margie could have said, this was the most unexpected but most thought-provoking. *Farm girl through and through, huh?*

He liked the high heels, but he liked the thought of blue jeans and bare feet even more.

He was thinking entirely too much about Callie Lincoln. Maybe because she was a gray area in his world of black-and-white rules. His first rule as a school principal was "Don't mix business with pleasure." In other words, he didn't want to attempt a relationship with a parent, an employee, or anyone connected to the school. That sorely limited the dating pool, because his second rule was "Find a wife at church." Unfortunately, all of the eligible females at church were either employees, connected to the school, too young, or too old.

Of course, he hadn't found his late wife at church; he'd found her at church camp. He smiled, remembering Susan Bingham as a camp counselor five years his senior and intent on acting so mature and haughty. It had all been an act. It looked as though he'd found another girl, woman, who knew how to act.

Callie had stayed with Darryl the entire time Deputy Young outlined Troy's accident. When the officer left, with Poppy still in the backseat and Troy white, shaking, and angry standing next to his father, Callie had rambled on about a typical kid mistake.

What would Susan have said about Troy's actions? What would Susan have done? Probably the same as Callie. She'd have emphasized that Troy hadn't left the scene because he was a bad kid or even because he was scared of Darryl. He'd left because he was a kid, and he'd panicked. Pure and simple.

But Susan would have grounded Troy for a year instead of two months.

Speaking of a year, Callie would be here only a year. She'd mentioned her temporary status more than once. She'd also mentioned some man named Richard Fletcher.

He could take on Richard Fletcher, invisible foe. He might even be willing to take on the challenge of proving Whiterock superior to Manhattan. It was Callie's refusal to let God back into her life that he feared. Satan was a worthy foe.

What to do? What to do?

Finally, after the last second-lunch student tossed away a half-eaten sandwich, Darryl returned to his office, gathered up some paperwork, and went to sit at Callie's desk. He'd man the phones and the door until she returned.

He was lost in the world of numbers when Callie pushed the buzzer on the entrance. "Mr. Meester, I'm back."

He walked to the door to let her in. He'd probably told her, "Call me Darryl," at least a hundred times, but she kept referring to him by his surname. It prompted him to call her Ms. Lincoln, even though he referred to the rest of his staff by their given names. It set her apart. It set them apart.

Holding the door open for her, he smiled. Smiled, because she looked stunning. She'd purchased a pair of light blue cotton pants and a flowered print shirt to go with them. On anyone else, the clothes would look frumpy. Why, Margie owned at least five outfits just like it, only in different colors. On Callie, the outfit exuded hints of outdoor picnics, games with young children, and laughter.

✉

As far as bad days went, it hadn't been the worst. Callie could think of more detrimental reasons for "having" to purchase a new outfit. She'd rushed to the nearest five-and-dime. Cotton and polyester weren't always her first choice, but in a pinch, they'd do. And she couldn't fault their comfort components. Once the last after-school care student left, Callie called home, excused herself from the family meal, and bundled Micah up for a night on the town. She'd been holing up for too long.

Rosie's Diner hadn't existed when Callie was a teenager. Big Al's had been the draw for the high school crowd. Rosie's was better. The fifties decor fascinated Micah, and in her new clothes, especially the polyester, Callie felt as retro as the red vinyl booth she occupied.

Jason handed over a menu and hurried to greet another

customer. The restaurant was full. Callie figured the Roths must be thrilled with the business now that twins were on the way.

"Mom, can I have a hamburger?"

"Whatever you want. We're celebrating." Callie leaned back in the booth and watched as Micah flipped over his menu, grabbed the four crayons provided, and started coloring.

"What are we celebrating?" he asked.

"My new job, you, happiness."

"Me." He lit up. "We're celebrating me. Why?"

"Because you're happy."

And he was. He loved his grandparents, he loved the farm, and already she could feel a closeness in their relationship that had been missing. The closeness Dr. Falk had noticed was absent and had the guts to be blunt about.

"I am happy," he announced, even as his favorite-colored crayon—blue—broke and fell under the table. "I'm happy that you're letting me order a hamburger." Ever since discovering that his old favorite, chicken fingers, was actually related to the chickens he fed every morning and the chickens he knew by first name, Micah had changed his eating habits. Callie could only guess at what his favorite meal might become once he realized that hamburger and Bessie the Cow had a lot in common.

Happiness. They were celebrating happiness.

Amazing.

She actually was happy in Whiterock, Alabama.

She actually enjoyed being a school secretary.

And motherhood was turning out to be the biggest blessing of all.

The bell above Rosie's door tinkled as a newcomer entered. Callie almost scooted down when she saw her boss and his son.

She didn't want to share her happiness with Darryl. He seemed only to have three items on his agenda this week: (1) Keep Troy busy, (2) organize the open house in a manner that will live up to Alberta's expectations, and (3) convince Callie to attend the teachers' morning prayer sessions.

"Do you mind if we join you?"

No was not an option since every booth and table in the restaurant were taken. *No* was not an option since Micah considered Troy more important than his Game Boy.

Micah scooted over and smiled up at Troy, who certainly didn't want to sit by Callie.

The booth had seemed plenty big before Darryl Meester took up more than half the space. Shannon, the waitress and Jason's stepdaughter, came over, giggled in Troy's direction, and asked if they were ready.

"What's your special?" Darryl asked.

Callie hadn't even looked at the menu, and now all she wanted to do was finish eating, hurry home, take off her clothes, and crawl into bed.

Shannon rambled off something about turkey, earning her a dirty look from Micah, who had toured the Golden Goose Farm earlier in the day with his first-grade class.

"I'll take that," Callie said.

"Me, too," Darryl agreed.

Both Troy and Micah settled for hamburgers. A moment later, Shannon brought their drinks, giggled in Troy's direction again, and hurried to another table.

"Troy's dating one of Shannon's best friends," Darryl explained.

Troy turned a shade of red Callie had never seen before.

After adding sugar to his tea, Darryl settled back and asked, "Has anyone prepped you on the sound system?"

Yup, Callie thought. *He's going to start with the open house, segue to Troy, and probably end with my errant church attendance.* Forcing a smile, she said, "No, not really. I'll see if Ms. Cavanaugh has time tomorrow."

"I'll be glad to teach you."

A cell phone sounded. Troy, already an unusual shade of red, proved that color can change in a wink. He turned purple.

"I thought I told you to turn your cell phone off while we were in the restaurant."

"I forgot," the boy mumbled. He took out the phone, looked at it, and miserably said, "It's Poppy."

Darryl shook his head. "Go outside. Five minutes."

Troy scrambled for the door. Then Micah did what a typical six-year-old was supposed to do whenever his mother was desperate for conversational assistance. He announced, "I have to go to the bathroom." It was two feet away. Not even Callie could gracefully announce that her son needed help.

That left Callie and Darryl sitting in the booth side by side, with no one across from them.

The Whiterock hotline would be buzzing tonight.

"Micah seems like a nice young man," Darryl remarked.

It was the right thing to say. Callie relaxed. "Yeah, I'm proud of him. He's been through a lot this year. He's turned out to be more of a trooper than I have."

"Kids have a habit of showing up their parents."

"How did Troy take his mother's death?" Once the words left her mouth, she wanted them back. It was an entirely too personal question.

Darryl didn't seem to notice her discomfort. "At first, I don't think he realized it was real. He seemed to be in a state of waiting. When I'd pick him up at school, he always looked surprised to see me."

Yeah, Callie had seen some of that. Not at school, but at home. Bill had always been the one to sit beside Micah and make sure he was doing his schoolwork, putting together puzzles, getting read to. Oh, all of the things a mother was supposed to be doing, too.

"Then he got mad. He went through a few months of very little talking. We went through counseling."

"We, I mean, Micah did, too."

"I know. I saw it in the notebook you kept."

"It helped me more than my son," Callie admitted.

"So you both went through counseling?"

"No, just Micah, but his counselor helped me, too."

"Why didn't you go through counseling?"

Luckily, at that moment Micah bounced out of the restroom and plopped across from them. He'd saved her. For Callie knew, as sure as she knew her name was Callie Lynn Lincoln, that Darryl had been about to say that counseling just might put her back in contact with God.

Chapter 6

An open house at a small school is a huge event. More than 90 percent of the parents attended. The too-conscientious parents showed up at six thirty even though the first event didn't begin until seven o'clock. They wandered the halls, admiring decorations.

Darryl tried to steer them either into the church auditorium or out onto the playground. He was somewhat successful. Callie was in the kitchen, helping Margie set out cookies, make punch, and set up more tables. She'd changed from heels to dainty white flats that accented a soft pink pantsuit. He'd never paid such attention to clothes before. His wife had hated to shop. He hated to shop, but maybe watching Callie parade in and out of the dressing room wouldn't be too painful. He was certainly willing to give it a try.

No, no, she's temporary.

After Monday's meal at Rosie's, the word *temporary* left a bad taste in Darryl's mouth. He found himself leaning toward a more permanent desire. Once the meal had been served and

Troy and Micah had relaxed, they'd shared a wonderful meal. Callie actually managed to get off the topics of work and Micah and share a few personal insights—insights that Darryl found interesting: She was a night person who lived in a morning-person world. She only wore heels because she was short and didn't like to look up at people. Her mother was teaching her how to crochet.

She artfully changed the subject every time he mentioned God.

He'd have to work harder to help her live up to the contract she'd signed that stated she was a churchgoer. He wanted to help her. Now, during the open house, was not the time.

The last few parents hustled into the church auditorium. Darryl walked up front with Callie. They sat in the first pew, side by side, and the evening began. One insight she hadn't needed to share the other night was her penchant for keeping track of tasks. Tonight as always, she carried her trusty clipboard and checked off each speaker after they'd performed the function she assigned. Pop-Pop opened with a prayer. Two kindergartners said the pledge and then led a flag song. Darryl stood up and welcomed the crowd before introducing his staff and teachers.

Finally, parents dispersed to find the rooms of their children. A few made their way to Darryl to either compliment or complain. Julie Matlock, the mother who campaigned against homework, made sure to find a moment to mention the overload of work her child faced each night. Mrs. Matlock was all of five feet and looked as frail as a wilting dandelion. But her voice was loud, and she had a habit of jabbing her right index finger at whomever she was addressing. According to Mrs. Matlock, little Michael had too many important after-school activities for there to be any time left for homework. Darryl felt not only maligned but exhausted when Mrs. Matlock finally went in search of the second-grade classroom.

"Looks can be deceiving," Callie whispered.

It took a moment for him to realize she was talking about Mrs. Matlock, because looking down at Callie, all he could see, think of, was her.

"Farm girl though and through," Margie had said.

It was only her second week, yet she had managed to put together a last-minute open house that equaled a veteran's. Even the most remiss parents had received the news that the open house was tonight. She stayed by Darryl most of the evening and jotted to-do notes on her clipboard. By the end of the night, he knew he was willing to take a chance on keeping her by his side forever. Unfortunately, he hadn't noticed his name on her to-do list.

✉

"My mommy sent you this." Roxanne Timberlake put a paper plate full of cookies covered in plastic wrap on Callie's desk.

Callie guessed they were the cookies Mrs. Timberlake had promised for last night's open house. They hadn't arrived because the entire family had the stomach flu.

"Thank you, Roxanne. Are you sure they're for me and not for your class?"

"They're for you because I threw up on you. I'm s'posed to say 'I'm sorry.'"

"Oh." Callie stared down at the cookies plopped on top of her desk. Roxanne had inadvertently brushed the cookies against Callie's coffee cup. A brown smudge of French vanilla cappuccino was spreading across the stack of papers awaiting attention on Callie's desk. She grabbed some tissues and blotted most of the stain.

No one had rewarded her with food back at her New York office. They'd been concerned with annual growth on assets rather than annual addition of fat on hips. But of course, no one had ever thrown up on her, either. She said the only thing she could. "Thank you."

Roxanne waited expectantly.

"Go ahead, have one," Darryl urged from his office doorway. He, no doubt, never had to worry about thunder thighs or flabby arms. He walked up to her desk, slid a cookie out from under the wrapping, and took a bite. "Yum."

If the way to a man's heart was through his stomach, no wonder Tina Timberlake had been married for twenty years now. That didn't mean Callie needed to indulge in the double-fudge creation that obviously melted in your mouth and then you licked off your hand. No, Callie knew that double fudge led to double chin. Tentatively, so as not to hurt Roxanne's feelings, Callie indulged in one. Just one. Then half of one.

It was all Roxanne needed. She grinned a toothless smile and ran off to the playground. "Ah," Darryl said, "a little chocolate never hurt anyone."

"Spoken like a true man," Callie retorted. She picked up the cookies, noting that a few papers were underneath, and walked into Darryl's office. Setting the cookies on his desk, she said, "They're all yours."

She lifted the corner of the plate, retrieved her stack of papers, and returned to her desk. What a morning. Her mother wasn't feeling well, her father had commitments in the next town, and Micah had followed her around the farm while she did her mother's chores and had rambled on for an hour about the joys of having a puppy.

"We're going back to New York in just a year," she'd reminded him.

He clearly didn't believe her, because he informed her that he had a name for the puppy and the perfect place for the puppy to sleep—in bed with him.

"Grandpa has two dogs. They can be yours," Callie tried.

"I want a dog to sleep with me."

"Grandpa never lets the dogs in the house!"

"He said he would."

Callie knew exactly what her father was thinking. *Keep Micah happy, keep Callie happy, maybe they'll stay.*

The Tuckers had six puppies at their farm. Apparently Grandpa had taken Micah for a visit. "Free to a good home" sounded like a bargain to Micah. And in her son's opinion, Alabama was a good home, a sweet home, while New York was a fast-fading memory.

This really wasn't what Callie needed. First, a son who was happily settling in to farm life. What if he were to take over the farm? That was not the kind of life she wanted for her son! It was too much hard work, too much chance—not enough excitement, not enough stimulation. And on top of that, a job that included calorie-laden temptations and a good-looking boss.

Settling down at her desk, she decided that as soon as Darryl left his office, she'd sneak one more cookie. The sugar rush would be enough to get her through the morning. Picking up her to-do list, she noted that "Pay Bills" was listed next.

And somebody had penciled in "Seek God."

She started to cross off the words but stopped. She only crossed off items if they were completed. She threw the list away and made a new one with "Pay Bills" written first. Roughly twenty different types of correspondence sat on her desk. Some parents actually put things in envelopes neatly labeled. Other parents simply wrote notes, stuck whatever was extra in the middle, and folded them. Then there were parents who simply paper-clipped money and stuck on a sticky note with a one- or two-word direction as to where the dollars should be applied. Callie had gone from client portfolios where she sometimes managed more than a million dollars to student lunch records where she sometimes tallied as much as ten dollars.

She went through the stack of papers in maybe an hour. After she recorded the last tuition payment, she sat back and looked around the office. Now that the open house was over, her days wouldn't be nearly so frantic. She could start trying to anticipate the rest of the year, start setting up a sensible, color-coded filing system, and—

"Ms. Lincoln," Darryl called.

She stepped over to his office. He held up a folder. "Alberta called. She thinks you might want to start working on the fall festival."

"Fall festival?"

"In our days, we called it Halloween."

Taking the folder, Callie peeked inside. She'd thought planning for the open house had been frantic. No, there was nothing frantic about the open house. The fall festival was the true definition of *frantic*, at least according to the size of this folder. And she had three weeks to put it together.

✉

Picking up the plate of cookies, Darryl set it aside. He'd take it home for Troy. Underneath, on top of his stack of papers, he spotted a red envelope. It hadn't been there when he'd first entered the office. Callie must have brought it in. It was probably a thank-you note or an invitation from one of the parents. It looked as if Callie had opened it. Actually, it looked as if Callie had run over it with her car. It was wrinkled and had brown stains on one corner, and if he wasn't mistaken, the chunky spot on another corner was dried nail polish. Not a color he'd noticed Callie wearing. It was the bright pink so many teenage girls wore. He knew this from experience now that Poppy Timberlake was spending time with his son.

Before he could peek inside the envelope, the phone rang. Pop-Pop was on the other end. The school board president didn't sound like his jolly self. After a few moments, Darryl knew why.

"Last night, a few of the parents expressed a concern," Pop-Pop began.

Usually Pop-Pop directed parents right to Darryl. What was different this time?

"Callie Lincoln's been in town three weeks and working for us two of those weeks. As you and I well know, she hasn't been to church in all that time."

Darryl sucked air between his teeth and blew it out in a loud gush. He'd been waiting for this information to erupt. He was trying to win her back to the fold, as were Margie and the teachers, but as of yet, Callie had resisted their attempts to reacquaint her with the Savior. "You know," Pop-Pop continued, "as Tom pointed out, it's in her contract that she's a faithful church member. That means she must actually attend. We need to do something."

"I'm working on it," Darryl said.

Pop-Pop chuckled. "I believe you are. She's a good kid, which is why I'm calling you instead of the other members of the school board. This matter will, however, be on the agenda for the next meeting. That's in three weeks. Let's pray about it."

Darryl had a hard time focusing both on the prayer and on the rest of the conversation. After his "Amen," Pop-Pop mentioned how much he'd enjoyed the open house and how this year the school really should do something about instigating a Grandparents' Day—Pop-Pop was a grandparent many times over—and how maybe Darryl was being a bit hard on Troy. Taking the driver's license away for two months was a trifle long in Pop-Pop's opinion, and since Pop-Pop was a personal friend of Clifton Merriweather, Whiterock's esteemed mayor, Pop-Pop knew the mayor was already over the incident.

Darryl wasn't surprised. For one thing, Mayor Merriweather had more money than the Kennedys. And for another, rumor had it that the mayor's daughter, Ellie, had hit a tree with said car just three days after Troy dented the door. Good thing her future husband, Zak, worked at a garage, as often as Ellie had trouble with cars. At least the family wouldn't have to worry about garage repair bills. Pop-Pop said that upcoming brides had a right to be nervous, just as newly-able-to-drive boys had a right to be nervous when on dates.

After hanging up the phone, Darryl helped himself to a cookie and chewed slowly.

What was the real reason behind Callie's lapsed church attendance?

Her parents were faithful. And everything about her suggested that she was a believer, from the gentle manner she showed to the children to the considerate and compassionate demeanor she used when dealing with parents.

She was overqualified for the job, and he loved it.

What he really wanted to do was give her a raise and attend church by her side.

The phone rang before he had any more time to mull over his concerns. He also believed the saying "Act in haste, repent at leisure." Today wasn't the time to stray from that belief. He set up an appointment with a textbook salesman, and after hanging up, he reached for the red envelope and slid out the piece of paper inside. His eyes scanned the handwritten poem quickly:

> *If I could gather my dreams, one by one, and hold them inside my heart, they would reflect you.*

Bright as the stars on a midsummer's night, your smile chases the clouds away.

Gentle as the rain that falls at midday, your voice reaches into my soul.

Sweet as the wildflowers that sweep through the valley, your laugh sends quivers through my heart.

In your eyes, I see my future.

It was just his luck to discover that his secretary shared his romantic feelings on the day he needed to threaten to fire her.

Chapter 7

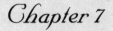

 One nice thing about teaching at a Christian school housed right inside a church was the accessibility of the minister. And Mondays were typically a slow day.

Darryl had prayed about Callie all weekend. He'd finally listened to the Lord's response and was now calling in the big guns—or rather, the big gun. At the end of the day, once he had ascertained that no one needed him, he went down to see Pastor Nelson. One of the biggest supporters of the school, Pastor Nelson was almost sixty, had five children, and had been the pulpit minister of the small-town congregation for almost thirty-five years. "Need me to endorse the school again?" the reverend asked after Darryl took a seat in his office.

"Anytime you endorse the school we appreciate it, but I'm here on a more personal matter."

"One of the students?"

"No, one of the staff."

Pastor Nelson steepled his fingers and looked thoughtful. "You're here about Callie Lincoln."

"You've been getting calls, too?"

"I get them first." The reverend sighed. "And Callie's father has been by to see me about three times already. He's worried. Plus, we've been praying for her during the elders' and deacons' weekly meetings."

"I'm praying, too." When Darryl first sat down, he'd intended to share the school board's concerns. Now he realized they were his concerns first. "Why isn't she attending church? Do you know?"

The reverend leaned forward. "This is not a breach of privacy since Callie hasn't been by to see me, and since her father would love to have some help with Callie. The way I see it, there are two reasons why Callie's neglecting her faith. One I'll bet you already know. She's mad at God. She liked it in New York. She was living her dream. She's mad that it was all taken away, that her husband was taken away, and she blames God. The other reason is she's afraid."

"That woman's not afraid of anything," Darryl said, remembering the phone call he'd overheard this morning. It was from Mrs. Matlock. The woman simply didn't want her child to have evening and weekend homework, ever.

Callie, without raising her voice or sounding condescending, mentioned a recent article that had appeared in the *Whiterock Gazette* about how well the second graders were performing at the Christian school; she reminded the mother of the waiting list; and she, as a personal testimony, related that Micah had the same amount of homework here as he'd had in his prestigious New York academy. Callie's final remark was that children learned more during their primary years than during any other year and that she appreciated how the teachers at Whiterock Christian rose to the occasion.

By the time the phone call ended, with Callie offering to withdraw the student—something Alberta never would have done—the parent was backpedaling. Darryl almost wanted to do a backflip and yell, "Go team!" Of course, offering to withdraw the student was a bit much, but Darryl liked everything else about the phone call.

"She is afraid," the reverend insisted. "Unlike you, she didn't have God to fall back on when her husband died. You knew Susan went on to a better place. Callie, who probably knows more about the Bible than the people complaining about her, knows that her husband probably wasn't going to heaven. He wasn't a believer."

Darryl felt a chill. In his family, it was his younger brother they all prayed about. It was his younger brother who'd almost cost Darryl his soul. Every day, Darryl said a prayer for him. But he'd never worried about Susan. He couldn't fathom how it would feel to lose a spouse and for the spouse to be truly *lost*. It was something he'd never had to think about. No wonder Callie was conflicted.

"I don't want to fire her," Darryl admitted. "Next to Alberta, I can't imagine a better secretary. Besides that, I like her."

He more than liked her; he'd known from the moment she stepped in his office that *special* didn't begin to describe her. He wasn't one to believe in love at first sight, either. Principals saw too many realities to believe in such fantasies. But the attraction he felt was very real. The poem proved it wasn't one-sided. He'd been praying for a helpmate. Now in addition, he was praying for Callie's soul.

"I like her, too." Pastor Nelson smiled and leaned forward. "Darryl, I bet you've heard of the KISS method."

Darryl winced. "Not that I dare say it in front of students. 'Keep It Simple, Stupid' just isn't something I want to hear chanted on the playground."

The reverend laughed. "I can understand that. Still, it's a phrase that deserves more attention. You've attended the men's breakfast now for two years. You've heard over and over how most of the unchurched are led to Christ."

"By friends," Darryl supplied.

"You really think it's any different for those who've fallen by the wayside?"

"No," Darryl said slowly.

"Callie needs a friend. Make her feel welcome outside of work. Talk to her about something besides tuition payments and tardies."

This was probably the least painful advice Darryl had ever received. He was actually being told, *asked*, by a man of the cloth to spend time with the woman who filled his dreams.

"I'll do it!" Darryl said. He knew just where to start. Zak and Ellie were getting married the next weekend. Troy would probably be sitting by Poppy. That left Darryl alone.

Alone, when he didn't have to be.

It wasn't where she wanted to be on a Wednesday morning. She was expecting a delivery of paper goods, plus the little Matlock boy had been absent since his mother's last phone call and Callie wanted to be at the front desk should he show. Yet here she was at the teachers' morning prayer session—against her will.

She wasn't ready, might never be ready. She'd been invited almost every day by Margie. Once Darryl added his voice, she knew avoidance was a lost cause. Darryl encouraged her to use this morning's prayer session as an opening to introduce the fall festival. Encouraged? Hah! He'd literally forced her. Why he couldn't just call a teachers' meeting was beyond Callie. But no, he'd practically grabbed her clipboard and threatened to type the prayer session at the top of her to-do list. It meant that much to him.

The man needed a life.

Now, sitting in the same chair she'd sat in the day she'd enrolled Micah, she realized she was acclimating to the school environment. That day, just a few weeks ago, her skirt had been too narrow at mid-thigh for her to sit comfortably. The new pantsuit she wore today didn't hinder her at all. She looked around the room at the other ladies. Only Mrs. Thomas wore a dress. Ms. Cavanaugh wore jeans. Boy, the school board had relaxed since Callie's student days.

Listening to the teachers lift up their students and families for God's care made Callie uncomfortable. No, it made her feel undeserving. A feeling she didn't know how to fix and didn't want to add to her list. She was doing just fine drawing closer to Micah and her parents; she had already paid off another debt; but she wasn't ready to face her demons, her guilt, her doubts.

After an "Amen" that Callie could barely echo, she'd cleared her throat and shared her ideas. Most of the teachers had tried-and-true ideas for what *they* would be doing for fall festival. Surprisingly, they all liked her ideas to upgrade Whiterock Christian School's fall festival with a dunk tank and an inflatable moonwalk. Afterward, Callie felt just as successful, just as important as when she'd supervised the daily trading activities of a team of outside brokers. That had been, what? Just a few months ago? *A lifetime ago.*

Heading back to her desk to relieve Darryl—when had she started calling him by his first name?—she stopped for a moment to appraise him before entering the room. He sat in the office reading his Bible.

She'd purchased a Bible for Bill early in their marriage. Would he have opened it if she'd opened hers? She'd never know. The church in Manhattan had been huge. She'd felt lost. The first time she'd attended, she'd sat by herself. Something she'd never done in Whiterock. Soon she missed a service, then two. Finally, she had stopped going altogether.

Had she ever asked Bill to go with her? Maybe once or twice. Then she'd given up.

Darryl didn't stand up when Callie entered. Instead, he smiled at her, a knowing smile. Just what he knew, she could only guess. "Do you need something?" she finally asked.

"As a matter of fact, I do."

She wanted her desk. Whatever he needed, she'd want to write it down and make sure it got done in a timely manner.

"I need a date to Zak and Ellie's wedding."

She said the first thing that came to mind, even though she knew what he was really asking. "I don't really know many single women in the area."

He responded with perfect wit. "I'm only interested in one."

Considering she'd written a love poem with the phrase *"If I could gather my dreams, one by one, and hold them inside my heart, they would reflect you,"* he had expected a bit more enthusiasm, along with eager acceptance.

What he hadn't expected was for her mouth to open in shock and for her to stand speechless until he said, "Well?"

"I—I—I. . ."

"You, you, you," he echoed.

The teasing worked, because she visibly relaxed and said, "I'd love to."

A few minutes later, sitting in his office, he remembered a saying of his grandmother's. If a day had gone particularly well, she called it a red-letter day. Fingering the love poem, he figured today counted as a red-envelope day.

They were definitely better than red-letter days.

Chapter 8

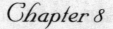

The last woman Darryl had taken to a wedding had been his wife. The drive to Callie's farm certainly gave a man time to think, but Darryl didn't need quite this much time. It made him aware of how the thought of dating scared him to death. He hadn't done it in almost seven years.

Maybe Troy had it right. Let it unfold the Sadie Hawkins way. Surely Callie, a woman who could pen such an awesome love poem, wouldn't mind instigating phone calls and nights at the movies or at the church's singles' events.

No, it would never work. She'd given the love poem anonymously, even trying to disguise her handwriting. No way would she leave herself vulnerable in the game of romance.

His Taurus hit a rut the size of a crater. He grabbed the steering wheel and slowed down. Just great. If he wound up with a speeding ticket, Troy certainly would have cause to debate the forfeiture of his driver's license.

Slowing down, Darryl almost stopped. He was in front of the Golden Goose Farm. He suddenly realized why it was a number one draw for the primary grades' field trips. He'd lived in Whiterock all this time, yet how little he'd explored! He hadn't made it past the Tracys' farm. It was white and had a wire fence with a NO TRESPASSING sign posted.

This was a road he intended to travel more, and not just because of its scenery.

Oh, if he were honest, it was definitely for the scenery—all five foot four of her.

Callie certainly lived in a beautiful area, and October was definitely the right time to see it. Trees laden with orange, brown, red, and yellow leaves lined the road. Fields were void of crops, but animals were in abundance, especially cows.

Maybe the reason Darryl continued to be a city—albeit small-city—boy had to do with smell.

He finally pulled up to the Barret Beef Farm. Micah opened the front door and raced out. "I'm not supposed to get dirty!" he yelled. Now here was a young man in his element. Darryl had watched Micah this morning as he followed his grandpa to the feed store, the hardware store, and finally the grocery store. They both wore denim overalls, and grandfather and grandson moved in synchronized harmony.

Tonight, the overalls were gone. Micah wore a long-sleeved, dark and light green shirt and a matching pair of green pants. He looked like he belonged on the cover of a young person's fashion magazine. Callie opened the screen door and waved. "Come on in. I just need to grab my purse."

He figured "Make Darryl wait for five minutes" was written on Callie's clipboard. The thought made him happy. Maybe he'd finally made it to her to-do list. Now he just had to figure out how to stay there permanently.

And how to put God there permanently.

Helen waved him in after Callie disappeared.

Wind blew, and a chill followed him up the steps. "I can't believe you drove all the way out here when Callie could have met you at the church," Tom Barret said, sticking out his hand. The twinkle in his eyes said he knew why.

"Want some hot chocolate?" Helen asked. Sitting on the couch in their living room, Darryl wondered if his son was going through the same torture over at the Timberlakes' house. Troy and his friend Randy were escorting Poppy and Mandy to the wedding. Randy had earned the right to be behind the wheel. He knew enough to avoid Mayor Merriweather's car.

"No, thank you. I'm not thirsty." Darryl folded his hands in his lap and looked around. The room oozed of comfort and use. The couch he sat on sagged in all the right places. A basket with crocheting supplies sat next to a rocker. Throw rugs dotted the hardwood floor. A large window looked out over the front yard. On one wall hung a large portrait of the family, including a man who had to be Callie's brother.

"That's Jeremy," Helen said, noting his perusal. "He's in Atlanta."

From a distance, Darryl could hear some discussion. Micah's voice carried.

"Micah wants to ride with you," Helen said. "Callie's vetoing the idea."

"Micah can ride with us," Darryl said. In a way, it would

be a good thing. It wasn't until after he'd invited Callie that he realized that as much as he wanted to woo Callie, intended to woo Callie, a wedding for a first date had a subliminal meaning he wasn't ready for.

Callie stepped from the hallway, Micah in hand. "Go with Grandma and Grandpa," she ordered.

"He can ride with us. I don't mind."

Micah's face lit up. For a moment, Darryl worried that he'd superceded Callie's parental authority. Luckily, her face lit up as much as Micah's. She wanted her son along. Good. If she cherished her son enough to include him on a first date—even one to a wedding—then maybe she could cherish someone else's son as much.

Both his and God's.

✉

Secrets were few in a small town, but obviously no one expected to see the school's principal escort the school's secretary to the wedding of the year. As Darryl parked the car in the already-crowded lot, Callie tried to hide her discomfort. It was such a change. When she lived here, the limelight had been her buddy. It had taken her away from the farm. It had put pom-poms in her hands, crowns on her head, and stars in her eyes. It had fueled her dreams of the future.

In New York, her job and family had been enough, and to her shame, she'd prioritized her job and family in that order.

Why had coming home made *home* so important?

Micah bounced in the backseat, straining against the seat

belt, ready to see his friends from school. "Jonah's the ring bearer! What's a ring bearer? I wanna be one."

Coming around the car, Darryl opened both of their doors. "You ready?" He took Callie by the arm in a loose and un-possessive hold.

Carefully, so she didn't twist her ankle on the uneven pavement of the parking lot, Callie stepped out and straightened the skirt of her emerald green dress. She'd purchased it right before Bill died, and when she'd pulled it out of the closet this morning, she realized the price tag was still on it. It wasn't a work dress; it was an out-on-the-town dress.

Micah willingly took her hand and then pulled both of them toward the door. "Have I ever been to a wedding, Mama?"

Mama? He'd called her "Mom" back in New York. The thought came quickly and stopped Callie in midstep.

"Are you all right?" Darryl asked.

The man probably wondered if he was out with a complete idiot. She hadn't been able to think of any intelligent, stimulating conversation in the car. She'd answered most of his questions in monosyllables, grateful that Micah was in the backseat and willing to jabber. Now here she was stumbling like a clumsy schoolgirl.

"Mama" is what she called her own mother. Micah had been listening. She'd gone from "Mom" to "Mama" in a matter of a month. And there, in front of the Whiterock Community Church with family and friends greeting them and nudging each other over the perfect match of Darryl Meester and Callie Lynn Barret, er, Lincoln, Callie suddenly realized that unless she acted quickly, she wasn't going back to New York.

Darryl seemed to pick up on her mixed emotions. He herded them into the foyer. They joined a line of well-wishers waiting to sign the guest book. A stack of gifts leaned against the wall. Callie noted that her family's gift already had a spot. She'd chipped in with her parents for a setting of silverware. Ellie's family had arrived in Whiterock about the same time as Callie's own, but while her great-great-great-great-grandfather lived off the land like the Piqua Shawnee Indians before him, Ellie's great-great-great-great-grandfather had lived off the buying and selling of the land, plus a little speculation and a whole lot of banking. In truth, Ellie's family was loaded.

"Hmmm," came a voice. Alberta Williams—in a wheelchair and sporting a look that said *I know what you're doing, I know what you're thinking, and I know just how I'm going to spread the news*—pulled up beside Callie. "I hear you're doing a pretty good job. Not thinking of making it permanent, are you?"

"Alberta," Darryl scolded. "You know we can't replace you."

"And I'm going back to New York," Callie said.

"Dad! We wanna go to Middletown after the wedding." Troy came up behind his father. "There's a movie that starts at nine thirty. Randy's dad said yes."

"Poppy and Mandy, too?" Darryl asked.

"They're asking for permission right now."

A squeal sounded from across the room. Callie recognized it as one of joy. "That would be Poppy," Darryl supplied. He glanced around the foyer until locating Mandy and her father. The look on Mac Kinsley's face didn't look so approving.

"I'm thinking it's harder to have daughters," Darryl confided in a low voice, "but sons are tough enough. I'll worry the whole night."

"Boys are a whole lot easier," Alberta agreed. "They get mad, yell, and get over it. Girls, now." She gave Callie a suggestive look. "They tend to hold a grudge." She laughed all the way across the foyer as she wheeled her way back beside her husband.

"You think she's trying to tell me something?" Callie asked.

"No, I think she's teasing you."

Callie wasn't sure.

Mac made his way across the room and stood next to Darryl. "Hello, Callie, Micah," he greeted. Then he asked Darryl, "So are you all right with this last-minute outing?"

"Troy seems to think he can make his midnight curfew," Darryl said.

Troy's face lit up. Until that moment, Callie realized, he'd been unsure of his standing.

"Mandy's curfew is ten."

"My curfew was ten, too," Callie remembered. "A couple of times, Mom made an exception. She called them gifts."

Mac shot a glance across the room. His look clearly said he'd rather give cards, flowers, a hug, anything else.

"Randy's a good driver," Troy said.

Mac made his way back to his daughter. A moment later she gave him a big hug.

"Mom, can I sit with Troy?" Micah's request took Callie by surprise. He'd been quiet during the interchange among the adults.

"Sure, squirt, you can sit with me."

Before Callie could protest, Troy and Micah joined the people entering the auditorium.

"Get used to it," Darryl advised. "You're losing him for an hour, an hour in which all you have to do is look across the room to see what he's doing. You can go grab him by the ear if you want to. Instead of attending the wedding reception, my son's getting in a car driven by a sixteen-year-old and driving to another town in the dark."

"I've got a few years," Callie squeaked.

"They go by fast."

He signed his name in the guest book and handed her the gold feather pen. She added hers and Micah's and then followed Darryl to the auditorium door. Glancing around the crowded room, she noticed Ms. Cavanaugh sitting next to Ms. Watkins. Good—Ms. Watkins needed friendship more than anything. Her name had been lifted up more than once during the three prayer sessions—all attended by Callie because Darryl claimed to be too busy to schedule a teachers' meeting. Just as Pop-Pop appeared to usher them to the groom's side—it seemed the bride's side was already full—Callie noticed the little boy sitting next to Ms. Cavanaugh. It was Michael Matlock. Callie searched for his mother and found her sitting alone in the back. For a moment, Callie almost appreciated the irony, but then she realized that she, more than anyone else, should understand what Julie Matlock was going through, was feeling.

Sometimes spending time with your child was more important than organizing his activities. Maybe she could suggest during the next prayer session that they lift Julie in prayer.

Callie sighed as she sat down beside Darryl. Could it be she was actually thinking about contributing something besides fall festival updates at the teachers' daily prayer session?

"Did you have a big wedding?" Darryl asked.

Glad to take her mind off her future, a future that probably would ape her mother's, she eagerly returned to the past. "No, we did the justice of the peace. It was quick, and neither of us wanted to take time off work."

"Susan and I did the whole shebang. She'd been dreaming of a big wedding since she was a little girl."

"I think all little girls dream of big weddings."

"You didn't."

"Yes, I did. But by the time I got married, my priorities had changed." Although she wouldn't have minded Ellie's elegant seed pearl and lace gown that looked as if it belonged to a former century. Little wonder the mayor's daughter would wear such a thing, since she and her soon-to-be husband, Zak, were both reenactors at Merriweather House. "The Wedding March" started, the procession began, and as Ellie joined Zak at the front, their smiles tender as they looked at each other, Callie thought what a handsome couple they made.

"Hey, you two." Margie and her husband scooted into the pew. "About time you got together."

That's when Callie started counting.

By the time Zak Blodgett and his new bride, Ellie, had left the reception and driven off into the honeymoon sunset, Callie and Darryl had been heralded with "So when did you two get together?" or its equivalent at least twenty times.

Chapter 9

Callie sat down at her desk and opened her calendar to Wednesday. She could easily devote the whole day to the fall festival and still not have enough time for preparations.

"What do you need us to do?" Troy asked.

Two helpers might be better than one if they weren't high school kids in the throes of a first crush. She set them to tearing the pages out of a perforated kindergarten math book. Troy was a natural. He tore with precision and grace. Poppy, a true Timberlake, managed to destroy five pages before Callie gave her something else to do.

Micah sat next to his "bestest" friend, Troy, and stacked the pages neatly.

"Poppy, answer the phone and take messages while I'm at the prayer session. Don't answer any questions except the simplest, and be polite."

Poppy jumped up. It was her favorite job, and one she'd done for the last three days while Callie attended the prayer session solely to update the teachers on the plans for the fall festival.

This Friday! The fall festival was this Friday!

Callie was almost glad Troy and Poppy were coming in during the early mornings. For Friday, she had a whole list of things for them on her to-do list. If the school wasn't housed in a church, she thought as she walked to the morning prayer session, she'd already be moving furniture and decorating the gym. But tonight's midweek service commanded a certain ambience that orange pumpkins and black cats didn't project.

Today the women convened in the third-grade classroom. The chairs were much more accommodating for narrow skirts and high heels. Three in a row. She'd attended three prayer sessions in a row, and she was starting to like them. Not that she would admit it.

When she'd mentioned Julie Matlock, Ms. Cavanaugh had chimed in with a few more specific requests, and then the prayer session almost got out of control as the teachers urged Callie to contribute more. She almost had.

The rest of the day flew by as Callie had known it would. Ten Band-Aids, two parent phone calls, and one trip to the bank later, she was ready to get back to work. She picked up her to-do list and checked off "Go to the bank."

Someone had added "Seek God."

This time she wasn't going to throw away the list. She'd just leave the item on there, unchecked.

Of course, that meant she had to reread it every time she glanced at her list.

The phone rang. She expected the Department of Health

and Welfare. It was time for their yearly visit. However, instead of a busy-sounding voice, she heard a deep baritone.

Richard Fletcher.

Darryl had always preferred Wednesday night services to Sundays. He'd always felt guilty about it, too. Singles' class usually comprised about ten hardy souls, and those in attendance usually were opinionated. He loved it. He'd learned fascinating details from Marvin Gillespie about how Jesus' last minutes on the cross must have felt. Back when Jason Roth had been single, he'd given a great talk on the Last Supper from a food handler's point of view. Just two months ago, Zak and Ellie together gave an insightful lesson about the rich young ruler.

Tonight promised to be the most interesting of all because Callie Lincoln had come to class and sat down right next to him.

"I'm glad you're here," he said.

"It's the to-do list," she whispered. "Someone wrote 'Attend service.'"

She looked nervous and guilty and out of place all at the same time. He'd seen other Christians come back to church after they'd fallen away. Some of them looked as lost as Callie did tonight.

Others looked thrilled to be back.

Clint Jarrot gave the lesson. Never before had Darryl witnessed God tie a lesson so closely to exactly what a wayward soul needed. Clint titled his lesson simply "Forgiveness."

Sitting next to Darryl, Callie kept a death grip on her pen

while writing down notes. The only other person to pay such rapt attention was Beth, Clint's girlfriend and future wife.

The singles class was quite a bit smaller than when Darryl had first joined. Of the ten attending tonight, four were engaged, two others were close to becoming engaged, and only four didn't have helpmates. A few weeks ago, Zak and Ellie still attended. A few months ago, Sam and Garrett still attended. A year ago, Jason and Nicole still attended. Darryl was beginning to think he'd missed the boat.

He knew exactly who he wanted to throw him a lifeline.

Callie Lynn Lincoln.

Class ended, and everyone dispersed to the auditorium. Darryl had hoped that Callie would stick by him for the mini-service that followed, but she headed for Micah and her family.

Darryl made sure she couldn't get away after that. He cornered her by the door. "Ice cream," was all he said.

Micah's face lit up.

"Come on, squirt," Troy said, followed by Poppy. "You can sit with us."

Micah's face lit up times two.

"Ah," Darryl urged, "you can't say no now."

Fifteen minutes later, sitting in a booth at Rosie's Diner, Darryl watched his teenage son woo Poppy while Micah sampled a little from everyone's dish. Chocolate from Poppy. Vanilla from Shannon. Mint chocolate chip from Mandy. Bubble gum from Randy. And praline pecan from Troy.

"He's going to have a stomachache," Callie said dryly.

"There are worse things."

"True," she agreed.

"So." He leaned forward. "What made you come to church tonight?"

"Decisions," she answered simply.

"Anything I can help you with?"

"No, I've already made up my mind. Now I have to live with the results."

She clearly had made up her mind, and she clearly didn't want to talk about it. He watched as she sipped her mocha malt and wished she trusted him more.

"Did you enjoy class?"

"I did. I remember when Clint was the kid from the wrong side of the tracks who was most likely to go nowhere. Funny, he stayed here and it looks like he's going somewhere."

"You went somewhere: New York."

She nodded. "I loved every minute of it. Until Bill died."

"I can't say Birmingham, for all its big-city appeal, impressed me much. I like it here where I know everyone and everyone knows me."

"You left Birmingham to escape Susan's memory, didn't you?"

He should have remembered there were no secrets in Whiterock. Of course she'd know.

"I wouldn't say it was Susan's memory, exactly, that prompted me to move. My leaving was just a lot easier on the family."

"Why?"

Only one person in Whiterock knew the complete story of the reasoning behind Darryl's migration: Pastor Nelson. The noise echoing throughout Rosie's Diner almost drowned out Darryl's words. "Well, I'm sure you heard that it was a member of the church, driving drunk, who was responsible for my wife's death."

Callie nodded.

"What you probably haven't heard, because I've never told anyone, is that the person who killed Susan was my younger brother."

"And you forgave him?" Callie whispered.

"Because I love him," Darryl said. "And if I didn't forgive him, he might never forgive himself. What if my hatred kept him drinking, kept him from repenting, kept him from going to heaven?

"Callie, if I hadn't forgiven him, it could have separated me from God."

The fall festival was a smorgasbord of people, events, and assaults on the senses. Students—present, past, and future—ventured into the school's gym and bought tickets for games and food. The aroma of the chili cook-off blended with the scent of too many bodies in one place and combated the rich smell of popcorn.

Callie sold tickets and tried to keep an eye on Micah. He had started the evening by going home with his bestest friend Jonah, because his real bestest friend, Troy, was too busy helping set up booths and tables to make time for a small being who so much wanted to help but only managed to get in the way.

Troy manned the inflatable moonwalk. His line was the longest. He'd ignored the "Dress like a Bible character" advice and instead was a dashing pirate who had mastered the word *arg*. Micah hadn't recognized him yet. Mandy, Shannon, and Poppy sat with Ms. Cavanaugh and painted faces. The girls had more paint on themselves than they managed to get on the kids.

Taking a sip of iced tea, Callie sold tickets to Mayor Merriweather and his wife. No doubt, the mayor was thinking about grounding himself in the school just in case his future grandkids attended.

"Want me to spell you for a while?" Alberta offered. "It's a perfect job for a wheelchair-bound volunteer."

Callie had witnessed Alberta trying to enter the gym, but a wheelchair was no match against children dressed in nonscary costumes and intent on winning one more piece of candy. "I'd appreciate that." Callie slid off her stool and scooted it aside so Alberta could maneuver behind the table. "You're looking good. Are they still telling you to stay off work for a year?"

"Why do you ask?"

"Just curious."

Alberta looked Callie up and down. "Girl, you never did know when you had it good. I can come back to work anytime. Don't you forget it."

After a trip to the ladies' room and a refill of iced tea, Callie wandered around the gym. She found Micah still in Jonah's company and quite happy. She followed a pack of sixth graders to the playground, where the dunk tank earned its place as the second-most-popular attraction—after the inflatable moonwalk, of course.

All week, Callie had staged a contest to determine whom the

students most wanted to see on the hot seat. To no one's surprise, Principal Meester was the number-one choice, followed by a sixth grader who had the bad habit of knocking other students down. The sixth grader refused.

Darryl showed up for his stint carrying a bottle of shampoo and a scrub brush.

He was wet, but not nearly as wet as he should have been.

He grinned when he saw Callie. "Where's the towel you were supposed to bring? A good secretary's supposed to be prepared for anything."

"A *good* secretary, huh?" She reached in her pocket and took out a ticket.

Here was something she'd never gotten to do in New York.

Darryl laughed when Pop-Pop took her ticket and handed her three balls. "If you're hoping for a raise," Pop-Pop advised, "I'd aim for his head instead of the target."

"There are some things more important than money," Callie said.

And suddenly, she meant it.

To live in New York, at least the way she wanted to live, cost more money than she could handle alone. It also took her away from friends, family, and yes, Darryl Meester.

A Darryl Meester who had taught her more about forgiveness and God with just a few sentences than she'd received in a lifetime.

It looked as though she'd be calling Richard Fletcher back and telling him she had changed her mind.

She threw the first ball. Her years as Whiterock High

School's head cheerleader paid off. She still had eye-hand coordination to brag about. Darryl hit the water with a splash and came up sputtering.

The crowd that had gathered to watch cheered wildly.

Darryl climbed back onto the hot seat.

Callie reached for the second ball.

Darryl held up his hand. "Wait!" Dripping wet and shivering because it was October, he put a hand over his heart, looked her in the eye, and began reciting:

> *"If I could gather my dreams, one by one, and hold them inside my heart, they would reflect you.*
> *Bright as the stars on a midsummer's night, your smile chases the clouds away."*

"Aw," murmured a few members of the crowd.

Callie almost dropped the ball. "Are you talking to me?"

He nodded.

She threw the ball. He hit the water a second time. The crowd didn't cheer. They held their breath.

Darryl climbed out of the water and back up the ladder to the hot seat. Once again, he settled down, held up a hand for her to wait, and recited:

> *"Gentle as the rain that falls at midday, your voice reaches into my soul.*
> *Sweet as the wildflowers that sweep through the valley, your laugh sends quivers through my heart.*
> *In your eyes, I see my future."*

First came silence, then a stunned giggle, which sounded as though it came from a group of teenage girls. Almost as one, the crowd turned to Callie to see what she would do.

"Looks like he's falling for you," Pop-Pop said.

"I always knew he was a smart man," Callie Lynn Lincoln said loud enough for the crowd to hear.

Then she dunked him again.

Chapter 10

The bell above Rosie's door tinkled as yet another refugee from the fall festival decided to continue on until the midnight hour. Callie handed Micah one of her French fries and waved when she saw her boss and his son.

"Do you mind if we join you?"

"I wouldn't have it any other way."

Micah scooted over and smiled up at Troy, who certainly didn't want to sit by Callie.

Callie had already looked at the menu and ordered. Now all she wanted to do was finish eating and find out what kind of a future she had with this man.

Before Darryl could open his mouth, a cell phone sounded. Troy grinned. "I think I'll take this outside."

Then Micah did what a typical six-year-old was supposed to do whenever his mother was desperate for time alone with the man of her dreams. He announced, "I want to go sit with Jonah and his mom and dad."

That left Callie and Darryl sitting in the booth side by side, with no one across from them.

The Whiterock hotline would be buzzing tonight.

Looking around the restaurant, Callie noticed Jason talking with his wife as she gently rubbed her stomach. Twins were in their future.

At a corner booth, Ellie and Zak looked at new home brochures. A house was in their future.

The bell above Rosie's door sounded. Sam and Garrett walked in. No booths or tables were available, so they took seats at the counter. They held hands while waiting for Shannon to take their order. A lifetime of together was in their future.

In all their futures.

Callie turned her attention back to Darryl.

Yes, she realized, she was staring at her future. Her blessed future.

In sweet home Alabama.

PAMELA KAYE TRACY

Pamela Kaye Tracy is a writer and teacher in Scottsdale, Arizona, where she lives with her husband and son. She was raised in Omaha, Nebraska, and started writing fiction while earning a BA in Journalism at Texas Tech University in Lubbock, Texas.

Her first novel, *It Only Takes a Spark*, was published in 1999. Since then she's published twelve more writings in suspense, romantic comedy, and Christian inspirational romance.

Besides writing, teaching, and taking care of her family, she is often asked to speak at various writers' organizations in the Phoenix area. She belongs to Romance Writers of America, The Society of Southwestern Writers, The Arizona Authors' Association, and the American Christian Writer's Association.

Epilogue

by Pamela Griffin

Epilogue

Two years later

As they did every year, parents and visitors flocked inside Whiterock Community Church to honor the students graduating from Whiterock High that May. Each of the students had brought their best schoolwork or anything they wanted to share of their school days to exhibit on tables along the back wall.

Seeing one another, Nicole and Jason, Ellie and Zak, Sam and Garrett, and Callie and Darryl exchanged greetings. They'd all become good friends since they'd joined a group for newly married couples at the church almost two years ago, and some of them knew each other from the singles group before that.

With her ten-month-old son, Taylor, in her arms, Ellie studied the tables. Zak walked beside her, talking with Jason and Nicole. Sam and Garrett stopped to admire Poppy's model of a castle. Shannon stood nearby, her face glowing pink from a woman's praise.

"I wrote that poem when I was a sophomore," Shannon said. "I wrote two, but the other got lost—"

"Thanks to me," Nicole inserted with an embarrassed wave.

Shannon grinned. "Yeah, thanks to Mom. But fortunately I liked the writing better on this one, and the other was a spare."

Ellie and Sam moved closer to read the handwritten note.

"It's my first and last attempt at Shakespearean poetry," Shannon explained. "A love poem. Looking back on it, some of the words I used were kind of lame for that time period, but my teacher seemed to like it. I got an A+."

"Really?" Ellie asked. "It's very good. Zak, come look at this. I wish I could write poetry like that."

"You've written some of the best poetry I've ever seen."

Ellie looked at him as if he were speaking Chinese. "I've never written a poem in my life."

"You're kidding, right?" Zak moved closer to Ellie, slipping his hands around her waist. His eyes widened as he looked at the poem. Sam edged closer; her mouth dropped open. Garrett stood to the side, his expression a mask of shock.

"Hey, what's with you people?" Shannon asked with a laugh. "You act as if you've never seen a love poem before. Oh, there's Mandy. I need to talk with her before she leaves."

Shannon hurried away, but the couples around the table barely noticed.

Sam recovered and tugged on the hem of her new linen top, a compromise between Mandy's spiked heels and her former line of baggy T-shirts. She laced her fingers between

Garrett's. "Thanks to that poem, our lifelong friendship turned into something even deeper," she whispered.

"If not for that poem," said Callie, patting her stomach, "I'd be in New York wearing a Miu Miu top instead of a maternity top."

"Oh, that's not true," Darryl protested. "That poem wasn't the first thing that inspired me to pursue you."

"Oh," Callie purred, "tell me again what or who I can blame for the 'love at first sight' bit you keep talking about."

"You can only blame yourself. You swept into my office, straightened my files, and put me on a to-do list. I didn't stand a chance."

Callie shook her head. "See," she said helplessly to her friends, "the only thing I can write is a to-do list."

"Shannon is really talented—I hope it's okay for a mom to brag." Nicole laughed. "I've convinced her to take a course in creative writing at college. One day she might even write a book. Sometimes it just takes a little nudge from an outside source to get things hopping."

"A nudge. . .from an outside source," Zak repeated in a dazed monotone. He chuckled and shook his head, looking at Ellie. "I guess that old saying really is true. God does work in mysterious ways."

"You, too?" Darryl looked up from staring at the poem, surprise on his face.

Zak's brows lifted. "I take it we're talking about the same thing." Zak gave a meaningful glance at the poem, then looked at Darryl.

"Yeah, looks like it. Without God's hand in things, I might still be a bachelor!"

The two men laughed as though embarrassed.

"What *are* you guys talking about?" Ellie asked.

"I think I know." Sam's face was also tinged with pink.

"Well, I'm sure glad someone does, because I'm totally clueless." Ellie shook her head and winced as her hair pulled, thanks to Taylor's hand wrapped in it.

"Why don't you let me take him for a while," Zak said. He lifted his son in his arms, carefully untangling Ellie's thick strand of hair from the child's sticky fingers. The boy gave a dimpled smile, much like his father's.

"It's getting late." Garrett put his arm around Sam's shoulders. "What do you say we all go out for a bite to eat?"

"Only if it's not doughnuts," Zak joked.

"Yeah, real funny." Garrett grinned.

"And no spicy food," Ellie added.

"I'll second that." Callie let out a smiling groan as she looked down at her seven-months-pregnant stomach. "By the way, how is Beth doing?"

"She's still having morning sickness, which is why she wasn't able to come, but otherwise both she and Clint are doing great. They've picked out sixteen possible names."

Callie laughed. "Well, they could either pare down to one selection or just plan on having a large family."

"We are." Ellie smiled up at Zak, and he gave her shoulder a squeeze.

"Ellie, you're not. . ." Nicole grabbed her arm.

"I am." Ellie's eyes sparkled.

"Oh, that's terrific!" Sam enthused, and the others agreed. "Now we have even more reason to celebrate."

"Micah is spending the night at my parents' place," Callie said, and Darryl smiled and nodded his agreement with the plan. "And Troy plans to watch a movie over at Poppy's house."

"Jason?" Nicole asked.

"I don't think your mother would mind watching the twins for another hour."

"If Ellie's parents weren't out of town on their second honeymoon," Zak said, "Ellie's mom would've claimed Taylor tonight. They dote on him, and it's because of him my in-laws finally accepted me."

Ellie smiled up at Zak. "I think my parents realized what a great guy you are long before Taylor came along."

He dropped a light kiss on her lips. "As long as you think so, that's all that matters."

"Why don't we make it my treat," Jason said, "and all meet at Rosie's Diner."

Everyone laughed and agreed. Arm in arm, the couples moved toward the door.

"Do you mind telling me what that was all about back there with the poem?" Ellie whispered to Zak as they took up the rear.

"I'll tell you later. But for now, let's just say it's a good thing for all of us that Shannon did her homework!"

"What?"

At her bewildered exclamation, Zak only gave her a big grin.

A Letter to Our Readers

Dear Readers:

In order that we might better contribute to your reading enjoyment, we would appreciate your taking a few minutes to respond to the following questions. When completed, please return to the following: Fiction Editor, Barbour Publishing, Inc., P.O. Box 719, Uhrichsville, OH 44683.

1. Did you enjoy reading *Sweet Home Alabama*?
   ❏ Very much—I would like to see more books like this.
   ❏ Moderately—I would have enjoyed it more if _____
   _____
   _____

2. What influenced your decision to purchase this book?
   (Check those that apply.)
   ❏ Cover   ❏ Back cover copy   ❏ Title   ❏ Price
   ❏ Friends   ❏ Publicity   ❏ Other

3. Which story was your favorite?
   ❏ *Head over Heels*   ❏ *Matchmaker, Matchmaker*
   ❏ *The Princess and the Mechanic*   ❏ *Ready or Not*

4. Please check your age range:
   ❏ Under 18   ❏ 18–24   ❏ 25–34
   ❏ 35–45   ❏ 46–55   ❏ Over 55

5. How many hours per week do you read? _____

Name _____

Occupation _____

Address _____

City _____ State _____ Zip _____

E-mail _____